MEET DR. MORELLE

MEET DR. MORELLE

A Collection of Chapters from his Case Book

By

ERNEST DUDLEY
The B.B.C. 'Armchair Detective'

WILDSIDE PRESS

If anyone can for a moment identify themselves or any other person with the characters or incidents in this book they are ideal subjects for a course of Doctor Morelle's psychoanalytical treatment.

Published by
Wildside Press, LLC
P.O. Box 301
Holicong, PA 18928-0301 USA
www.wildsidepress.com

Wildside Press Edition: MMIII

CONTENTS

TO
MY FATHER
BUT FOR WHOM THIS MIGHT NEVER
HAVE BEEN WRITTEN.

CHAPTER I

THE CASE OF THE LADY WITH THE LORGNETTE

Extract from the *Medical Directory* (current year):
MORELLE (Christian names given) 221B, Harley St., W.1. (Tel.
Langham 05011)—M.D. Berne (Univ. Berne Prize & Gold Medal-
list) 1924; F.R.C.P. Lond. 1932 (Univ. Vienna, Salzburg, Carfax,
U.S.A.); Phys. Dept. Nerv. Dis. & Lect. in Neurol. Rome Academy,
1929; Lect. & Research Fell. Sorbonne, 1928; Carfax, U.S.A. Fell.
Med. Research Counc. 1930; Research Fell., Salzburg Hosp. 1931;
Psychiat. Carlos Hosp. Rome; Psychiat. Horgan Hosp. Baltimore;
Pathol. Rudolfa Clin. Berne; Medico-Psychol. Trafalgar Hosp. &
Clin. Lond.; Hon. Cons. Psychiat. Welbeck Hosp. Lond. Author,
" Psychol. aspects of prevent. treat. of drug addiction," *Amer. Med.
Wkly.*, 1932; " Study of analysis in ment. treat.," *Ib.*, 1930; " Ner-
vous & mental aspect of drug addict.," *Jl. of Res. in Psychopathol,*
1931; " Hypnot. treat. in nerve & ment. disorder," *Amer. Med. Jnl.,*
1930; etc.
Extract from *Who's Who* (current year):
MORELLE (Christian names, but no date, place or details of
birth given). *Educated*: Sorbonne; Rome; Vienna. M.D. Berne,
1923 (for further details of career as medical practitioner see *Medical
Directory*—current year); Lecturer on medico-psychological aspects
of criminology to New York Police Bureau, 1934; Lecturer and
medico-psychiat. to police bureaux and criminological authorities
of Geneva, Rome, Milan and Paris, 1935-1937. *Published* miscel-
laneous papers on medical and scientific subjects (see *Medical
Directory*—current year). *Writings for journals* include: " Auguste
Dupin versus Sherlock Holmes—A Study in Ratiocination,"
London Archive & Atlantic Weekly, 1931; " The Criminal versus
Society," *English Note-book, Le Temps Moderne & New York
Letter,* 1933; etc., etc. *Address*: 221B, Harley St., London, W.1.
Recreations: Criminology and fencing—European fencing champion
(Epée) Switzerland, 1927-28-29. *Clubs*: None.
Entry in Doctor Morelle's personal diary, dated March 5th, year
not indicated:
" Today a young woman answering to name of Miss Frayle
entered my employ. I fear my inherent good nature persuaded
me to offer her the post of assistant in my research and laboratory
activities and act as secretary. She would appear to suffer from an
astigmatic condition of the vision and wears spectacles which do
little to enhance her somewhat unprepossessing appearance.
However, she appears to be a willing worker and possesses a self-

effacing personality. Whether these characteristics are the result of low intelligence and moronic mentality I am not certain. I fear it to be the case. No doubt the young woman will shortly commence to presume upon my generosity and grow inefficient—or by her timorousness and anxiety to please irritate me beyond endurance. In any event it would appear I shall not be long before having to dispense with her services, and my magnanimous gesture will be finally discharged."

Not to have compiled a case-book would have been unusual in any practising medical man: the recording of particulars relative to his patients being a mere matter of routine. When one regards Doctor Morelle as somewhat above the average physician, the inclination is to expect that during such a wide and singularly varied career he must have compiled a fairly extensive case-book. One incidentally of more than ordinary interest. And in fact *his* case-book runs into several volumes. In them is recorded in his characteristically neat and meticulous handwriting the minute and precise details of every case with which he has been associated.

To say they make an intriguing contribution to the study of human nature could hardly be described as overstatement. From the moment he began his career as a medical practitioner Doctor Morelle has concerned himself only with the unusual, the bizarre. In these pages are crystallised all the frailties and foibles, the ever-insoluble mystery of the human mind and soul. Each case it seems adds yet another chapter to the remarkable history of human, inhuman or subhuman conduct. Therein is set down the illuminating if somewhat disturbing glimpses into such subterranean twistings of the brain, such tortuous writhings of the spirit as pass belief.

Professional ethics apart the Doctor has, of course, no desire that his memoirs shall remain other than secret. They are recorded purely for the study of medical colleagues, other men of science and anthropologists, to whom, as he is far from unaware, they are of inestimable value. There are other reasons besides why his memoirs may not be the subject of public scrutiny. In a number of cases those involved have been personages of importance, some of whom are still alive. In one or two instances political issues were involved, there were men in high places who entrusted the Doctor with the safety of their honour and careers so they might be disentangled from the sinister skeins in which they were caught. His integrity they knew was never in doubt. *

*A leading U.S.A. newspaper syndicate, learning of his vital intervention in the somewhat surprising case of a certain Grand Duke, offered Doctor Morelle a fantastic sum for the " inside facts." The Doctor's rejection of he offer was as may be imagined couched in no uncertain terms !

8

Again there are other cases whose publication to the world at large would bring distress to those persons still living who had been, indirectly or directly, implicated. And while Doctor Morelle's attitude towards his fellow-creatures is perhaps most accurately described as one of benign contempt, at no time has he sought deliberately to do harm to someone defenceless and unable to retaliate.

There are, however, a number of chapters from his memoirs which he has of late felt might, without indiscretion, be exposed to the public eye. This new attitude has in fact been brought about (though he would never be prepared to admit it) by some recent successes in authorship. He had been prevailed upon to write several articles for a journal and periodical or two on more popular aspects of forensic medicine.* The attention with which his writings were received, the flow of praise and adulation accorded him he secretly found most gratifying. Though not for an instant of course did he appear to hold anything but the loftiest disdain for this admiration. At any rate he has now become somewhat surprisingly cognisant of the right of the general public to certain avenues of knowledge which he feels he alone may open up to them. As a result of this new frame of mind: these chapters from his secret memoirs.

The incidents described in the following pages, the names of the protagonists, identifiable details and circumstances have been judiciously altered. But in their essence, in the presentation of these aspects of the cupidity and cunning of men and women; the records of murderous avarice, hatred and human pathos, the stories are unchanged. The same as when with unerring eye and sure step Doctor Morelle, accompanied by the fluttering Miss Frayle, unravelled the dark problems and brought to them the light of his cold logic and powers of scientific ratiocination. It might not be inappropriate to begin with the strange affair which he has indexed as "The Case of the Lady of the Lorgnette." For it was this case which introduced him to Miss Frayle, and she in turn who introduced him to the lady in question, or rather to that unfortunate being's corpse.

It was at a late hour one moonless and rather misty night when the Doctor was proceeding somewhat briskly along Chelsea Embankment. He had just left the house of Sir Burton Muir, the eminent K.C. and a small party of friends with whom he had been dining. It had been a pleasurable evening, good food excellently cooked and served, good wine; together with a flow of conversation befitting the intellect of guests and host. Doctor Morelle had as was his habit made brilliant contributions to each various topic of

* See files of *London Journal, Science Quarterly* and *Edinburgh Magazine.*

discussion, scoring points with his sardonic shafts of humour. He had left before the others, having in mind some work awaiting him unfinished in his laboratory. Now having decided to take a little exercise before ultimately hailing a taxi he was walking quickly along the Embankment in the direction of Chelsea Bridge.

Somewhere down river a ship's siren hooted mournfully and the Thames running past was dark and forbidding. The mist swirled chill and raw across the Embankment which seemed quite deserted. But as he strode on, his mind full of the research problems with which he presently proposed to grapple, Doctor Morelle passed the figure of a young woman leaning against the parapet. He might not have noticed her so insignificant a figure she made, but something, a certain tenseness about her attitude caused him to throw her a passing glance. A few paces on he paused to light a cigarette. As he flicked a flame against the tip of his Egyptian Le Sphinx he glanced back, and snapping the cap of his lighter into place swiftly retraced his steps.

" You know," he said to her, and his tone was level and charged with a sardonic quirk, " I don't think I should! "

She gave a startled gasp. " Oh! . . ." His swift and noiseless approach had taken her utterly unawares. He regarded her. She was small and slim, pathetic in her shabby clothes, and she stared up at him wide-eyed through horn-rimmed spectacles which were perched awry on her nose. The look of desperation in her face gave way now to one of forlorn misery and wretchedness.

" Drowning's a cold and dismal affair only a fool would choose," he murmured.

" I'm not going to — " Her attempted denial faded into a broken whisper, and she turned away to stare down at the dark waters. Unmoved he watched the tear-trickle run down her nose and splash onto the parapet. He said:

" I can suggest several other ways of committing suicide, much more pleasant." He paused as if to decide for her which method might prove most acceptable. Then he sighed, and with a tone of disappointment, added : " Regrettably, however, it would be wrong of me to name them."

" Please—please leave me alone. . ."

He had no intention of acceding to her request until his curiosity had been satisfied. Insinuatingly he said : " Should I—er—call a policeman? "

Her face jerked up to him in terror. " No! Oh, don't! "

" Very well. But in return you must tell me something. Who are you? "

She said hesitantly : " My—my name is Frayle—Miss Frayle."

" And what—Miss Frayle— " and now he smiled thinly, " apart

from contemplating putting an end to your life—do you do? "

" I'm—" she corrected herself with a little shudder, " I *was* a secretary-companion."

" Your employer I presume having dispensed with your services?" The reply was a whisper he only just caught. " She's dead."

" Oh. . .? " he queried after a brief pause. She began to dab her face with her handkerchief and blow her nose. Now she spoke hurriedly, blurting out the words as if anxious to get rid of them: " I went out just now to post the letters—I do every evening—and when I came back I found her. . ." Her voice rose hysterically. " I didn't do it! I didn't—! "

He cut in quickly, deceptively soft-voiced. " What happened then? "

" I—I lost my head . . . The way she looked! Oh, it was horrible! " She shuddered violently, her face contorted at the remembered horror. " I rushed from the flat."

" Without waiting to call a doctor—or inform the police? "

She heard the coldness in his tone, and burst out: " I daren't! You don't understand. They'll say I did it—she was always telling people—her friends—once even the hall-porter—I hated her, I wanted to see her dead; " She broke off, and then added pathetically, " She wasn't very nice sometimes. She was— "

Again he cut in. " Supposing, Miss Frayle," he suggested, " you and I go back to the flat together? "

" Oh, no! " she gasped, terrified. " I can't—I couldn't face it—! "

He surveyed the glowing tip of his cigarette. Without looking at her, without raising his voice: " I think it would be better for you if you did as I say."

Her reaction to the implied threat behind the quietly spoken words was almost violent. " No, no—! "

She might not have spoken, Doctor Morelle glanced at the mist swirling about them, gave a somewhat over elaborate shiver and added: " Besides, I am finding it a little chilly."

" I won't go back —! " Her voice rose stubbornly. " You can't make me — " She broke off with a strangled gasp as a bulky figure loomed up suddenly and a deep cockney voice obtruded itself.

" Here, here—now— " said the newcomer paternally.

" Ah, good-evening, officer," Doctor Morelle greeted him imperturbably.

" Anything the matter? " the policeman inquired, scowling slightly at Miss Frayle as if to imply that it must be she and obviously not the other who was responsible if anything was untoward. Miss Frayle tried to melt behind the Doctor. " Er—nothing—it's nothing— " she murmured.

11

"Lot o' noise about nothink!" observed the policeman agreeably and gave Doctor Morelle the benefit of half a grin.

"Perhaps I may explain. I am a doctor, this young lady is my patient, and she is somewhat hysterical. A nervous case, you understand, officer?"

The officer nodded with fullest understanding. He had a daughter of his own, "difficult" young woman she was. Worry of her mother's life. "Oh. . ." he said. "I see." And nodded more vigorously.

"I'm just about to conduct her home." And to Miss Frayle in that insinuating tone: "Am I not, Miss Frayle?"

There was only one answer she knew. Knew also that he realised she knew. She glanced up at his saturnine face shadowed by his soft black hat. Out of the tail of her eye she caught the glint of official buttons and trembled. After all, she told herself, the other had said he was a doctor. Perhaps he really was. She tried to reassure himself but with sinking heart had to admit he was like no other doctor she had ever met. Nothing kindly and gentle about him. This tall and gaunt, almost sinister figure with the sardonic smile and penetrating, mesmeric eyes.

"Yes . . . Yes . . ." she answered him in a whisper. "We'll go now."

The policeman grunted approvingly and Doctor Morelle observed in an undertone: "I thought you'd be sensible!" He raised his voice and said briskly, "Now come along. . ." And taking her arm pressed it as an indication she was to lead the way. Involuntarily she obeyed and turned towards the direction from which he had come when he had first passed her. As they moved off together, the police-officer called out heartily: "Good-night, sir."

The Doctor condescended to throw him a brief "good-night" over his shoulder.

Several minutes later they arrived at the front entrance to Bankside Mansions. It was a typical block of flats of the smaller type, with a short flight of steps running up from the pavement to the doorway. The double doors were still open and Doctor Morelle paused at the entrance to survey the small foyer beyond.

"Here we are," said Miss Frayle unnecessarily.

"The porter is still on duty." He turned to her. "Did he see you come out?"

"No. . . I used the back stairs, not the lift. We're only on the second floor." They had spoken in low tones, for the porter whom Doctor Morelle had observed was standing by the lift-gates expectantly awaiting their approach. They went in.

"'Ello, Miss Frayle?" the porter greeted her cheerily, but with a note of slight surprise. "Good-evenin', sir." He was an undersized, sandy-haired man, aged about forty-five. He wore a dark uniform, but no cap. There was a cigarette-stub peeping from behind one ear. As they stepped into the lift Miss Frayle made a forlorn attempt to brighten up.

"Good-evening," she said, but her smile was unconvincing.

"You looks a bit done-in, Miss," commiserated the porter, clanging the lift-gates together and pressing the button. The lift whirred upwards.

"The young lady was taken ill in the street," said Doctor Morelle.

"Oh, dear," exclaimed the other sadly, shifting his gaze from Miss Frayle and staring at her companion. After a pause during which the Doctor gazed abstractedly into space, the man said: "I didn't notice yer go out, Miss."

She began to answer him, stammering to find a non-committal explanation, but Doctor Morelle covered her confused fluttering, asking slowly: "You've been on duty here all evening, have you?"

"S'right. I'm just goin' orf now. My missus sometimes gets them attacks," with a nod towards Miss Frayle. "Verdegris, the doctor calls it. . . Second floor!"

The lift stopped, the gates opened and they stepped out.

"Well, I 'opes yer'll be better in the morning, Miss."

"Thank you."

"Mr. Dacre ain't arrived yet," he went on, as he closed the gates after him. "Expect he will presently. Good-night," and he disappeared from view.

Doctor Morelle turned to her. "Who is Mr. Dacre?"

"Her nephew. She was Miss Dacre," she explained. Her face lit up slightly. "He's very kind." She frowned. "I'd forgotten he's expected tonight. Oh, it'll be awful for him — "

"And you lived with her alone? Except when he came?"

"Yes."

They stood in front of a door painted pale green with a chromium number on it. She refrained from saying: "This is the flat"—somewhat to his disappointment—instead produced a key and turned it in the Yale lock. He followed her into the small hall, closing the door behind him. She went on ahead of him, while he stood and gazed round with apparent disinterest. On his right was a miniature hall-stand holding a woman's overcoat, hat and umbrella. Beyond it a door, closed; another door beyond that, slightly ajar. On his left was a large window, then a passage, probably leading to the kitchen and bathroom; past that another door, closed. The floor was carpeted; there were two or three prints on the walls and a bowl of flowers in a corner.

"You left the light on," he said.

13

She was about to enter the room directly in front of her, the door of which was half-open. She turned and said apologetically: "I know. I must have forgotten when I rushed out."

He took off his hat, placed it on a chair, with his walking-stick alongside and his gloves. "This—this is her room," she whispered. "I—I must have left the light on here, too."

He moved towards where she stood, irresolute. If he noticed her face was white and that she was visibly trembling he gave no sign. "She always locked her bedroom door when she went to bed."

"What was she afraid of?"

"Her jewellery. She kept it in her room."

"The door is half-open now. Was it like that when you came back after posting the letters?"

She nodded. "The light wasn't on."

"You have already explained you must have omitted to switch it off when you made your precipitate exit."

Again she nodded dumbly. Then moaned: "I—I can't go in again."

"You must. Follow me." He preceded her into the bedroom. He stood at the foot of the bed for a moment, then moved swiftly round to Miss Dacre. She was dead and her end had been a violent one. A brief, cursory examination was all that was necessary to show she had been smothered to death. He stood up, lit a cigarette. Behind him a weak, shaky voice said: "Oh, it's too horrible."

Without giving her a glance he snapped:

"Then sit down and look the other way."

Feeling sick and faint Miss Frayle obeyed. It seemed to him apparent a pillow had been used to suffocate the woman; he was about to bend to examine one which was disarranged from the others when something soft and warm brushed against his leg. With an exclamation of slight surprise he glanced down.

"What —? Whose cat?"

"Miss Dacre's." She called to the animal, purring loudly now. "Pharaoh, come here?"

A flicker of amusement showed on Doctor Morelle's lips. "Pharaoh?"

"She believed cats were the reincarnation of Egyptian gods," Miss Frayle explained.

"He has a very dark complexion for an Egyptian!" was his dry comment. Suddenly he stooped to examine something on the floor. He did not touch the object, but noted it had fallen as if dropped from the dead woman's left hand which drooped over the side of the bed.

"That's her lorgnette," offered Miss Frayle helpfully as she stroked the cat now curled at her feet.

14

"I had already surmised that myself," he replied. He went on, half-aloud: "The cord's broken as if wrenched from her neck."

"You mean, there was a struggle?"

"No doubt your deduction might be correct!"

A thrill of excitement momentarily replaced her trepidation and apprehension. He added without a glimmer of amusement in his face: "Would you not care to wrap the exhibit in my handkerchief?"

Her spectacles nearly slipped off her nose as she hastened to obey his suggestion. If she heard it she did not heed the sardonic note in his voice as he murmured: "Carefully, in case there may be some finger-prints on it! Now, place it on that table."

She could hardly speak with excitement. "You—you think it might be a cl-clue?" she stammered.

"Not for one moment! Merely that you seem to attach such importance to it!"

Her face fell. "Oh . . . Well, perhaps I'd better sit down again and mind Pharaoh."

"That might prove of some positive assistance, Miss Frayle. Or perhaps you could —?" He broke off. "Just a moment," he said and crossed the room. "The window is slightly open, I perceive."

"That's unusual . . . She always kept it closed at night."

"Unhygienic!" he remarked, opening the window wider and peering out. "It leads to the fire-escape. It would have been a relatively simple matter for someone to force the catch and enter and exit this way."

"You mean the murderer?"

"He would hardly have called in merely to say 'good-night'! I wonder if her jewellery has been removed—? No matter for the moment." He gazed round the room abstractedly as he moved over to her. "You say she always locked herself in at night? Wouldn't she open the door to anyone?"

"Only sometimes to her nephew. He looked after her business interests. If he came in late from the City when he was staying here she'd want to talk to him perhaps about business."

"I gather Miss Dacre was a woman of means?"

"She was well-off, yes. But—but rather mean."

He fixed his eyes upon her. With a chill running down her spine she saw that his pupils perceptibly expanded and contracted. They gripped her with an almost sinister fascination, so that she was compelled to rivet her gaze on his. After a moment, when she felt she was about to succumb to a mesmeric trance, his eye-lids flickered down and he turned his head to knock the long ash from his cigarette.

"You didn't like her very much, did you?" he murmured without

15

looking at her. She drew a deep breath to steady her voice. I didn't,"
she said quietly. " But I wouldn't—wouldn't have done that."

He replaced the cigarette between his lips and expelled a spiral
of smoke ceilingwards. " I should like to question the hall-porter."
" I'll get him."

" That was what I was about to request," he said. " However,
you have anticipated my wish." He gave her a bleak smile that
seemed to her quite terrifying. " I'll go now," she said quickly.

He called after her: " Place the cat in another room. See it
does not contrive to escape."

The hall-porter when he arrived accompanied by Miss Frayle was
suitably impressed with the horror of the tragedy. He had changed
the jacket of his uniform for a worn sports-coat, and had removed
his collar and tie. He mumbled an apology for his appearance,
explaining he was preparing for bed when Miss Frayle had called
him. " Poor lady, wot a terrible thing to have happened," was his
comment when acquainted with the circumstances of Mrs. Dacre's
death. He seemed sincerely affected. " One of the nicest tenants
we have—er— " he corrected himself self-consciously " —had."

Doctor Morelle's gaze rested on a spot somewhere above the
other's head. Nevertheless he had not failed to register the man's
pallor and a nerve that twitched at the corner of his right eye. He
was trembling slightly, too.

" Before we call the police," he said, " perhaps you might care to
answer one or two questions? "

" Er—well, there ain't much I can say. You see— "

" You look somewhat shaken."

" Well, I— "

" It must be an awful shock for you," Miss Frayle put in sympathetically, and then catching the Doctor's chill look upon her,
realised her temerity in speaking and fell into abashed silence.
The porter glanced at the bed—the body had been covered by a
sheet by Doctor Morelle—and nodded glumly.

" Yes, it is," he said.

" Doubtless it is an unnerving experience. Partake of a cigarette,
it will help to restore your equilibrium." And the Doctor extended
his thin gold cigarette-case.

Gingerly the other took a Le Sphinx. " Oh, thank yer,
sir—er—Doctor." And: " Oh, thanks ever so," as Doctor
Morelle held out his lighter.

" Now . . . tell me, you have been on duty all this evening, I
seem to recollect you declaring? "

" Since tea-time."

" Can you also recollect what persons used the lift while you
were in charge of it? "

16

"There wasn't very many." He pondered for a moment. "Let's see . . . It was just after I come on I took Miss Jarrow up to her flat on the third. About five o'clock that'd be . . . Then half-an-hour later, I suppose, I brings Mr. and Mrs. Farrell down from the fourth . . . Little arter six I took Mr. Riley up to three—he was visitin' Mr. Woodham, tenant of the flat there, often does . . . And then . . ." He paused, scratching his head.

"It would appear no one unknown to you made use of the lift? "

"No." The answer was definite.

"How about the stairs? " Miss Frayle said. "Mightn't somebody have— "

The Doctor's voice was like a whip-lash. "I am not incapable of conducting my own interrogation, Miss Frayle."

She mumbled an apology, blushing and fiddling with her spectacles. The porter coughed in a sympathetic effort to cover up her embarrassment, and eyed his cigarette. "Posh cigarettes, these, all right," he said. "Don't often smoke one like this," and tried a half-grin to relieve the tension. All of which was lost on Doctor Morelle, who was not even aware either of them had said anything.

"You took Miss Frayle down when she went out to the post? " he pursued.

"'S'right. About ten that was."

The Doctor did not condescend to glance at her for corroboration of this. The other went on: "Out about fifteen minutes she was, then I brings her back up here again. 'S'right, ain't it, Miss? "

Miss Frayle nodded mutely.

"The—er, ah—stairs? "

"I tell yer nobody could've used them without me seeing 'em. Even the times I'm in the lift I keeps me peepers peeled. Been one or two burglaries round these parts, lately there have, so I— "

"You seem positive no one could have visited any of the flats, and this one in particular, without your cognisance? "

"Eh? " The man gaped at him without understanding for a moment. Then it sank in. "No," he declared. "No one could have, and that's a fact. Stake me life."

"I imagine the lift may be operated by remote control? "

"Oh, yes. So if me or the other porter 'appens to be orf for the moment, anyone wantin' it can call the lift and work it theirselves. But we're usually around when the bell rings."

"And the porter who was on duty before you? "

The other laughed confidently. "He wouldn't let no one up without arskin' 'em their business. More'n his job's worth. No. I'm no deteckertive, but it strikes me somebody from one o' the flats must have done the pore lady in." He tapped the ash off his cigarette with an aggressively knowing air. Doctor Morelle

17

regarded the grey ash in the ash-tray momentarily and then eyed the cigarette which the other had returned to his mouth.

" I think we may count ourselves fortunate that you are *not* a— " he paused almost imperceptibly to emphasise the correct pronunciation " — detective! "

The man shifted uncomfortably. As if there was a somewhat unpleasant odour offending his sensitively chiselled nose, the Doctor turned away from him and addressed Miss Frayle: " During your brief absence just now," he said, " I took the opportunity of ascertaining that there is a tradesman's entrance from the kitchen. It opens onto the iron staircase which connects also with the fire-escape." He inclined his head to the window and then regarded her unblinkingly.

She stared at him uneasily. Was he waiting for her to speak? she asked herself, fidgetting nervously with the collar of her dress. She decided perhaps he was expecting her to say something. " Yes—that—that's quite right," she stammered, and then stopped, awaiting his cold rebuke.

" I am gratified to learn," he murmured sardonically, " that you are not entirely devoid of your articulatory powers! "

Miserably, Miss Frayle looked at him through her spectacles. Whatever she said or left unsaid, did or did not do, it was bound it seemed to be wrong so far as he was concerned. The first glimmerings of a realisation that there was nothing she could do about this state of affairs began to break in on her consciousness. She could not know she was in fact establishing a basis for a philosophy upon which she was in future to rely.

He was speaking again. She strove to concentrate upon what he said. Her desire to please him was so obvious it would have been pathetic—to anyone but Doctor Morelle.

" I ascertained furthermore," he was saying, " that the kitchen-door opening onto the iron staircase was locked and bolted on the inside." He paused to draw at his cigarette and slowly expelled the smoke. " What," he queried, " does that convey to you? "

She goggled at him helplessly. " To—to me? " she said. He nodded. She creased her brow. " The door was locked and bolted on the inside," she repeated slowly. " I—I'm sorry, but I can't see anything special in that. It always was locked and bolted at night."

" Quite right, too," put in the porter.

" Unless," she went on hopefully, " it means that no one could have got into the flat that way while I was out? "

He rewarded her with fleeting quirk of his thin lips. " Precisely, my *dear* Miss Frayle," he said. But she couldn't decide whether his over-emphasised term of affection was meant in a kindly way or as sheer sarcasm. She concluded it must be the latter.

" I can't see as it could mean more'n that, neither," the other man volunteered.

" Your opinion was not solicited," came the instant rejoinder and at that moment they heard a faint humming sound.

" Someone usin' the lift," explained the porter at once.

" It's probably Mr. Dacre! " she exclaimed.

" Ar," said the man and made as if to move to the bedroom door. Doctor Morelle shot a glance at Miss Frayle's agitated face and snapped: " You think so? " then to the other: " Remain here! "

" Why? Wot—? "

" Do as I instruct you! "

" Here, wot the blazes—? " The man's tone was truculent, though he stood irresolutely staring at the Doctor.

" In point of fact," was snapped back at him, " you will find yourself unable to do otherwise! The cigarette you have been smoking contains a narcotic which completely paralyses the nether limbs."

The porter gulped, speechless, terror-stricken. Beads of perspiration glistened on his face. He stood as if rooted to the spot. Doctor Morelle turned to Miss Frayle, who stood with mouth agape: " Quick! Bring my walking-stick. Close the front-door. Switch off the hall-light and return here. Move—! "

Miss Frayle shot out of the room as if from a catapult and was back in an instant. The whine of the lift grew louder. He took his walking-stick from her without a word and motioned her to one side. As the lift jerked to a stop and they heard the gates slide open, he switched off the light and swiftly but quietly closed the bedroom door. They were in darkness. The sound of the porter's laboured, puzzled breathing was broken by Miss Frayle gasping: " Doctor! What—what are you going to —? "

" Sssh! Quiet! Not a sound from either of you! "

She subsided, and the porter who was about to protest against such swift and unexpected happenings, groaned and was also silent. There was a moment's pause, then the sound of a key turning in the Yale lock. Miss Frayle shivered with apprehension. Perhaps it was not her nice Mr. Dacre, after all. Perhaps it was—she hardly dare allow the idea take shape—perhaps it was the murderer, returning to the scene of his crime. A phrase she had once read came back to her, ill-remembered, but something to the effect that murderers always return to the scene of their dark deed.

The front door opened and closed. Footsteps approached, then a voice called out: " Miss Frayle . . . ! " It was nice Mr. Dacre after all. She relaxed with a little smile and drew a breath to call out to him, when a hand was clamped over her mouth. Doctor

19

Morelle's voice hissed in her ear: "Keep quiet! *Don't answer!*"

Again the newcomer's pleasant voice was heard: "Miss Frayle! Are you there—?"

There was a slight pause as if he was making sure there was no reply, then the bedroom door opened and the light snapped on.

"What —?" Dacre began, staring first at Doctor Morelle, who stood leaning negligently on his walking-stick, then at the porter, who tried to grin that he wasn't at all responsible for such proceedings.

"Mr. Dacre —" stammered Miss Frayle as his gaze rested on her. But that was as far as she got, for the Doctor's soft: "Good-evening" swung his eyes back to him. He was a tallish, pleasant-faced young man, frowning now and nonplussed. Suddenly he saw the shape on the bed, and a quick glance at their faces brought from him a gasp of inquiry:

"Oh! . . . What—what's happened?"

With a quick movement he was at the bedside. "Oohh—!" A great cry of distress and shocked, broken tones: "The poor thing—! Oh . . . the poor thing—!"

"This must be a terrible shock to you, I know—" Doctor Morelle said quietly.

Dacre shot a look up at him, a penetrating glance, and his voice was belligerent. "Who are you?"

Miss Frayle began: "Mr. Dacre, I—I—if you'll let me explain—"

The Doctor brushed her aside. "I am Doctor Morelle," he said with great dignity, great simplicity. "Miss Frayle—er—called me in."

"Oh . . ." Dacre gestured towards the bed. "When did this—this happen?"

"Death occurred between forty and fifty minutes ago . . . As a result of suffocation." He glanced down suddenly as something warm and soft brushed against his legs. He fixed a cold stare on Miss Frayle. "I thought I instructed you—?" he began, but she broke in.

"I'm so sorry! I couldn't have closed the door properly on him. I'm *so* sorry . . ." She called to the cat. "Pharaoh, come here—" Purring loudly the animal walked slowly over to her.

Doctor Morelle turned to Dacre. "The facts in this—er—unfortunate tragedy may be elucidated quite simply." He spoke slowly, enjoying the full flavour of the attention that was now rivetted on him. He paused and calmly swept their faces with his gaze until again he was speaking to the young man. He allowed a faintly derisive smile to play about the corner of his mouth, and taking a Le Sphinx from his cigarette-case, lighting it, said:

20

"But I feel sure, Mr. Dacre, you would not wish to be bored by my recapitulation of those facts? "

Miss Frayle noticed his grasp of the walking-stick tightened as Dacre took a pace forward, his jaw set. "What the devil d'you mean? " he demanded.

Without taking his eyes off him, the Doctor spoke to the porter: "Go into the sitting-room," he said, "and telephone the police . . . It is all right, you will be able to move now, the effects of the narcotic have worn off."

Muttering the man started for the door.

"Keep back—! " Doctor Morelle rapped out the words as Dacre lunged forward at the porter. As he spoke there was a scrape of steel and the blade flashed from his walking-stick, its point at the young man's chest. Dacre stepped back, his face suddenly haggard and grey, a wild, trapped look on it.

"Blimey! A swordstick! " exclaimed the porter and dived into another room where he could be heard urgently telephoning Scotland Yard.

There was a moan and a thud behind Doctor Morelle as Miss Frayle collapsed in a dead faint. Doctor Morelle, however, did not take his eyes off the dangerous figure he held pinned in the corner. Somehow he seemed to convey the impression that even had he been able with safety to turn his head, he would hardly have bothered to do so.

Doctor Morelle lit his Le Sphinx and said:

"Waiting outside the flats until the moment he saw Miss Frayle go out to the post, Dacre slipped, by way of the tradesman's entrance, up the iron staircase. He entered the flat by the kitchen-window, which he had carefully studied and learned how with the aid of a thin, strong penknife he could contrive to open from the outside. By knocking at his aunt's bedroom in the usual way he was by that unsuspecting woman admitted."

He was addressing his elucidation of Miss Dacre's murder to the Divisional Inspector. They were in the sitting-room of the flat. Dacre had been removed, after breaking down and confessing to the crime. In the bedroom the police-surgeon had made his examination; and photographers and finger-print experts were completing their work. Miss Frayle, somewhat recovered from her faintness but bemused and terribly tired, sat listening to Doctor Morelle, trying hard to take in what he was saying. The Divisional Inspector raised an expectant eyebrow and the Doctor proceeded:

"After Dacre had smothered her with the aid of the pillow, he took the jewels—the motive for his crime—and made his exit through the bedroom window, deliberately leaving it open to create the impression the murder was an outside affair. He had closed the kitchen-window behind him. Unfortunately for him, however, he committed one error."

He paused again, this time to heighten to the full the dramatic effect of his next words. The Divisional Inspector however took this opportunity to observe sententiously: "They always do!"

The Doctor eyed him coldly. "He omitted to lock the bedroom door behind him," he went on, an ill-tempered note in his voice, "and gave away damning knowledge of his error when he returned later. For . . . thinking Miss Frayle to be absent he walked directly into his aunt's room, *without pause to knock or even test whether it was locked.* Had Dacre been innocent of any knowledge of his aunt's death he would certainly, believing her to be alive, have gone through his habitual procedure before entering the room." He allowed himself a sardonic smile of triumph as the Divisional Inspector stared at him in open admiration.

"By God, that was smart of you!" the other exclaimed. "Damned smart!"

Doctor Morelle gave a slight shrug and knocked the ash off his Le Sphinx.

Miss Frayle said: "I still don't understand about that drugged cigarette you gave the porter . . ."

He spread his hands in an indulgent gesture. "The cigarette was, of course, perfectly innocuous. I fear I was prevaricating when I informed him it was a paralysing drug. I merely wished to prevent him from revealing to Dacre that we were in the flat."

She said:

"But it *did* paralyse him—he couldn't move a step!"

"Merely auto-suggestion, my *dear* Miss Frayle. His will-power is considerably under-developed, and I found him a singularly easy subject on whom to demonstrate the—er—shall we say—peculiar gifts I happen to possess!" And with wonderfully assumed casualness Doctor Morelle crushed the stub of his cigarette into the ash-tray.

CHAPTER II

THE CASE OF THE SOMNAMBULIST'S SECRET

Miss Frayle glanced briefly at her diary, was about to close it when her eyes widened behind her spectacles, her mouth made an O of incredulity. She glanced again at the page and made a rapid mental calculation. It was true, she had been with him a year. With a long sigh she leant back in her chair and stared out of the window.

Her thoughts retraced themselves over the past months. It seemed ages ago—and yet it might have been only yesterday—when she first met him. Anyway it had been a year unique in her experience. Unique, she told herself, in the experience of any young woman. A year she was not likely to forget. Moreover she was beginning to arrive at the uncomfortable conviction that the year beginning and each one succeeding it would be equally strenuous, hectic and disturbing, equally nightmarish.

Doctor Morelle was like that. His magnetic personality not only attracted all with whom he came into contact (while it simultaneously repelled some) it also attracted Trouble. Miss Frayle spelt it in her mind with a capital " T " because it wasn't ordinary trouble. Not at all the kind she had associated with a doctor's practice, such as awkward patients, urgent midnight telephone calls and so on. Nothing like that about *him!* No, it was always Trouble that was queer and sinister.

Like that business about the Grey Parrot. With anyone else it would have been psittacosis or something. Not very nice for the poor parrot and upsetting for its owners, of course. But when the Doctor investigated the Grey Parrot affair it turned out to be much worse than anything like that. She repressed a shudder as she thought about it. A horrid, fantastic business. She had nightmares about it still.*

She supposed she was being rather unjust to the Doctor. He wasn't really the cause for awful things happening, it was silly to pretend he was. But if only he wasn't so interested in anything unusual, so—she searched her mind for the word—so bizarre. That was it. If only he would just deal with ordinary cases the same as any other Harley Street doctor. She got up and went to a shelf of books that chanced to catch her eye.

The titles alone were enough to frighten one. In German, French and Italian, with words like *Kriminalanthropologie und Kriminalistik; Médecine Légale, Technique Policière, Criminelle,* and so on . . . The walls of the study were lined with books devoted to such subjects ; there were filing-cabinets crammed with information on the same theme. The Doctor had one bookcase which ran from floor to ceiling locked, and on an occasion when she had asked the reason for this precaution, his reply had sent chills down her spine. Once or twice a morbid curiosity had prompted her to glance at the thick dossiers ranged behind the glass, but they bore only index-numbers for titles. She often thought they really contained nothing

---

* The sinister machinations which Doctor Morelle discovered behind the death of a certain financier's African grey parrot must at present remain secret. One of the chief actors in the case is still alive.

frightening at all, and the Doctor's answer to her question about them had simply been another example of his twisted, sardonic sense of humour. All the same even if she did happen to possess the key she wouldn't have opened the bookcase for a thousand pounds.

The telephone broke into Miss Frayle's dubious speculation on the contents of a thick volume bearing a long and sinister sounding title in Spanish.

"Hello . . . This is Doctor Morelle's house. Yes. Oh, yes. Ten-forty to-night at the hospital. I'll tell the Doctor, and will you please convey his thanks to Sir Andrew? Thank you so much. Good-bye."

She replaced the receiver and made a note in the Doctor's diary. It was an invitation from Sir Andrew Ridley, the eminent brain specialist, for Doctor Morelle to witness an operation that night. It was an invitation he had been awaiting for the past few days, for the operation was in the nature of an experiment, a new drug being used in connection with it. It was the drug and its effects in which the Doctor was particularly interested. He had been a pioneer in the research work upon it. As a result of his exhaustive study and experiments he and Ridley both felt that a revolutionary discovery had been made which would be of inestimable value in the case of certain more delicate brain-operations. Ridley was most enthusiastic about the possibilities of the Doctor's new-found preparation, and was determined to put it into practice upon the first opportunity. That opportunity had now arisen and the surgeon had sent a message asking that Doctor Morelle should be present.

As Miss Frayle scribbled the note the study suddenly darkened and she glanced up to see the sky above the houses opposite was overcast. In a moment there came a gust of wind and a spatter of rain drove against the windows. She frowned and then hurried along to the laboratory where Doctor Morelle was engaged upon some other research work, this time in connection with the final stages of a blood-test experiment.* She wanted to inform him of Sir Andrew's news, while there were a number of other appointments of which to remind him. Apart from these an empty inner sensation proclaimed to her the not unimportant fact that it was approaching lunch-time.

Doctor Morelle was however destined not to be present at the operation to which he had been invited, nor was he to witness the completely successful response of the drug he had discovered to the test to which it was subjected. This disappointment was perhaps

* See his *Positive Evidence in Bloodstain Classification* (Manning & Hopper), London. (Also published by Karter, New York, and translated into Spanish and French).

THE CASE OF THE SOMNAMBULIST'S SECRET

counter-balanced by an exciting if somewhat sinister chain of incidents which were set in motion at about the time he should have been setting off for the hospital.

The rain had continued all day and rattled now with unabated fury against the curtained windows. Miss Frayle stood at the study-door, holding it open with one hand, while with the other buttoning the top of her rain-coat. She gave an anxious look at the figure bent over the mass of papers on the wide desk, apparently oblivious of her presence. Hesitatingly she drew a deep breath and stammered:

"Doctor Morelle—"

"What is it—what *is* it? " he snapped without raising his head.

"You—you're due at the hospital at ten-forty, and it's gone ten-fifteen already."

He looked up at once, his expression almost sinister in the glow of the desk-lamp. He turned to the clock in front of him. "Ten-sixteen! And the operation scheduled for ten-forty . . . Why was I not informed it was so late? "

Rising, he thrust the papers to one side with a gesture of irritation and eyed her accusingly. "Do not stand there goggling at me, answer my question! " She opened her mouth to explain this was the fourth time she had reminded him in the last fifteen minutes of his appointment, but knew she might as well save her breath. "And might you not agree," he went on relentlessly "that if you removed that agonised expression of self-abnegation from your face and obtained a taxi, it would facilitate my arrival at the hospital? "

"I'll see if I can find one cruising past."

"Thank you! " he replied sardonically. Then in a tone full of self-commiseration: "As you have omitted to bring my coat and hat I will procure them for myself." Miss Frayle gave him a look and hurried away. Returning a few minutes later she found him waiting, tall and dominating in a long overcoat, his walking-stick under his arm.

"I've got a taxi," she said with breathless triumph. "It's outside the door."

"I did not imagine you had prevailed upon the driver to bring it into the hall! " he said.

"I was lucky to get it, a night like this. It's still raining."

He surveyed her glistening coat with over-elaborate surprise. "Really? " he murmured. "I was fully under the impression you had been spraying yourself with a watering-can of the horticultural variety! " Pulling on his gloves he snapped: "Come along! I have something more important to do than listen to your obvious ineptitudes."

She followed his gaunt figure, closing the front door behind
25

them. They stood on the step and bent to the rain-gusts. The taxi-man opened the door and the Doctor motioned her to get in while he gave the address. As he was about to direct the driver, Miss Frayle gave a piercing scream and backed agitatedly out of the taxi, stumbling and half-falling onto the pavement.

"Oh—! Oh, Doctor Morelle—! "

He caught her arm and prevented her from collapsing altogether. She was moaning now hysterically. "Good heavens! What is it —? " he snapped.

The taxi-man lurched across in his seat and said hoarsely: "Blimey—! Wot's up—? "

She managed to gasp: "In—in there! Something—a—a—body!"

"Body? "

"Body! " echoed the driver, nearly falling out of his seat in astonishment. "Body, did she say? Oo's—? "

"Oh! " moaned Miss Frayle. "I—I touched its face—! " She shuddered with horror.

"Switch on a light, driver."

"Yes, Guv'nor." The man obeyed and clambering down, came round to join them. "Must be seein' things! " he started to grumble, then broke off with a grunt. "Blimey! " he exclaimed, "she ain't!"

Eyes narrowed the Doctor regarded the interior of the taxi and remarked: "If you wish to faint, Miss Frayle, do so elsewhere. One inanimate form is sufficient for the moment." She reeled to the luggage-space beside the driver's seat and sat there, her head between her knees. The rain trickled down the back of her neck.

"Wheeeyew! " whistled the taximan through his teeth. "Dead all right by the looks of him! "

"Hmm . . . Paper-knife driven into his heart."

"Messy sight, ain't it? All that blood on his evening shirt—lucky none of it's got on my floor. But how the devil did he get into my cab? "

"The answer to that question remains to be ascertained. If, meanwhile, you would assist me to carry him into my house."

"Yes sir." The man, still puzzling, pushed his cap back and scratched his bald head. "Yer see," he went on in explanation, "you were first fare I 'ad ternight, since I left me rank."

"Open the front-door, Miss Frayle," the Doctor called, snapping her into action. "Come on, come on! "

She stood up, shivered as the rain ran half way down her back and as if in a trance obeyed. The driver said: "Shall I take the feet, Guv'nor, and you 'is head? " Together they carried the body within, the rain beating at them. They placed the dead man in the consulting-room.

26

A little later Doctor Morelle, having concluded his examination came into the study and placed the paper-knife, wrapped carefully in a handkerchief, on his desk. Miss Frayle stared at it in fascinated horror. She and the driver had been waiting for the Doctor, and the taximan now sat up and cocked an inquiring eye. "Pulled it out, did yer?"

Doctor Morelle made no reply, but thoughtfully lit an inevitable Le Sphinx. After a moment he said: "Your surmise then, driver, is that while you left your vehicle, which was alone, on the rank—? "

"Just popped into the pub round the corner, I did."

"Someone—the murderer, or murderers, presumably, must have deposited the body— "

"That's right, bunged it in me taxi. Blimey, bit of a sauce, eh, Miss? " He turned to Miss Frayle who was blinking at them through her spectacles. Doctor Morelle contrived to curb his impatience with the man's garrulity. He proceeded smoothly: " All forms of identification have been carefully removed from the deceased. Nothing in his pockets offers any clue. One thing, however, I did observe— "

" I noticed that while his clothes were slightly damp, the soles of his shoes aren't a bit wet or muddy—was that what you were going to say, Doctor? " It was Miss Frayle who somewhat recovered from the shock she had suffered now made the interruption, taking the words out of his mouth.

"I do wish you would mind your own business! " he snapped at her. " I am supposed to— "

"Crikey! " suddenly exclaimed the taxi-driver, banging his cap on his knee, " that's it! I remember now—! "

"What," asked Doctor Morelle irritably, " have you recollected?"

" I seen that bloke afore! That scar on his cheek . . . Yes, that's right! Blimey! Why 'e come out of an 'ouse opposite my rank, and I took him down to the City."

Miss Frayle gave a squeak of excitement. " A house by your rank? "

" S'right. Coupler days ago. It was that scar wot reminded me."

" In which case it might facilitate his identification if you drove me there forthwith," the Doctor observed.

" Okay."

" Come along, Miss Frayle . . . "

The rain had slackened to a drizzle when they drew up outside a medium-sized house standing back slightly from the road. A narrow strip of garden on either side isolated it from the other houses, and two or three trees and high shrubbery helped to screen it from passers-by. Opposite as the driver had said was a taxicab-rank in the middle of the wide road. The rank was deserted. Miss Frayle and Doctor Morelle stepped out of the taxi, and after he had said something in an undertone to the driver, they both made their way to the front-door. The wind soughed in the trees and the rain dripped mournfully against the dark, untidy foliage.

Suddenly the Doctor paused abruptly. He had caught a movement at a ground-floor window, the flash of a man's face, white against the darkness. Then the curtain had been quickly drawn again. Miss Frayle, meanwhile, noticing nothing ascended the steps and pressed the bell. She turned as he joined her.

"Have you rung? " he said.

Unable to resist the chance of getting a little of her own back, she answered: "Oh, no, Doctor! I guessed whoever's at home must be psychic! "

"Then perhaps you might care to ring again," he said with elaborate politeness. She rang twice, long shrilling rings whose echoes within came back to them. There was no reply. Doctor Morelle tapped his stick on the edge of a step, his eyes narrowed speculatively. After a moment he stepped down and crossed to the window. The window at which the mysterious face had appeared. He gave it a brief survey and quickly raised himself onto the wide sill two or three feet from the ground. He took a narrow torch from an inside pocket. It was an ordinary type window, the upper and lower frames secured in the middle by a catch. The light from his torch enabled him to examine it through the glass and he gave an exclamation of satisfaction. He eased the blade of a thin penknife along the centre join. After a moment's pressure there was a sharp click as the catch sprang back.

"What are you doing, Doctor? " Miss Frayle stood below, looking up at him, eyes wide behind her spectacles. He gave her a sardonic glance, pressed against the lower half of the window and as it squeaked upwards said: "Effecting an entrance by way of this window, my *dear* Miss Frayle! "

"Oh, but we can't go in that way! Someone might see us! A policeman, or— "

"What a timorous creature! Very well, you remain behind and whistle if danger approaches! "

"The house seems very dark and quiet. Perhaps the taxi-driver was mistaken, or—not telling the truth. Anyway there seems to be nobody here."

He merely looked back in the direction of the road. The sound of the taxi-engine ticking over could be heard. He smiled enigmatically and said: "Are you accompanying me or remaining behind? "

"I—er—I suppose I'd better come with you."

"I warn you—" he began darkly.

"I know," she said quickly. "There may be trouble. All the same I'll feel safer with you, and anyway I'm tired of the rain trickling down the back of my neck! . . . I can't whistle either! "

"Let us enter," he said, holding out his hand. She grasped it and stood beside him. "Follow me." And pushing the curtain aside, he landed lightly in the room. A moment later and she half fell in, banging her head on the window and bringing from him an unsympathetic chuckle.

"It's awfully dark."

"A moment and I will ascertain the whereabouts of the light-switch.". A door showed up black against the lighter coloured wall, and he moved over to it unerringly.

"You must have eyes like a cat! " she said.

They were in a well-furnished room, and moved noiselessly on a thick, richly purple carpet. She blinked in the sudden strong light and a fresh wave of panic and doubt assailed her. "Suppose the police *do* catch us? "

"I imagined you had considered that before you joined me on this burglarious exploit! "

"But it's your fault. You told me to— "

He silenced her protest with a warning wave of the hand and silently opened the door. She followed him into the wide hall. He switched on the light. In the heavy silence that lay over the house, a grandfather clock was ticking away somewhere. It sounded abnormally loud.

"Everything's so quiet," she breathed.

"Still as the tomb! " He said it deliberately to frighten her. He felt her gasp convulsively and clutch at his arm. With a sardonic smile he. turned to her. She was staring, eyes like saucers at something ahead of her. He followed her gaze. At the top of the staircase leading down into the hall stood a figure.

"What—what—? " gurgled Miss Frayle incoherently.

"Do control yourself! " he snapped irritably.

"Coming downstairs—Doctor, look—! "

"A somewhat curious apparition."

"It's—it's a woman—! "

"Attired one might suppose in a not unbecoming negligee! "

"She looks so strange . . . her eyes—! "

"Hmm . . . A remarkable example of somnambulism. Keep quiet."

Miss Frayle gulped and clutched his arm more tightly. "You —you mean she's walking in her sleep? "

"Precisely, Miss Frayle. Watch . . . She is descending as if with some definite purpose."

"What shall we do if she comes this way? "

29

They were talking in whispers. Now the woman reached the foot of the stairs and seemed to be about to approach them. Miss Frayle hardly breathed the question. Suddenly the woman stopped and turned slowly.

" She is proceeding across the hall."

They watched her move slowly but purposefully towards a door. On reaching it she stopped then opened it and went in. There came the click of the switch as she snapped on the electric light.

" Oughtn't we to do something? " asked Miss Frayle anxiously.

" Wait here a moment. Possibly the creature will be coming this way again."

She shuddered. " It's so creepy! "

" Sssh—! Here she comes now . . ."

" Still sleep-walking! "

" Going back upstairs. No doubt returning to her room . . There she goes."

" It's uncanny."

The woman reached the top of the staircase and disappeared from view.

" She's left the door open," said Miss Frayle, pointing to the shaft of light that came from the room the sleep-walker had just left.

" We might investigate now and ascertain what, if anything, it was attracted her there," said the Doctor. " Come along."

She followed him and stood just behind him as he paused in the doorway. It was a small library, also used as a study as the heavy, carved desk at one end showed. It was this which at once caught Miss Frayle's attention.

" Look! " she gasped. " Sitting there—! "

Doctor Morelle crossed the room. " Hmm . . . curious attitude," he murmured. " I fear we shall never wake *him*."

Miss Frayle stared at the inert figure slumped over the desk, a bullet-wound in his temple. Drops of blood had run down onto his evening shirt. " He's dead," she whispered and suddenly felt violently sick. " Oh—! " she moaned, " I think I'm going to faint—! "

" Do not be so foolish! " he snapped irritably. " Sit down—put your head between your knees! " She managed to reach a chair and fell into it, then proceeded to follow his advice. She felt terrible. " This is no time for hysterics," she heard him saying, as if from far-off, his voice cold as ice. Then he was murmuring to himself: " Obviously self-inflicted . . . Death must have occurred only a short while ago . . ."

He found the revolver beside the dead man's chair, where it had fallen from his hand. He was about to pick it up for a closer examination, when Miss Frayle gave a gasp of alarm and a man in

30

butler's attire stood in the doorway. His heavy face wore a scowl of interrogation.

"What are you doing here?" he demanded belligerently, coming towards them. He stopped with a horrified look as he saw the figure at the desk. "Colonel Mason—! What—what's happened—?" he choked.

Doctor Morelle said: "I am afraid he is dead."

"But—but—? What—?" The man's shocked dismay was painful to watch. "Oh, this is terrible—"

"He has been shot, as you perceive."

"Murdered—?"

The Doctor gave him a quick look. "Why should you imagine it is a case of homicide?"

"I—I—don't know. I—I—what else could it be—?"

"It might be an accident. It might be *felo-de-se*. As it happens it is the latter."

"Suicide?"

"That conclusion is compatible with the evidence before me."

The butler's gaze travelled from the Doctor to Miss Frayle and back to the Doctor again. "How—how did you get in here?" he said at last.

Doctor Morelle glanced up casually from the writing-desk and regarded him coolly. "I believe someone here wishes to see me," he murmured after an almost imperceptible pause. "I am Doctor Morelle." He took a Le Sphinx from his cigarette-case and tapped it carefully. Miss Frayle goggled at him. She was utterly at sea. He inclined his head towards the hall. "As you would no doubt observe if you went into the other room our mode of ingress was somewhat unconventional. Miss Frayle did, however, ring your bell several times—without effect."

"I—er—I—Colonel Mason never told me he was sending for a doctor," he muttered.

"Could it be someone else requires my aid?"

"There's Mr. Lovell," was the uneasy reply. "But he's out."

"How about the lady?" murmured the Doctor through a cloud of cigarette smoke.

The man's uneasiness grew. "Mrs. Mason? Oh—er—she's asleep."

"I see."

At that moment a voice raised inquiringly was heard from the hall: "Who's there? Is that you, Markham—?" The owner of the voice came in. He was a middle-aged man of medium height. He wore a double-breasted evening jacket with a carnation making a crimson splotch on his lapel. He stopped as if he had received a blow.

31

"Good God—! Colonel Mason—! " He came forward with a hoarse cry.

"The Colonel's dead, sir," said the butler. The other was trembling violently. He turned and demanded: "Who are you? What are you doing here—and this young woman—? "

"I am Doctor Morelle. Here at the—er—invitation of Mr. Lovell, I believe. This is my assistant, Miss Frayle."

"When did Mr. Lovell ask you here? "

"About twenty minutes ago." He turned blandly to Miss Frayle. "You *weren't* quite sure of the name, were you? "

She gulped, then stammered: "Er—no, I wasn't, was I? "

"Though you did say, if you recall," he insinuated, "it was a name like Lovell, did you not? "

Her head was reeling, but she contrived to say mechanically: "Oh, yes; Lovell, or Novell, or Govell—something like that. It was rather difficult to catch over the 'phone."

"And you found Colonel Mason—like this when you arrived? "

"Precisely."

"Oh . . . "

"Says it's suicide, sir," put in the butler.

"Suicide? But— " The man broke off and stared at the inert figure. He passed his hand in bewilderment over his brow. "I'm his secretary," he said jerkily. "My name's Dale . . . This is terrible. Terrible. You're—you're sure it's suicide? "

"I have no doubt at all."

"I'm afraid I don't understand about Mr. Lovell," the other said dazedly. "Mr. Lovell does live here—he's Colonel Mason's cousin—but he went out for a luncheon appointment and hasn't returned." He said to the butler: "Mr. Lovell's *not* come in, has he, Markham? "

Doctor Morelle caught a fleeting look exchanged between the two men before the other replied: "No, sir."

Dale said: "So I fail to see—er—Doctor, why he should have telephoned you to call here."

Might he not have telephoned on Mrs. Mason's behalf? " asked the Doctor quietly, and observed the flicker of uneasiness that appeared in Dale's eyes.

"Mrs. Mason isn't ill. She's asleep. Besides even if she was suddenly in need of a doctor, how could he know if he hasn't been back? "

Doctor Morelle conceded that point with an inclination of his head. But his eyes were narrowed as he abstractedly tapped the tip of his cigarette. He said: "Mrs. Mason is a victim of somnabulism, is she not? "

Dale started. "You saw her? "

32

" She came in here before we did."

" She was walking in her sleep," Miss Frayle said unnecessarily. The secretary gave a groan of dismay. " This is unbearable—! "

" Should I tell Mrs. Mason, sir—? " The butler hesitated, then went on. " Perhaps it would be better if— "

" No, no! Don't disturb her yet."

" Very good, sir,"

" I'll ring if I want you, Markham."

" Er—yes, sir." The man made to go, then paused. " Shall I close the window in the other room? "

" What? "

" The window, sir, I—er—I believe it's open. I—er—I didn't hear the Doctor ring, and so they came in by way of it."

Dale glanced sharply at Doctor Morelle, who however seemed to consider any further explanation unnecessary.

" Close it, Markham. Close it, of course! "

" Yes, sir."

" Oh . . . "

" Yes, sir—? "

" If Mr. Lovell should return before the Doctor—ah—goes, let him know he is here."

" Very good, sir." There was a further exchange of looks between them and the butler closed the door after him. There was a moment's pause. Then Dale said slowly: " Doctor, there's something I'd like to ask you . . . Do you believe Mrs. Mason did this—while she was sleep-walking? "

Doctor Morelle regarded him. " I have already intimated to you," he said, " that her husband died from a self-inflicted wound."

" I know. I was wondering if you really believed that—or if you thought— "

" Apart from the other evidence which I have taken into account, Miss Frayle and I were in the immediate vicinity when in her somnabulistic state Mrs. Mason entered this room. We can both vouch for the fact that we heard no sound of any shot fired."

Miss Frayle looked at him suddenly. " Of course! " she exclaimed. " That *proves* the poor woman couldn't have done it! "

" Thank you, Miss Frayle! " observed Doctor Morelle with a sardonic smile. He said to the other: " Your question does, however, raise a not insignificant point."

" Yes? " Anxiously.

" Why do you imagine Mrs. Mason should wish to murder her husband? "

There was a deathly silence. Then: " He made her life a hell! " Doctor Morelle raised his eyebrows a fraction.

Dale went on: " Are you going to fetch the police? "

"I fear that will be necessary."

"*You won't* . . ." came the grim answer, and with a sudden movement the man bent and picked up the revolver. Miss Frayle gave a squeal of fright. "Oh—!"

The Doctor eyed the white, twisted face behind the gun. "Calm yourself, now!" he murmured.

"Don't move, either of you, and put up your hands!" Miss Frayle raised hers with such alacrity that she knocked her spectacles off. She stood there, blinking short-sightedly, too terrified to retrieve them. "Come on, Doctor Who-ever-you-are! Put your hands up!"

"The name is Morelle—Doctor Morelle—and your attitude will not help matters—"

"If you don't raise your hands, I fire!"

"Perhaps I should point out that I am something of an expert on firearms, and that the one you are holding now happens to be unloaded."

"What—?" Dale crumpled, his mouth gaping stupidly. Doctor Morelle smiled thinly.

"If you will just place it on the desk? . . . Thank you. And Miss Frayle, you may return your spectacles to their appropriate place now."

"Thank you, Doctor—"

"Anyone might imagine," Doctor Morelle said smoothly, "that *you* were in love with Mrs. Mason . . . And not as I surmise to be the case, the absent Mr. Lovell."

Dale stared at him like a man seeing a ghost. "How—how did you know?" he said in a low voice.

"That Mr. Lovell was enamoured of Mrs. Mason?"

The other nodded.

The Doctor glanced at his watch. His ear caught the sound of what might have been a taxi-engine fading away into the distance and an enigmatic expression flickered across his face. "By the way," he said, "I wonder what is delaying him?"

"Mr. Lovell?"

"Mr. Lovell."

"Yes . . ." Dale licked his lips nervously. "I expected him back before this. Probably the rain may have held him up or something."

Miss Frayle glanced quickly at Doctor Morelle. He seemed to be engrossed in a picture on the wall immediately behind the desk. She said brightly: "It's been raining all day . . . Hasn't it?" But they were paying no attention and her voice trailed off.

Suddenly the Doctor stepped forward. "Is this a photograph of Mr. Lovell?" he asked. "In flannels and blazer?"

34

Dale glanced at the wall and nodded. "But how did you guess? You've never seen him before, have you?"

Doctor Morelle gave him a non-committal look. Without turning his head, he said: "You recognise him, Miss Frayle, do you not?"

"Except that the scar doesn't show," she answered, after a moment's scrutiny.

"No . . . the scar is not visible. Is it, Mr. Dale?"

"Umm? Oh, the scar? No, it wouldn't show in that picture." He frowned uneasily and was about to say something more when the door opened. It was the butler again.

"Did you ring, sir?" he asked, and Miss Frayle sensed a sinister purposefulness in the manner in which he closed the door. Trembling apprehensively she glanced at the Doctor. Somewhat to her surprise he was fixing the butler with a sardonic grin.

He said: "It would appear your hearing is more acute when one does *not* ring for you, than when one does!"

The man made no reply, but turned questioningly to Dale. Doctor Morelle said: "However, since you seem anxious to be of some service, I suggest you find a covering to place over the deceased until the police arrive."

The man looked at Dale again, who nodded. "Yes . . . do that, Markham. It will look better . . ." The butler went out. The Doctor had turned his attention to a black metal contraption beside the writing-desk.

"Colonel Mason's dictaphone," said Dale.

"I perceive it has an attachment by which one may hear what has been spoken onto the cylinder . . . It might be interesting to listen."

The other said nothing. Doctor Morelle pressed the device which operated the machine. The cylinder started to revolve, and in a moment a voice, slightly distorted by the mechanism, could be heard:

"*Friday evening . . .*" said the voice. "*Reminder to make appointment with Gresham tomorrow . . .*" There was a pause. Then: "*Reminder to ask Dale to go into details of North Western Railway shares . . .*"

"Can you hear, Miss Frayle?" asked the Doctor in the next pause.

"It's uncanny," she whispered.

The voice again: "*Reminder to tell Dale to obtain documents relating to Fletcher and Morgan Company . . .*"

"That is Colonel Mason's voice?" queried Doctor Morelle.

Dale nodded. "Yes. He must have been using it this evening; making notes for some business he planned to work on tomorrow."

35

"I had somehow imagined that to be the case," the Doctor replied smoothly.

"A—a voice from the grave . . ." Miss Frayle said. She stared at the dictaphone and shivered.

"A somewhat melodramatic observation, not to say morbid!" Doctor Morelle said. The voice had stopped. All that could be heard was the scratch of the needle on the revolving cylinder. Doctor Morelle stopped the machine. "I would prefer you to exercise your imagination more profitably," he went on. "What for example have you deduced from this little exhibition of mechanical ingenuity?"

Miss Frayle's face was a blank. "Wh—what?" she stammered.

"I might have known!" was his only comment, and he turned to Dale.

"I'm afraid I don't see that it proves anything," he said, with a puzzled frown.

"Does not the fact that Colonel Mason was this evening making plans in a normal way for tomorrow postulate that he did not anticipate his approaching demise?"

"Why, yes."

"Precisely. At what time would you say did he use the dicta-phone to-night?"

"Oh, before dinner. He never worked later than that."

"We have to ascertain therefore what it was caused him to take his life during the two or three hours after he had quitted this room to change and dine. Have we not?"

"I—I suppose so . . . Yes."

The butler re-entered and placed a sheet over the dead man. Miss Frayle looked away, feeling sick again. Somehow she felt the figure looked more gruesome now than it had appeared before. She noticed with a sudden apprehension that the butler after completing his task closed the door and stood as if guarding it. Doctor Morelle, however, appeared to be unaware of the man's presence. His attention seemed attracted to the writing-desk. Suddenly he moved to it and picked up an envelope from two or three others stacked against a heavy inkstand.

"Curious," he murmured abstractedly. "This envelope, like the others here, would seem to have been opened with the aid of a paper-knife. And yet," he paused studiously to run an eye over the desk, "no implement for that purpose would seem to be evident."

Neither Dale nor the other spoke. Doctor Morelle raised a saturnine face and went on coolly: "It would also appear from the cut edges of the envelope that the—er—absent paper-knife was—shall we say—an adequately sharp instrument . . ."

"Put the damned letter down!" Dale exclaimed thickly. "What's it got to do with Colonel Mason's death?"

"I was not at that moment thinking of Colonel Mason," said the Doctor softly. At that moment the door-bell rang.

"Who the devil—?" began Dale, and Doctor Morelle murmured: "Possibly Mr. Lovell has returned, and has forgotten his key?" He added, with a glance at the butler, who had already made as if to answer the ring: "I am gratified to note that your hearing has become normal!"

The bell rang again. "Go and see who it is, Markham!"

"Yes, sir."

In a moment he was back, followed by a police-sergeant and a constable. In the background hovered the taxi-driver.

"'Ere we are, sir!" he grinned cheerily at the Doctor. "Gave yer fifteen minutes like yer said, then went and fetched the cops—!" He coughed with mock embarrassment, winked at the two policemen and corrected himself. "Sorry! *Perlice,* I should've said!"

While Miss Frayle blinked unbelievingly at the new arrivals, and the butler stood indecisively looking from one to the other, Dale made an attempt at bluster. "What the blazes is the idea?" he barked. The police-sergeant, who had been staring at the white shape by the desk, turned to Doctor Morelle. He was negligently tapping a shoe with the end of his walking-stick. He raised his eyes as the sergeant began to speak and anticipated the question.

"Your inquiries will no doubt begin, officer, with Colonel Mason's suicide and the circumstances surrounding it. I should like to point out, however, that this unfortunate tragedy is inter-related with the death of Colonel Mason's cousin, a Mr. Lovell, whose body at this moment reposes in my consulting-room."

"The man's mad!" exclaimed Dale, his face twisted with rage and fury. "Mad, I tell you—!"

Breathless, goggling at the scene, Miss Frayle caught a movement from the butler, as he stepped forward aggressively. The constable, however, motioned him back, and the man checked himself. The taxi-driver who had now obtained a clear view of the sheet-draped figure, blurted out: "Blimey! another body . . . 'Ow many more of 'em!"

Imperturbably—he might have been dictating a letter to her, Miss Frayle thought—the Doctor proceeded. "Therefore, officer, pursuing your inquiries you will in due course find it necessary to question Mr. Dale here as to what knowledge he has regarding the murder of the aforementioned Mr. Lovell. In the event of a not unnatural desire on his part to evade some of your more leading questions, I feel confident I am in a position to furnish all the relative answers—"

37

" I tell you my cousin hasn't come back yet! " Dale's voice rose.
" He went out to lunch, and— "

" In his evening clothes," queried Doctor Morelle through a cloud
of cigarette-smoke.   He smiled thinly as the other's jaw sagged.
" That was the apparel he was wearing when found in the taxi— "

" S'right! " put in the driver.

" When therefore you declared he had not returned home from
his luncheon appointment I knew you were prevaricating—you had
obviously instructed your butler to assist in the deception.   Con-
ceding the possibility, remote though it might be, that Mr. Lovell
had returned, changed his clothes and gone out again without
either of you being aware of the fact, it would have been
impossible," his voice was raised a fraction in emphasis, " for him
to have quitted the house of his own volition without his shoes
becoming wet and muddy in the rain! "   He paused to savour the
dramatic effect his words had upon them.   The silence was electric.
He went on: "The conclusion to be inferred was obvious.   He
must have been carried out of the house."

He blew a spiral of smoke ceilingwards.   " We come now to the
late Colonel Mason," he went on, " and the connection between
his and Mr. Lovell's demise.   The evidence supporting my theory
that Colonel Mason committed felo-de-se— "

" Suicide? " said the police-sergeant.

" Precisely . . . The evidence is irrefutable.   We next ask ourselves why he took his own life.   He is a man of fifty years of age
or so, of some means," he indicated the surroundings with a wave
of his walking-stick, " and still actively engaged in business.   His
secretary, Mr. Dale, cannot advance the suggestion that financial
difficulties or business anxieties drove him to death."

He paused for Dale to speak.   The man remained silent.

" But his attitude did suggest the fear that Mrs. Mason might in
fact have murdered her husband.   What prompted that fear?   I
postulate that Mrs. Mason's affections were, or were about to be,
transferred elsewhere.   To whom?   Why not Mr. Lovell?   As you
may ascertain from that photograph he was a not unhandsome
man.   Someone also nearer Mrs. Mason's age.   She as most of us
here are aware is young, attractive no doubt.   Of a somewhat
neurotic temperament she revealed the secret she shared with
Lovell to her husband—probably spoke the other man's name
during one of her somnabulistic states.   To-night Colonel Mason
charged Lovell with alienating his wife's affections.   Bitter words
were exchanged.   A blow was struck.   A body was removed and
deposited in an empty taxi across the way— "

" S'right," said the driver.

" Remorse overtook Colonel Mason," went on Doctor Morelle,

38

inexorably, "remorse and fear of the consequences . . ." He indicated the white figure, "The rest you know. No doubt Mr Dale will in due course acquaint you with the facts as to who assisted in the disposal of the body—he or the butler— "

At that moment Dale rushed the door. The constable stopped him, however, with a neat punch to the jaw, and almost with the same movement snapped the handcuffs on him.

"Accessory after the fact," the sergeant said heavily. The taxi-driver who was enjoying the situation enormously had edged himself towards the writing-desk. Eyes popping with curiosity he picked up the revolver Doctor Morelle had placed there. The Doctor saw the action and rapped out a warning:

"Put that revolver down! "

But the driver had squeezed the trigger. There was a loud report and a hole appeared in the ceiling.

"Blimey! " ejaculated the taximan dropping the gun as if it were a hot brick. The sergeant picked it up quickly.

"Here, here! " he said censoriously. "Better let me take care o' that, before you shoot someone! "

Miss Frayle was staring open-mouthed at Doctor Morelle.

"But—but you said it was unloaded," she stammered.

He surveyed her sardonically. "Did I? " he queried. "Dear me! I fear I must have been bluffing . . ."

Came a long drawn out sigh from Miss Frayle, and she slumped to the floor in a dead faint. Doctor Morelle regarded her with a slight frown, examined the tip of his Le Sphinx and said to the taxi-driver: "I think you had better take us home." And he stubbed out the cigarette.

CHAPTER III

THE CASE OF THE CHEMIST IN THE CUPBOARD

"Quickly—the acid, Miss Frayle! "

Miss Frayle rapidly scanned the row of test tubes and bottles.

"The small phial—next to the iron sulphate—" snapped Doctor Morelle, his hand outstretched impatiently.

His peremptory command flustered her for a moment. She snatched the phial and caught it against a large container of distilled water. There was a crash and tinkling of broken glass. Without a word and with incredible quickness the Doctor took Miss Frayle's hand and placed it under the full force of the cold water tap. Then he examined it carefully.

39

"You are singularly fortunate. You might have sustained a very nasty burn."

Miss Frayle readjusted her glasses and regained her breath.

"I—I'm sorry, Doctor Morelle," she managed to stammer. "It slipped and—"

"I am not incapable of perceiving you do not appear to exercise full control over your digital extremities! Has the acid splashed your clothes at all? "

"No—just the corner of my overall."

He seized a bottle of alkaline solution and applied it liberally to the part of her overall indicated. Then he turned out the Bunsen burner beneath the retort which had been emitting a pungent odour.

"That brings our little experiment to an abrupt conclusion for the time being at any rate," he said with a chilling glance at her.

"I'm so sorry, Doctor," she apologised again.

"I think your expressions of regret might well take a practical form, Miss Frayle. Perhaps you would care to procure another phial of acid for me."

"If you'll tell me the name— "

"I'll write it down. It's just possible that Mr. Jordan may be of some assistance to me. You know his shop? "

"The little chemist's shop in the turning off Welbeck Street? Will there be anyone there at this time? "

"Mr. Jordan resides on the establishment. You will ring at the side entrance. I have written the formula on this card of mine—you will present it to Mr. Jordan with my compliments."

She took the card upon which he had scribbled his requirements. He went on:

"I am confident he will have a sufficient supply to enable me to carry on with my work to-night. So that if you will hasten, Miss Frayle, I should have time in which to complete the experiment I am engaged upon before retiring for the night."

Miss Frayle hurried off, while Doctor Morelle lit an inevitable Le Sphinx cigarette and then divested himself of his white coat. In a moment he had returned to his study to make some notes.

Despite its undistinguished frontage, Miss Frayle had no difficulty in finding Mr. Jordan's chemist shop. She made her way to the side door which was in a narrow entrance between the shop and a garage. She rang three times, but there was no response. No sound of any movement within. She knocked loudly. It was then she realised that the door was not firmly fastened. Her first knock sent it slightly ajar. She banged the old iron knocker again, but there was still no reply. After a pause she stepped inside with some idea of perhaps finding Mr. Jordan in a room at the back.

A strong smell of antiseptics greeted her as she hesitated for some moments, trying to make up her mind whether to call out or not. She called quietly at first: " Mr. Jordan? " Then louder But no reply.

At the far end of the tiny hallway, she noticed a flight of stairs. Thinking the chemist might be occupied in an upstairs room and perhaps slightly deaf, she decided she had better investigate further. It was a choice between that and going back without the precious acid. She decided she could not face the sardonic rebuffs from Doctor Morelle if she should return empty-handed.

Very gingerly, she began to climb the stairs. It was only a short flight, opening on to a small landing which was crowded with crates, packing cases and cardboard boxes of all descriptions. She tapped on the door immediately facing her, and as there was no reply, tried the handle, feeling more and more like a person intent upon some guilty purpose.

The door opened to reveal an unusual-looking room. It was a combination of warehouse, laboratory, office and living room. Nearest the door were still more packages and shelves containing innumerable bottles, whilst under the window was a large sink and bench, obviously used for dispensing. In the wall opposite were large cupboards, and near the fireplace was a table upon which were the remnants of a hasty meal. Two or three chairs made up the rest of the furniture.

It was growing dusk, so she snapped on the electric light switch by the door. This, she felt should convince anyone that she did not seek concealment, and that her presence in the place was not for some dishonest motive.

The only sound emanated from an old-fashioned, noisy wall clock, and once again Miss Frayle stood nonplussed as to what she had better do next. Then she caught sight of the telephone perched on a roll-top desk in a corner near the fire. If she rang up Doctor Morelle and explained the position, she argued to herself, perhaps he would suggest some other chemist. Or he might even have some idea where Mr. Jordan was likely to be found. At any rate, those saturnine features would not be visible at the other end of the wire. She was assailed by doubts once more. Suppose Mr. Jordan came in and found her using his telephone? Well, she would have to explain that's all, she told herself. It would be embarrassing, but a vision of the Doctor awaiting her return with increasing impatience spurred her to action. She went over to the instrument and dialled.

In a moment there came Doctor Morelle's familiar tones: " Yes? "

" Oh Doctor Morelle, it's me," she stammered. " I mean it's ' I '

41

—Miss Frayle— " She hastily corrected her grammatical error and prayed he hadn't noticed it. All he said was:
" I am not incapable of recognising that the sounds impinging on my ear emanate from your vocal chords," his voice crackled over the wire. " From where are you telephoning? "
" Mr. Jordan's. I'm upstairs in his laboratory. He isn't here."
" Then where is he? "
" I—I'm afraid I don't know."
" Who admitted you then? "
" I knocked and rang, but no one answered. I tried the side door and as it wasn't locked I went in. I called out, still no reply. Then I thought he might be working upstairs so I came up. But no one's here at all." She drew a deep breath. " I've telephoned to know if you would like me to wait till Mr. Jordan comes back or— "
Doctor Morelle heard her break off with a sharp intake of breath, then give a terrified scream.
" Miss Frayle! "
There came another scream, which died into a moan. Followed a clattering thud, as if the telephone receiver had fallen.
" Miss Frayle—what is it! Answer me—what happened? " He waited a moment or two, then murmured to himself. " Confounded nuisance she is! . . . Here am I waiting to proceed with my experiment . . . Frightened by a mouse no doubt! . . ." He flashed the receiver bar impatiently . . . " Hello? . . . Miss Frayle? . . ." After one more attempt, he replaced the instrument.
" Ah, well," he snapped to himself, " I suppose I had better go round and revive her."
It was now dark outside, and he might have had some little difficulty in finding the chemist's side door, but for the fact that he had his narrow examination torch with him. The door was as Miss Frayle had found it, half-open. He walked in quickly, called: " Is anyone there? " Then made his way swiftly upstairs. By his torch he could see the door slightly open at the top of the stairs. He went in, found the switch and flooded the room with light, to reveal Miss Frayle lying crumpled by the desk. In her fall, she had somehow contrived to wrench the telephone receiver from its cord, and the useless instrument lay on the floor. He picked it up and placed it on the desk, then turned his attention to Miss Frayle. She was still unconscious. Her face was ashen. He picked her up and laid her flat on an old couch that ran along one side of the room. Then he opened the window. Within a few moments she began to show signs of recovery. She moaned once or twice, then opened her eyes and blinked at him. She pushed her spectacles which had fallen awry back into position. Fortunately they had not been broken.

42

"Oh, Doctor, I must have fainted . . . I'm so sorry . . ."

"Why apologise? " he retorted with heavy sarcasm. "You are little more than semi-conscious at any time! " She passed her hand over her forehead in bewilderment, then struggled into a sitting position. He steadied her. He continued:

"However, perhaps you can recall what caused you *completely* to lose consciousness? "

She looked up at him in utter bewilderment for a moment. Then suddenly her eyes dilated with horror behind her spectacles and she swung her feet to the floor. She clutched at his arm:

"Where—where is it? "

He regarded her narrowly.

"Where is what? "

"The body! It fell out of that cupboard over there." She shuddered, and for a second looked as if she might be about to faint again. "It was horrible! Horrible! "

"Come, come! " said Doctor Morelle sharply. "Pull yourself together! As you can see, there is no body anywhere."

Miss Frayle blinked short-sightedly.

"But I saw it! While I was 'phoning you, the cupboard door over there started to open—it's open now— "

"Cupboards have opened before now as a result of traffic vibration from the street."

"That's what made me scream," she went on, not listening to his suggested explanation. The picture of what she had seen was too vivid in her mind. "When the door had swung open, the man fell out—and I fainted."

"Can you recall what he looked like? "

"His face was ghastly . . . there was blood on the side of his head . . . his hair was grey . . . he had a moustache . . . oh, it was terrible! " She shuddered once more. "Do you think it might have been Mr. Jordan? " she asked.

"He could answer to that very incomplete description," he agreed, but there was doubt in his voice. He said smoothly:

"There is, however, an aspect of this case which interests me particularly, Miss Frayle. Briefly it is how you managed to distinguish this man's appearance in the dark."

Miss Frayle sat straight upright with a jerk.

"In the dark? "

Doctor Morelle nodded, a sardonic expression on his face. "Yes, my *dear* Miss Frayle. When I arrived here this room was in complete darkness. While it may have been only dusk when you arrived here, still it would not have been light enough for you to observe—"

"But I put the light on when I came in," she said. And added quickly: "Otherwise, how would I have seen to telephone? "

He regarded her closely. There was no doubt about the certainty with which she spoke. She went on:

"Somebody must have come into the room while I was unconscious—and moved the body. And *they* switched off the light when they went out."

"H'm, that would have been possible, I suppose." He conceded the point reluctantly. He was annoyed that her explanation would cause him to abandon his theory that Miss Frayle had been suffering from some stupid hallucination. "I wish you would adjust your spectacles, instead of blinking at me in that astigmatic fashion," he snapped suddenly.

They had slipped again in Miss Frayle's excited vehemence. She put them into position once more. Meanwhile the Doctor was carefully examining the cupboard she had indicated. He discovered a small, dark, wet stain that might have been blood.

He surveyed the rest of the room. Standing on a small cupboard near the sink he found a bowl containing two or three goldfish. "Somewhat incongruous," he mused. "Mr. Jordan's laboratory would appear to be adequately equipped." His gaze rested upon a collection of test-tubes and various chemical apparatus. To his experienced eye they told him the chemist had obviously been engaged in research work of some nature.

He moved over to the table and gave a cursory glance at the remains of Mr. Jordan's tea, which had been laid on a check cloth covering only half the table's surface. He was about to pass on when he noticed a cigarette-end almost concealed by a folded evening newspaper. It had apparently burnt itself out on the edge of the table.

"Do you recall noticing this before?" he asked Miss Frayle, pointing to the cigarette end. She shook her head.

"Then perhaps you will assist me to look for an ash-tray."

Puzzled by his request, Miss Frayle nevertheless obeyed. They searched every likely place during the next few minutes. At length, having failed to find any ash-tray, he murmured:

"It would appear indicative that Mr. Jordan is—or was—a non-smoker. That might, in turn, suggest he recently entertained a visitor who did smoke."

"Yes—yes, that would be it," agreed Miss Frayle enthusiastically. "Perhaps we could trace the man that way—if we could find out the make of cigarette—" she concluded somewhat vaguely.

"I had already ascertained the name of the manufacturers of the brand in question," replied the Doctor with a frosty smile. "As, however, I imagine they sell the better part of a million a day of this particular brand this knowledge would not seem to be of much assistance to us!"

44

Miss Frayle subsided.

Doctor Morelle continued to survey the room in search of some sort of clue. Finally, he went to the window. With some difficulty he managed to open it to its full extent, and stood looking out on the yard of the garage below. It was moonlight. "I wonder," he mused, "if the body could have been removed by way of this window?"

Miss Frayle joined him and too looked out.

"It isn't very high from the ground," she said helpfully. He nodded and thoughtfully lit a cigarette. "It is just possible that man cleaning his car down there may have noticed something unusual."

"I'll call him," said Miss Frayle promptly, and proceeded to do so. The man looked up and replied in a cockney accent. He wore overalls, but there was a taxi-driver's hat perched on the back of his head.

"Wot's the trouble?" he asked, looking up from his work.

"Er—do you—have you . . . ?" Miss Frayle became incoherent, not knowing what question would be quite the one to ask. Doctor Morelle unceremoniously edged her aside.

"During this evening, have you, by any chance, observed a person or persons descending from this window?" he said.

The man eyed him quizzically, then pushed his cap even further back on his head.

"No, guv'nor, I ain't seen no person or persons. I ain't seen nobody. But then I been inside the garridge this last 'alf-hour, cleaning up the old taxi. I reckons to give 'er a sluice twice a week, and it's usually about this time, on account of business bein' a bit slack. So I takes this opportunity to— "

"Quite so," Doctor Morelle cut short the garrulous explanation.

"I can't say as I've ever seen anybody climb out o' that window," pursued the taxi-driver. "But wiv' that spout," he waved in the direction of where a rain-spout might be, "it shouldn't be much trouble—especially to one of these cat burglars. Why—is there anything wrong?"

"Nothing wrong" replied the Doctor and pulled down the window.

"There would not appear to be any egress in that direction," he murmured.

"Wasn't he smoking a cigarette?" asked Miss Frayle. "I saw the glow of it I'm sure."

"That fact alone would not necessarily implicate him in this affair," replied the Doctor acidly. "At this moment, there are possibly five million people in London, including the murderer, smoking a cigarette. Even I am indulging in the pernicious habit!"

With a saturnine smile he flicked the ash of his Le Sphinx. Then he leaned against the edge of the table and surveyed the room once more. Miss Frayle regarded him anxiously.

"What are you going to do now, Doctor? Don't you think we ought to notify the police? "

"All in good time, my dear Miss Frayle, all in good time! First, I wish to consider the evidence so far manifest. There are several quite amateurish aspects of this case which should not render the mystery particularly difficult to elucidate."

"Well, I don't quite see that we're getting much further . , Perhaps if the police could examine some fingerprints or— "

"Such elementary routine, while it may serve to fire your somewhat fevered imagination, would merely hinder the process of deduction at this stage."

He took out his magnifying glass and examined another blotch on the floor, just outside the cupboard from which Miss Frayle had seen the body fall. For the greater part uncovered, the floor was marked with stains of all sizes and descriptions, but this particular one seemed to be fresh, and also had the appearance of blood.

"No doubt a slight effusion from the wound when the body fell," he murmured thoughtfully. "If only you could have contrived to retain control of your senses at that moment, Miss Frayle."

"But I've never seen a body fall from a cupboard like that before, Doctor! " she protested.

"I hope you are now satisfied. But that is of no assistance to me in discovering the identity of— "

He was interrupted by a ring at the side-door bell.

Miss Frayle jumped. "Oh—what's that? " she cried.

His mouth twisted into a smile. "Merely the result of electrical impetus upon a mechanical device, actuated through pressure applied by a human agency upon another mechanical device! "

Miss Frayle goggled at him through her spectacles as one word magniloquently followed its predecessor.

"You mean it's the door bell? " she managed to murmur at last.

"Precisely, Miss Frayle! "

He stubbed out his cigarette.

"Who is it, I wonder? " she asked.

"That," he said suavely, "may be ascertained by proceeding to the door in question and opening it."

"I'll go." But he motioned to her to remain where she was.

"I would rather you remained here—and sat down," he said.

"Thank you, Doctor." She gave him a grateful look. "I *am* still feeling a bit shaky."

"Do not misunderstand me," he replied quickly as he made for the door. "I am merely anxious to avoid the irritation of your

46

again losing that little consciousness with which you are normally endowed! "

Miss Frayle, however, no longer appeared to be paying attention. "Listen! " she whispered, her eyes widening. "Whoever it is, they've got tired of waiting."

There was a sound of footsteps ascending the wooden stairs.

"Alfred—you there? " called a man's voice.

Doctòr Morelle, who had paused at the door and stood waiting, made no reply.

Miss Frayle breathed: "It's a man! "

"Brilliant, Miss Frayle! " the Doctor said without taking his eyes off the door.

In a moment the door opened. A short, thickset man, wearing a bowler hat stood there. He removed it to reveal light, almost sandy hair. His eyebrows seemed to be non-existent, and he boasted a straggly sandy moustache. His blue suit was rather shabby, and inclined to be shiny at the elbows. His rather bleary eyes were somewhat shifty, and as he saw them he appeared to assume an air of confident ease which seemed to require of him not a little effort.

"Hello, what's all this? " he exclaimed heartily, as he came into the room.

"Good evening," replied the Doctor smoothly, waiting for a further explanation.

"Isn't Alfred—Mr. Jordan here? " demanded the visitor.

"I fear I cannot tell you." Doctor Morelle surveyed the new-comer with narrowed eyes calculated to make anyone feel uncomfortable.

"He—he's disappeared," Miss 'Frayle said.

"Disappeared? " repeated the man. "How d'you mean: ' disappeared? ' I expect he's popped out to see one of his pals, more likely than not. Or a customer, maybe. He's sure to be back soon. You see he was expecting me. I'm his brother-in-law, by the way. Green's my name."

"I am Doctor Morelle, and this is my assistant, Miss Frayle."

Green nodded.

"Have you been here long, Doctor? "

"Some considerable time. I—er—wanted a particular acid from him at rather short notice. But he seems to have vanished in some-what odd circumstances. A cigarette? "

Green shook his head.

"No thanks—don't smoke. Funny old Alfred isn't here. It was rather a particular matter of business I wanted to see him about. I wonder if he got my message wrong? Thought he was to meet me round at my place? "

47

He raised the hand holding his bowler and scratched his sandy head.

"This is a blooming nuisance! Taken me half-an-hour to get here, and now he's out. I wish I knew if he'd gone to my place." He gave Doctor Morelle a genial grin, who coldly ignored it, and went on to suggest:

"I suppose there is no possibility of telephoning your residence in order to ascertain whether or no he is there? "

"Er—yes—could do that—if his 'phone here had been working."

"Doubtless there is a call-box within easy reach? "

"Just round the corner, there is as a matter of fact."

"We will go out together," said Doctor Morelle. "If you will excuse me a moment . . . "

He went to the window and flung it open. The taxi-man was busily polishing the radiator of his cab.

"You again, guv'nor? " he grinned, looking up.

"Would you bring your taxi round to the front immediately? "

"Okay—couple of shakes! Just give me time to get me coat on . . . "

The Doctor closed the window.

"But why do we want a taxi, Doctor? " Miss Frayle asked, a puzzled expression on her face.

"For the purpose of transit to the nearest Police Station," replied Doctor Morelle deliberately.

She glanced quickly at Green who had swung round at the last two words.

"Police Station? " he repeated. "What's on your mind, Doctor?"

Doctor Morelle showed no sign of perturbation. "I have an idea the mystery of the missing Mr. Jordan will very soon be elucidated," he replied evenly. "Elucidated by me, of course—after which it will be merely a matter of form to hand the culprit over to the appropriate authorities"

"Anyone would think there's been some sort of crime," the other expostulated. "Just because old Alfred pops up the road— "

"If you will come down and make your telephone call, perhaps you may be able to give us some further information regarding Mr. Jordan's movements? "

"Yes—all right—I'm ready," agreed the other, moving towards the door. "I hope nothing *has* happened to him " he went on. "But I'm sure you're taking it too seriously."

"Possibly," said Doctor Morelle curtly, turning to Miss Frayle.

"Perhaps you will wait here for the taxi-driver and direct him to the telephone box? We shall be awaiting him."

"Yes—of course, Doctor Morelle."

The Doctor followed Green down the narrow stair. Miss Frayle

48

came after them. They went out through the side door and Doctor Morelle and the other went off. She waited at the front of the shop until the taxi appeared.

The Doctor and Green reached the call-box, and the man went inside to make his call.

While he was speaking on the telephone, the taxi drove up, Miss Frayle opened the door to find the Doctor waiting quietly smoking a cigarette.

"Have you really discovered the murderer of Mr. Jordan?" she asked him in a whisper with a hurried glance at the man in the call-box.

"Indubitably, my dear Miss Frayle. He is at present quite busily occupied inside this telephone box." She gasped and he proceeded smoothly: "We may have a little difficulty in persuading him to visit the Police Station. However—"

Miss Frayle interrupted him. "Don't worry about that, Doctor Morelle! We shall have no trouble at all!"

He gave her a quick, quizzical look.

"I am afraid I fail to comprehend you, Miss Frayle. Perhaps you will kindly—?"

Again she interrupted him. This time a triumphant smile lit up her face.

"There isn't much to explain, Doctor," she said. "Simply that I've brought a policeman with me!"

And she indicated the stalwart figure of a police-constable who was at that moment clambering out of the taxi.

It was over an hour later that Miss Frayle, waiting in the study of the house in Harley Street, heard the front door open, and Doctor Morelle came in. She rushed into the hall to greet him.

"Did he confess?" she gasped excitedly.

"Pray control your exuberance, Miss Frayle," he replied calmly, divesting himself of hat and coat with maddening deliberation.

"But the man Green—did he kill his brother-in-law?"

"Of course." Doctor Morelle led the way into the study with Miss Frayle hurrying after him. He seated himself in the chair at his desk.

"The mystery proved quite simple when reduced to its elementals," he said, taking a Le Sphinx from the skull which had been ingeniously made into a somewhat macabre-looking cigarette-box.

"Under pressure, Green confessed he had paid a visit to his brother-in-law shortly after eight-thirty this evening, quarrelled with him over financial matters and struck him down. This occurred just at the moment you arrived at the side door and rang the bell.

49

Of course, you heard nothing—even if your mind had been alert! "
he added sardonically. He went on: "Realising there was no
time to be lost, he pushed Jordan's body into the cupboard and at
the same time secreted himself there."

Miss Frayle shuddered. "How awful—if I'd known that horrible man was in there . . ."

The Doctor lit his cigarette. "It must have been a cramped
space," he continued through a cloud of cigarette-smoke, "hence
the door burst open, with the result that you fainted. During your
period of unconsciousness, Green dragged the body to another
room, from where it has now been recovered. My rapid arrival
upset his calculations, and he left the premises, planning to return
later to dispose of the body. Then he recalled he had left his
cigarette. He *did* indulge in the tobacco-smoking habit after all—"

"Yes, I know," she smiled.

"Indeed?" His eyebrows were raised in inquiry. "May I ask
how you formed that opinion."

"I noticed nicotine stain on his moustache."

"Yes, yes, quite obvious, of course!" Doctor Morelle said, in a
tone of annoyance. "That roused my suspicions, too. He was
fearful the remains of the cigarette would incriminate him and he
returned hoping to regain it. My suspicions were confirmed by his
complete lack of surprise when he referred to the telephone being
out of order. This inferred he must have been in the room earlier
in the evening to have observed this fact." He paused dramatically:
"*In the room between the time you used the telephone and my
arrival!* How otherwise could he have known so conclusively it
was damaged? "

Miss Frayle nodded vigorously. "Of course! " she said.

He said with a thin smile: "And now, my *dear* Miss Frayle . . .
I am anxious to resume my experimental work in the laboratory
at the point where unfortunately our attention was distracted."

She looked at him with a slightly dazed expression.

"But—but Doctor," she stammered, "the acid? "

He paused with his cigarette half way to his lips. "Do you
mean to inform me," he said, his voice sharp and bitter, "that you
have omitted to obtain another phial to replace the one you so
carelessly broke? "

She goggled at him. "Well—I—I—Yes, I didn't— " She broke
off floundering.

"Really, your careless inattention to your work is most repre-
hensible— "

"I'm so sorry, Doctor," she apologised. But even as she spoke
she realised it was no good. She could not prevent that flow of
pompously precise words of censure that began to fall from his

THE CASE OF THE MISSING TREASURY OFFICIAL

lips. Miss Frayle sighed resignedly and sat down to wait until Doctor Morelle finished the tirade directed against her.

CHAPTER IV

THE CASE OF THE MISSING TREASURY OFFICIAL

A vacation in the accepted sense was rarely in the scheme of things so far·as Doctor Morelle was concerned. True, for an odd week or two during the year he was not to be found at the house in Harley Street, but those weeks were never spent in complete isolation from all things scientific. Rather did he prefer to utilise the time away from London on some special research. Research, for example, in a branch of science which he had little opportunity of pursuing in the midst of his many activities and investigations which kept him busy most of the time.

When he intimated to Miss Frayle they were to devote the middle fortnight in July to a journey to the small Ægean island of K——*, she asked in her shy, tentative manner what inquiry he proposed to make there. In vain, she sought to recall any mention of the island in correspondence—or even a telephone call. She could think of none, and when he urbanely assured her that he had decided to visit K—— because he liked it at that time of year, her spectacles almost slipped off her nose in a sudden joyful anticipation of a real holiday at last.

But the Doctor had not informed her why he liked K— in July. It had nothing to do with the uninterrupted sunshine, or the soft warm breezes, or even the incomparable blueness of the ocean around its sandy beaches.

They had scarcely established themselves at the main hotel on the island before the truth was out. Doctor Morelle introduced her to a bulky specimen case which he had unpacked immediately. He proceeded to inform her they would be spending the greater part of their time in search of certain fauna which were to be found on the rocks in the hot July sun instead of taking refuge in the crevices and fissures which concealed them for the greater part of the year.

Assuming that K—— would prove to be a miniature Lido, Miss Frayle had brought high-heeled shoes and two new dresses which she felt were most appropriate. On hearing the Doctor's plans for their stay she swallowed her chagrin and with commendable

* It has been thought wiser not to divulge the real name of the island in question.

commonsense hurried out and purchased a serviceable ready-made skirt and short-sleeved shirt, together with a pair of sandals. In the days to come she was to congratulate herself time and again upon her foresight in making this rapid decision.

Clad in a pair of flannels, an old shirt and a large Panama hat, Doctor Morelle proved absolutely tireless. Hour after hour he scrambled over jagged rocks, occasionally pausing to peer through a magnifying glass which he carried in his hip pocket. He lectured Miss Frayle unceasingly upon the habits of crustacean life which she had never known to exist. She remained unconvinced that she was any the happier for the knowledge imparted to her by the energetic Doctor. For the first day or two, she simulated some interest in the various specimens, even managed to ask what she thought were several intelligent questions. At the end of that time, however, she was more concerned with her freckles and sunburn to worry very much about the various data relative to such insignificant creatures with their long Latin names and to her, uninteresting histories.

Doctor Morelle seemed as usual, either quite unaware of or indifferent to her boredom. He continued his scientific harangues as if he were conducting a party of students. Every day, the routine was the same, and they arrived back at the hotel just in time to take a bath and change for dinner, after which Doctor Morelle would disappear to pore over the specimens he had captured that day, and make copious notes concerning them. Left behind in the hotel lounge, Miss Frayle would drowsily listen to the small orchestra until she could repel sleep no longer. She would sleep to dream often of myriads of nightmarish versions of the odd creatures which had fascinated Doctor Morelle during the day's scramble over the beach and rocks.

One evening at dinner, Miss Frayle noticed a strikingly attractive woman eyeing the Doctor speculatively. She was dark and exotic-looking, and sat at a conspicuous table by one of the windows. She was alone. Miss Frayle sighed, not without a trace of envy as she observed her well-moulded high cheek-bones, long lashes and perfectly proportioned nose. She noticed the woman looked across at the door every time anyone entered, as if she expected a companion to join her. No one had done so, however, when Miss Frayle and the Doctor adjourned to the lounge for their coffee.

The little orchestra was playing a soft melodious folk air with a romantic lilt which Miss Frayle hummed to herself as she sipped her coffee. The Doctor eyed her over his Le Sphinx with an expression of annoyance. He was anxious to discuss certain discoveries he had made that day, though he was, of course, perfectly aware Miss Frayle was quite indifferent to these researches. He

52

was about to interpose a cutting remark which would dissolve her not unmelodious accompaniment to the orchestra when a waiter appeared, hesitated a moment, then came across to them with a note. He stood in anticipation as Doctor Morelle tore open the pale mauve envelope, asking as he did so:

"Who gave you this?"

"That lady over there, Doctor Morelle," the waiter indicated with a movement of his head the woman whom Miss Frayle had noticed earlier. She was now having coffee in a corner. She was still alone. The Doctor threw a narrowed glance in her direction.

"H'm," he murmured, unfolding the single sheet of notepaper, "I am not under the impression I have made her acquaintance."

"Well, she's certainly been trying to make yours!" put in Miss Frayle, who had been watching the proceedings with some interest. "I've noticed the looks she's been giving you."

He turned and swept her with a sardonic look.

"I am gratified to learn of the interest you have taken upon my behalf," he said.

Miss Frayle, too intrigued with the situation, remained for once unabashed.

"What's in her note? she asked. "Perhaps she wants to show you the ruins by moonlight!"

"I have no interest in expeditions of an archæological nature," he assured her seriously. He assumed an air of indifference and seemed about to return the note to the waiter without reading it.

Miss Frayle sighed.

"Do read it!" she urged.

"Curiously enough, ruins have never appealed to my intellect," mused the Doctor, as if considering this phenomenon for the first time. "There is no doubt a psychological reason—but that would of course defy the comprehension of a minor intelligence such as yours, my dear Miss Frayle."

His voice trailed into a murmur. The waiter, abandoning all hope of a reply to the message, withdrew. Very deliberately, Doctor Morelle laid the note on the table and tapped the ash off his cigarette. After a moment's pause he picked up the note again. Miss Frayle noticed his eyes narrow and a wary expression flicker over his saturnine features.

"'Dear Doctor Morelle '," he read quietly, with a slight frown. "'Forgive this presumption, but I am in great distress, and know you can help me. If you will, follow me out into the hotel court-yard. I will explain everything. Believe me, Lola Varetta '."

"The notepaper's got rather a nice faint perfume," remarked Miss Frayle.

"Thank you, but my own olfactory organ is not completely

insensitive and is capable of detecting the aroma to which you refer! "

"What are you going to do? " she said, ignoring his familiarly pompous sarcasm.

He replaced the note in its envelope and puffed thoughtfully at his cigarette. "It is, of course, always difficult to ignore an SOS, however obscure its origin," he murmured.

"And besides she *is* very lovely . . ."

"My dear Miss Frayle, feminine pulchritude makes an impression upon me so infinitesimal it might well be described as negligible."

"All the same," she persisted, "you're going to follow her! "

He smiled at her thinly: "And I presume that if I do you will be able to pride yourself upon an intimate knowledge of human reactions? "

He drank the rest of his coffee slowly. Suddenly Miss Frayle said in a whisper: "Look! She's going out now! "

He said slowly in a studiously absent tone: "I think, however, you might postpone any observations upon the problems of human conduct until a more propitious moment." And he rose to his feet. Miss Frayle set down her cup quickly.

"Doctor Morelle—are you going? "

"An acute observer like yourself should have no need to ask such a question! " he retorted.

"She's gone in the direction of the courtyard! "

"You grow more observant each *year!* "

"I'd better come with you," she said determinedly, standing beside him.

"Do indeed. Let us find her together in the—er—trysting place she has chosen."

Glancing at her worried face and eyes apprehensive behind her spectacles, he chuckled sardonically, and led the way in the direction in which the woman had disappeared.

The courtyard was small, and black shadows lay on one side cast by the brilliant moonlight. The air was sweet and heavy with the scent of flowers.

"Is that you, Doctor Morelle? " came a soft, liquid voice from out of the shadows. It possessed the merest trace of a foreign accent. Miss Frayle thought it held a somewhat caressing note which filled her with a vague sense of irritation.

"Good evening," murmured the Doctor.

"Oh, how can I thank you! " cried Lola Varetta, impulsively, coming forward into the moonlight, her hands outstretched.

"This is my assistant, Miss Frayle."

Said Miss Frayle politely: "How do you do? "

The woman halted. "Good evening," she responded with much

less enthusiasm, which did not pass unnoticed by Miss Frayle. A tiny smile appeared at the corners of her mouth and hovered there.

"It would appear that you are in need of help, Miss Varetta? " said the Doctor.

In her emotion the other's hand went to her slender white throat. "It is terrible—terrible! I am almost out of my senses."

Doctor Morelle surveyed her for a moment. He murmured: "Tell me quietly and calmly."

Lola Varetta clutched his arm dramatically.

"Ah, Doctor!—how wonderful, how soothing your personality. The instant I saw you to-night, I realised your strength of character and your noble mind. I knew if only I could gain your help . . . And then when the waiter told me you were the great London doctor, the Great Doctor Morelle . . . ! "

Miss Frayle gave a little cough. Surely he can see she's just an adventuress telling the old, old story! she said to herself. But the Doctor gave no sign that he was in any way embarrassed by this fulsome flattery. On the contrary, a gratified expression seemed to flicker over his saturnine features. Or perhaps it was just a trick of the moonlight.

"You were telling me that you were in some distress," he reminded her.

"Ah yes! It is my brother—he is lost—or—or dead! "

"Lost? But surely on a small island of this nature that would be somewhat difficult? "

"You do not understand. My brother should have returned from the Bullion Vaults by now. He was to have met me here at the hotel. I have a premonition— "

"Bullion Vaults? " He cut into the rapidly rising note of hysteria in her voice.

"Yes." She spoke more slowly, calmed by his tone. "He should have returned this evening from the Bullion Vaults at the usual time. They are at the Treasury, my brother is a Treasury official. I telephoned there several times, but no answer."

"When did you last telephone? "

"About an hour ago."

"But surely a night-watchman is on duty? "

"Still there is no answer. That is why I feel certain something is wrong."

"You say you telephoned your brother several times?"

"Yes . . . First about four-thirty and an official told me he was not in. I thought perhaps he had gone out to tea at one of the ministries, so I did not telephone again until after six o'clock. He had not returned then. The official I had spoken to before was just leaving. He said my brother had told him when he went out

55

that he would return a little later. He could not understand what had delayed my brother. Again I telephoned, as I have told you, about an hour ago. Oh; what should I do, Doctor Morelle? Please, please help me! "

"Why not get the police? " It was Miss Frayle who, somewhat to her surprise, found herself making the suggestion. She promptly stammered and then fell silent, fiddling with her spectacles 'in embarrassment at having spoken at all. Lola Varetta seemed momentarily to be taken aback by the question.

"Perhaps I had better explain," she murmured, after some hesitation.

"That," replied Doctor Morelle crisply, "would be an excellent idea! "

"You will understand, Doctor . . ." she hesitated again, then went on. "My brother is a little unpopular with the police authorities. There was a big forgery case recently in which he was called to give evidence—he is something of an expert in such matters. As it happened, his evidence was not favourable to the police as they had anticipated. Their prisoner was not convicted." She spread her hands expressively—"They have not forgotten! So I do not wish to involve my brother in an enquiry which may turn out to be of no importance. That is why I ask you to investigate. The police are—" she forced a wan smile—"how you say, not very clever. They would be clumsy and stupid. But you, you are discreet and so clever."

She gave him the full benefit of her smile, and her eyes shone with admiration.

Miss Frayle gave a little cough that might have been a discreet comment, or merely caused by a tickling in her throat. Doctor Morelle glanced at her sharply.

"Where are the Bullion Vaults? " he asked Lola Varetta.

"On the other side of the town," she replied quickly. "I have my car ready. We could drive there at once." She sensed the possibility that her appeal for help had not fallen on stony ground. "Oh, Doctor! " she exclaimed. "You are so wonderful—! "

"Very well, let us proceed," he cut in hurriedly. "I feel sure, of course, your brother has merely been detained." He turned to Miss Frayle: "No doubt you would appreciate a drive in this—ah— romantic moonlight in any case. Would you not? "

"I think I might enjoy it very much," she replied in a tone which was somewhat non-committal. He eyed her with a sardonic smile.

"You would like your assistant to accompany us? " the woman asked with a show of surprise. "In case there may be some danger? " she insinuated.

56

"I think there may be some danger if I don't," answered Miss Frayle quickly and with surprising finality. She had already made up her mind. The entire story was a concoction from start to finish!

Lola Varetta's car proved to be a large, expensive-looking one, scarlet in colour. It purred through the narrow moonlit streets. Doctor Morelle sat, at her inescapable invitation, beside the glamorous creature, who handled the wheel skilfully. Miss Frayle was in the back, straining her ears to catch every word of their conversation. It appeared, however, to consist of little more than a cross-examination by the Doctor on the habits and routine of the missing brother. A few minutes brought them to the Bullion Vaults. It was an old building of ornate type of architecture. It loomed massive and darkly forbidding in the shadows of the narrow street in which it was situated. Lola Varetta stopped the car outside the front entrance, and almost before the sound of the engine had died away she had hurried up the broad steps and tried the heavy studded door. It was locked.

"You see! It is locked!" she cried.

"Hardly surprising in the case of a Bullion Vaults," remarked Doctor Morelle dryly. He stepped back and surveyed the front of the building for any sign of life. All the windows were dark.

"I presume there is some sort of side entrance?" he asked. "A smaller door reserved for employees?"

"I—I do not know—"

"Let us investigate."

Followed by the woman and Miss Frayle, he led the way round the side of the building and down an even narrower street. There were indeed two smaller doors, but the first they tried was locked. The second, however, stood half-open. A breath of chill air seemed to meet them. The Doctor paused for a moment and eyed the entrance thoughtfull. He lit a Le Sphinx before observing: "Presumably, we may enter!" Taking a small torch from his pocket he led the way into a bare looking small and chilly vestibule

Miss Frayle shivered. "It seems very quiet in there—and dark." she whispered. She and the woman stood looking round uncertainly. ₁There were three doors leading from the little hallway, all of them closed. There was a small reception cubicle in a corner near the door they had just entered. Doctor Morelle flashed his torch inside it. It was empty.

"Something is wrong!" gasped Lola Varetta. She appeared obviously very scared. "That door should have been locked." She pointed to the door of the street. "Something has happened to my brother!" Even Miss Frayle thought her distress was genuine. She herself was not feeling particularly happy. There seemed to be an

57

atmosphere of chill foreboding about their surroundings. She wished she was back in the hotel.

"Come now, calm yourself," murmured Doctor Morelle. "Perhaps if you would both remain here while I investigate a little further—"

He was moving in the direction of the right-hand door when it opened suddenly and a wide beam of light from a large torch swept over them. When the light had moved from his eyes, the Doctor could discern two men had appeared. They were wearing police uniforms. One of them carried an old-fashioned portmanteau. The leading man addressed them sharply in the island tongue. When Doctor Morelle answered imperiously in English that he did not speak that language, the second man spoke:

"What are you doing here, and who are you?" he said in harsh accents. It was he who carried the torch and he waved it aggressively.

Lola answered coolly, and in English for the benefit of her companions: "I am calling for my brother—Captain Varetta of the Treasury Staff."

The man surveyed her. "Captain Varetta would not be here at this hour," he said with a meaning smile. "You say he is your brother, eh? And tell me, please, how are we to know that? You have opened that door—you and these people with you may be thieves—"

"A party of thieves intent upon robbing your vaults would hardly consist of one man and two very harmless women!" murmured Doctor Morelle. "And please refrain from shining that torch in my face. I find it extremely trying to the eyes."

The man ceased shining the torch haphazardly. He looked at his companion questioningly, as if awaiting a decision. The other came forward a pace.

"I am afraid," he said in halting English, which they found difficult to follow. "You stay here until I make further inquiries. Please do not leave here. Please!" He turned to the other man and spoke sharply. "You stay outside the door—come!"

The two men in uniform went out into the street, closing the door after them.

"Are we imprisoned?" asked Miss Frayle apprehensively, the moment they had gone. The Doctor silenced her with a look. Cautiously he approached the window and appeared to be listening intently. Then he suddenly opened the outer door through which the men had made their purposeful exit. He came back, threw his cigarette to the floor and crushed it with his heel.

"As I had apprehended. Both have disappeared!"

"Both?" echoed Lola Varetta.

"Disappeared!" gulped Miss Frayle, goggling at him through her spectacles.

"Do you mean they were not—real policemen?" cried the other.

"I entertain that very strong suspicion. Had they been, why did they not, for instance, demand from us some means of identification?" He glanced at Lola Varetta.

"But their uniforms—?" stammered Miss Frayle.

"My dear Miss Frayle, you really must refrain from such ingenuous acceptance of the obvious. Does it not occur to even your simple imagination that it might be possible for determined persons anxious to impersonate minions of the law to procure uniforms very similar to, if not actually, those of the police?"

"But how could they—?" Lola Varetta was beginning to ask further questions when he once again waved a hand for silence. "Listen!"

From the front of the building came the unmistakable sound of a powerful motor engine.

"My car!" exclaimed Lola. "How dare they! ..."

Doctor Morelle made a little gesture of resignation.

"I fear it is too late now to take action," he murmured. "Apart, of course, from telephoning the police. The *real* police," he added with a faint smile. "Perhaps you would be good enough to do so from the nearest call-box. I seem to remember observing one just outside this building. Do not concern yourself unduly. Your vehicle will be recovered." As she turned to do so, he called after her: "For the time being, it will be sufficient to report the theft of your car."

She nodded. "Yes, yes, I quite understand, Doctor Morelle. Of course ..." She hurried out.

The Doctor turned to Miss Frayle. "The theft of her car seems to have taken her mind off the whereabouts of her brother," he remarked. "Which may be as well."

"What—what do you think has happened to him?"

"That, my dear Miss Frayle, is a matter for my immediate investigation." He moved to the door through which the two men posing as police officials had made their appearance. "Would you care to remain here and await Miss Varetta's return? Or accompany me?"

Miss Frayle gulped.

"I think I'll come with you, Doctor Morelle."

"There may be a body or two," Doctor Morelle warned her with a thin smile.

"I—I'd rather be with you," she admittedly nervously.

He regarded her with raised eyebrows and, in a tone of over-elaborate surprise, said: "Indeed?"

Miss Frayle said, as if to explain her admission: " I—I don't think she likes me . . . "

" I see! " And with a sardonic glance at her he went swiftly through the door. She followed him, keeping as close behind him as possible, wondering what it was this time, what it was she could have said which, it appeared, had offended him.

No sooner had he proceeded a few steps along the passage than the Doctor saw a reflected light in the distance. He hastened in its direction, to reach a short flight of steps. These led to a cellar where the light was burning. It was similar in appearance to any underground room in a bank or safe deposit vaults, with its long rows of files. There was also an ancient copying press, a badly scarred desk and an odd chair or two.

On the opposite side of the room, Doctor Morelle saw what he sought—a formidable iron door, resplendent with the coat of arms favoured by the makers of the strong room.

" This is, I feel, the Bullion Chamber," he informed Miss Frayle, as he strode over to examine the door.

" If it is, I don't see how we can possibly break into it! " said Miss Frayle, whose confidence had returned somewhat, for that seemed to be his intention.

" No? " he replied. " Nevertheless might we not attempt a not unconventional method of gaining admittance! " He swung his weight on the handle, and the massive door slowly opened outwards to Miss Frayle's astonishment.

" It—it couldn't have been locked! " she gasped, pushing her spectacles, which, in her excitement had slipped awry, back into place. The Doctor for once made no attempt to administer one of his invariably crushing replies. He was intent upon the figure of a man leaning against the bars of the inner gate. Obviously it was the night watchman. The man was conscious though he appeared somewhat overcome by the heavy atmosphere in the strong room, which had only one small ventilator. However, the outside air which now found its way into the Bullion Chamber seemed to revive him. By the aid of the light from the outer cellar Doctor Morelle could discern an inert form in a corner. A gasp from behind him signified Miss Frayle had seen it too.

" Who—who is that? " she breathed.

The night watchman, groaning and with a dazed expression, answered her in broken English.

" It is—Captain Varetta." He went on speaking with difficulty. " I am the night watchman. I came on duty at six o'clock this evening. All was quiet. Then Captain Varetta returned for some papers. That would be about seven o'clock. I was saying good-night to him—just outside in the passage there—when two men in policeman's uniform suddenly appeared and attacked us. They threw us in here and imprisoned us behind these bars."

Doctor Morelle nodded.

"We have, in fact, just seen two men sucn as you describe. We shall have to find some way of extricating you," he added, eyeing the heavy lock from which the key had been removed. "I fear I am powerless to unlock this."

"Ah, the scoundrels took the key! Doubtless they have robbed the other bullion rooms as well," the man said with a dejected expression.

"I see you consoled yourself and helped to pass the time by smoking," observed Doctor Morelle, glancing through the bars and noting the stubs littered around the floor.

"I was so upset—it helped to quieten my nerves. I smoked all I had—there were only three."

"Better take one of mine till we can find somebody to let you out." The Doctor handed him his case through the bars, and offered the flame from his lighter. The man accepted the cigarette gratefully.

"Thank you—thank you—" he murmured, inhaling deeply. "When I recovered consciousness—it would be about half-an-hour ago, I found myself in here with—with Captain Varetta." He looked at the inanimate figure in the corner. "He was already dead," he said soberly.

"So I had already perceived," said Doctor Morelle. "He appears to have suffered a fatal blow on the head." He paused for a moment to gaze at the body. Then he asked: "What are your instructions in an emergency such as this?"

"Telephone the police. The number is N004801."

"N004801," echoed Miss Frayle automatically.

"Is there a telephone near at hand?"

"There is a switchboard in the second room along this corridor."

Doctor Morelle turned to Miss Frayle: "Perhaps you will telephone the police. I do not have to instruct you to advise them to come immediately." But Miss Frayle had hurried off almost before he had finished speaking. She was not unhappy to quit the scene of the violent and murderous attack which had resulted in Captain Varetta's death, and the prospect of doing something useful calmed her shaky nerves.

The police arrived ten minutes later to find Doctor Morelle and Miss Frayle reviving Lola Varetta. She had collapsed at the sight of her brother. She had rushed into the Bullion Vault before Miss Frayle could intercept her to break the news more gently. When the officer in charge of the several policemen who had arrived had liberated the night watchman, Doctor Morelle said to the former:

61

"I want you to examine the contents of Captain Varetta's pockets." He indicated the dead man, and he and the officer together carefully examined his clothing. Their search revealed a wallet, a gold watch, a silver pencil and fountain pen, a handkerchief, keys, some small silver and two or three personal letters.

"Nothing much there," commented the officer.

Doctor Morelle nodded thoughtfully. He turned to the night watchman and suddenly snapped:

"Be good enough to turn out your pockets!"

The man looked surprised, but with a look at the police officer he slowly obeyed. There were a few coins, a handkerchief, a penknife, a notebook and an envelope containing identity papers.

"That is all?" queried Doctor Morelle.

The man nodded. "But yes," he said with an attempt at a smile. "What else should there be?"

Looking a trifle puzzled, the officer turned deferentially to the Doctor: "I do not understand what you expect to find?" he said.

"No? Then perhaps you will be good enough to examine the floor of this strong room."

Very mystified, the others obeyed.

"What do you find there?" queried Doctor Morelle.

"Only three cigarette ends," was the baffled reply.

"That is all the evidence necessary," murmured the Doctor, "to implicate this man—" he indicated the night watchman, whose jaw sagged—"in the murder of Captain Varetta and the theft of the bullion which was removed by his confederates to-night!"

Doctor Morelle calmly proceeded to light a Le Sphinx while the others stared at him in amazement. The night watchman was the first to recover from his surprise, but as he made a move to escape, Miss Frayle gave a warning cry and the man was forcibly restrained by three policemen, and a pair of handcuffs clamped on him.

The Doctor puffed luxuriously at his cigarette. "And now," he said, "I must attend to the deceased's sister."

Under the influence of a prescription given to her by Doctor Morelle, Lola Varetta had at last sunk into an exhausted sleep. With an expression of satisfaction, the Doctor turned to Miss Frayle:

"Miss Varetta will sleep now. Tomorrow I will visit her again—" They were in her own bedroom of her villa overlooking the shore. "I fear that unless she takes my advice, which I shall of course persuade her to do, she may suffer a bad breakdown in health."

"Poor woman. What a terrible thing to have happened!" He

nodded. "I shall have to call at police headquarters for a few minutes in the morning first. Then, after I have visited Miss Varetta here I shall be free to continue my researches into the life and death of those crustacean creatures which I pointed out to you this morning, Miss Frayle. You will recall the species in particular which I suggested bore a certain resemblance to human beings, in that some types appeared almost to be guided by good intentions and others by evil intentions, and all met a similar fate that seemed designed for them? . . . "

When they arrived back at their hotel, a message awaited Doctor Morelle asking him to telephone a number. He returned five minutes later.

"As I expected, the man has confessed," he said to Miss Frayle. "His two confederates have been overtaken by a police launch heading for the mainland."

She was very tired by the night's events, but not too wearied to ask:

"But I still don't see how you discovered the night watchman was mixed up in the crime."

"Merely a matter of logical application to all the essential facts in the case. The man claimed to have regained consciousness some thirty minutes prior to my opening the door of the Bullion Chamber. During that time he smoked three cigarettes—you may recall there were three remains of them on the floor. But neither I nor the police officers found any spent matches. On searching the deceased and the night watchman, furthermore, neither proved to possess either matches or lighter." He paused, then said softly: "How then did the night watchman ignite his first cigarette? "

Miss Frayle gasped.

"You mean he must have got a light from one of the two men—before he was locked in the strong room? "

"Precisely. Which fact pointed to his story being false—and his implication in the crime. As he has confessed, he was in actuality party with the other two men to an elaborately planned robbery. Out of this Captain Varetta's murder—unpremeditated no doubt—was a result."

Miss Frayle shuddered:

"How terrible! "

The Doctor went on smoothly: "As I shall now be able to dispense with my visit to police headquarters, I feel it would be beneficial if I made an early start for that part of the shore I was investigating. No doubt you will wish to accompany me, Miss Frayle? "

Her heart sank at the prospect.

"Immediately after breakfast, do you not agree? " his voice

went on remorselessly in her ear. " An early breakfast . . . "
 She had been looking forward to enjoying a late breakfast in
bed. She stammered, started to ask him if he might not prefer to
start off alone. The words stuck in her throat.
" You wish to say something? "
" I—I—that is—". She gave up. " Oh, all right, Doctor
Morelle," she said.
" Good-night, Miss Frayle."
" Good-night, Doctor . . . " And Miss Frayle sighed heavily
and stumbled wearily upstairs to bed.

CHAPTER V

THE CASE OF THE VANISHING FILM-STAR

Miss Frayle only occasionally visited a cinema, not that she did not
enjoy seeing films, but Doctor Morelle's scathing criticism of them
dissuaded her somewhat from going more often.
" Ah, yes, my *dear* Miss Frayle," he would murmur sardonically
whenever she advised him she planned to spend an hour or two at
a picture-house, " indulging in that curious form of escapism so
welcomed by the masses." And he would sigh with over-elaborate
concern. " Aware as I am, of course, of your extraordinarily
limited intelligence, nevertheless I cannot refrain from expressing
my amazement that even you actually find enjoyment in such a
form of so-called relaxation."
" Oh, but it's quite amusing— " she would try to defend herself,
but he would cut her protestations short.
" While here in this house," he would continue, " you have access
to the most engrossing literature written— ". He would cough
with an attempt at modesty that caused her to blush with shame on
his behalf and proceed. " —Some of the volumes I have contributed myself would capture your interest far more than any puerile
rubbish projected upon a cinema-screen. But no, you would prefer
to waste your time with hundreds of other cretinous creatures witnessing a shadow-show accompanied by mechanically recorded
dialogue and music . . . "
He would cease as if the subject was too pitiably beneath his contempt for him to waste further words. And Miss Frayle always
went to see the film she had in mind just the same.
One morning the telephone rang and she felt a thrill of excitement when the voice at the other end asked her if Mr. Sam Keller
could speak to the Doctor. Sam Keller, she knew, was the famous

film producer, the man who had come all the way from Hollywood to build up the British film producing branch of his American company. He had already constructed enormous studios at Elstree which swarmed with Hollywood technicians and directors—and some of the most glamorous stars. Sam Keller, the man who could take over an entire floor of the Savoy for himself and his secretaries and retinue ; who picked up the telephone and spoke to New York and Hollywood as easily as Miss Frayle might speak to one of the Doctor's patients. Sam Keller, who brought over his own stable of trotting ponies (though he had no time ever in which to watch them trot) ; Sam Keller, who could pick you out from a crowd and with a wave of his magic wand put your name up in lights all over the world and pay you millions of dollars a year.

Naturally, when she gave the name to Doctor Morelle he disclaimed any knowledge of it. When she gave him some idea of his importance and explained that the great film producer wished to speak to him personally he gave her a contemptuous glance and told her to say he was out.

" His secretary says it's urgent," she said.

" I am out."

" But he may be ill. Dying," she persisted.

He threw her a frosty glance and resumed his work on the contents of his note-book and the other papers before him on his desk. Miss Frayle shrugged in despair and returned to the telephone. She was back in a moment.

" Mr. Keller has spoken to me himself," she said. " It is a matter of some importance to him upon which he would be very grateful for your advice . . ." The Doctor might not have been aware of her presence. She went on : " Mr. Keller also asked me to tell you he is a personal friend of Mr. Paul Van Piper of New York."

Doctor Morelle brought up his head quickly.

" Why did you not advise me of that fact at once? " he snapped, and went swiftly to the telephone.* Miss Frayle followed him, wishing fervently she could have summoned up sufficient courage to have asked the Doctor how she could possibly have known about Mr. Keller's friendship with Mr. Van Piper until Mr. Keller had told her so himself.

" Doctor Morelle? " a pleasantly soft voice with a Californian accent greeted the Doctor over the telephone.

" Doctor Morelle speaking."

" I want to ask you about poisoning."

* Doctor Morelle had saved the life of Paul Van Piper's wife, a beautiful New York heiress. The story of this extraordinary and macabre case may be included in a later collection of the Doctor's memoirs.

"What precisely do you wish to know? "

" Well, you see, Doctor, I'm at the moment producing a film called ' The Wonderful Hour '."

" A highly original title I feel sure! " Doctor Morelle could not refrain from making the sarcastic comment. The other, however, seemed not to detect the sardonic note in the Doctor's tone.

" You like it? " Keller asked. " Fine! I thought it up myself." He went on: " Well now, the point is this—we've just started to film a scene which builds up to a terrific climax in which the girl takes poison. Belladonna."

" A deliriant often favoured by women of a somewhat hysterical and neurotic nature," observed Doctor Morelle.

" Er—something like that," said Keller uncertainly. " I said to make it Belladonna because I liked the sound of the name."

" Would you mind informing me exactly in what way all this can possibly concern me? "

" You see, after the woman's taken the poison—the woman in the film, that is—we want to make sure she reacts in the right way."

Doctor Morelle permitted himself a mirthless chuckle.

" My dear Mr. Keller, any handbook on elementary first-aid will give you all the facts you require concerning the symptoms—widely dilated pupils, delirium . . ." He broke off with some irritation. " Really, you're wasting my time. Go out and purchase the first book you can find on the subject. You will discover the reactions to an overdose of Atropa Belladonna set forth in detail. A child could understand it."

" Maybe," said the other grimly, " but Lilli Lagrande is no child! "

" Lilli who? "

" Lilli Lagrande, star of the picture—she plays the part of the woman who's got to take the poison."

" If, as I gather from your tone, this person is unable to conform to the instructions given her regarding the performance of a simple action, then surely the obvious procedure is to secure someone else with a trifle more intelligence," advised Doctor Morelle with some impatience.

Keller chuckled.

" You don't quite understand. Lilli is one of my big stars. Her pictures clean up. But she has to have every line, every movement, every turn of the head hammered into her. Now d'you see what I'm driving at? "

" I must confess I am not very well acquainted with your business methods, Mr. Keller."

" Look, she won't take any advice on all this poison stuff from the director of the film. Says he knows nothing about it. She

66

won't even let me try and show her. But if I take a big doctor down to the studios—somebody like—well, like the great Doctor Morelle, for instance—she'll just eat out of your hand."

"That eccentric experience I have no wish to enjoy," replied the Doctor, not displeased, nevertheless, by the other's flattery.

"Now, Doctor," pleaded Keller. "You can name your own fee—all expenses paid—and whatever figure you say I'll double it. It'll only take you a couple of hours in the morning. It may sound a crazy notion to you, but it's important as hell to me."

Doctor Morelle hesitated before deciding to give a negative reply.

"You're the only man in the wide world can help me," urged Keller, "just as you were the only man who was able to help our mutual friend that time . . ."

The Doctor could not repress a thin smile at the other's anxiety, and the reminder of one of his greatest triumphs caused him to pause a moment longer in reflection.

"Very well," he said in a tone of great reluctance amounting to condescension.

"That's great! I'll send a car to pick you up at ten in the morning."

Miss Frayle, who had contrived to follow the gist of the conversation with suppressed excitement, could hardly refrain from applauding the Doctor's decision.

The following morning as they drove in the luxurious limousine past the imposing entrance to the Excelsior Studios at Elstree, Doctor Morelle observed rather acidly to Miss Frayle: "I trust this visit will afford you an opportunity to become disillusioned concerning these motion-pictures which you are continually eulogising, instead of expending a little concentration upon more edifying matters."

"Oh, yes, Doctor Morelle," she replied, having heard not one word he had spoken. She was far too absorbed in her surroundings, and thrilled with the exciting possibility that perhaps one of Hollywood's glamorous images viewed hitherto from the darkness of a cinema might appear startlingly in the flesh before her gaze. She fiddled with her spectacles, polishing them in eager anticipation.

They entered a large, modern white building, and were conducted at once to Mr. Keller's office. Surrounded by chromium-plated furniture and rugs and curtains which must have cost a small fortune, Doctor Morelle concluded the film-producer was a man not without certain good taste. He had the rather disconcerting habit, however, of keeping a light-coloured Fedora hat perched on the back of his head. He was relieved to see that he did not have a cigar stuck in his mouth.

Keller seemed very glad to see them, and proposed to conduct them to the "set" right away. Before they left the office, he depressed a switch and spoke into the instrument on his desk:

"I shall be on Stage Number Four—and don't interrupt me! "

Yes, Mr. Keller," came the tinny reply. As they came out in the corridor, they heard several loud speakers announce:

" Mr. Keller's on Number Four! . . . Mr. Keller's on Number Four . . . ! "

"A little premature, surely," suggested Doctor Morelle.

"Take no notice of that—it's customary in the motion-picture business to keep your name in front of folks, or they're liable to forget you're about! " he explained mildly with an almost apologetic smile.

They came into the open air, crossed a square and entered a huge structure covered with long sloping roofs. A red electric bulb glowed outside the door, and several notices adjured their silence. These instructions Mr. Keller ignored, talking the whole time in his smooth, soft accent, as they picked their way through a wilderness of electric cables and odd " props " towards the group of actors on the brilliantly illuminated set. The building reverberated with the banging of workmen's hammers, until a voice called:

" Quiet! "

Whereupon a little man in a loud tie and a louder pullover leapt to his feet and shouted energetically:

" Quiet on the set! "

The hammering ceased, and immediately silence fell upon the crowd of technicians, actors and others grouped around the garishly illuminated scene.

" Lights! "

The brilliant lighting was approximately trebled.

" Roll 'em . . . Camera! "

Miss Frayle watched with bated breath while the two sun-tan complexioned actors sprang into life, followed by the long arm of the ubiquitous microphone and an ever-following camera while they moved round the set.

Just as she was becoming interested in the scene, a voice called: "Cut! "

The little man in the bright pullover leapt up again and yelled: " Save 'em! "

Five arc lamps snapped into darkness, and again the pandemonium of hammering broke out. Miss Frayle goggling, found it hard to believe that out of the apparent muddle and chaos before her and which seemed to prevail on every side, could anything evolve which she, in company with cinema patrons the world over would pay to see.

She glanced at the Doctor. His saturnine features wore their most supercilious expression as he gazed with studied disinterest at nothing in particular.

"That's Lilli Lagrande," whispered Miss Frayle to him when Keller had left them for a moment to speak to the director of the film. "She's French . . . and that's Anthony Bell with her . . . the papers call him the new British star." She had seen them both in several films and felt a thrill as she recognised them. The Doctor hardly deigned to glance in their direction.

"By a cursory glance at their respective crania, I should say they were both of a singularly low order of intelligence," he murmured unkindly, and deliberately employing, as he well knew, only a small degree of accuracy.

After a moment there were more shouts for silence, the lights came on again in all their brilliance, the man in the multi-coloured shirt shouted. Miss Frayle watched the petite blonde and glamorous French star, brought to England after a dazzlingly successful stay in Hollywood, whence she had gone after her triumphs in French films. At the moment she was going through the antics and emotions befitting a society butterfly who has fallen in love with a poor but handsome young sculptor. Anthony Bell, with appropriately stream-lined profile and dark crinkly hair, portrayed the sculptor. As Lilli Lagrande passionately declared she had at last found true love in his arms, Miss Frayle heard a cockney voice, a man's, mutter behind her:

"Conceited little pup, he is," said the voice.

Another man voiced a cockney agreement. "S'right," said the second voice. "All 'e thinks of all the time is gettin' 'is pretty-pretty dial in the papers! "

"Ar," said the voice number one. "Fair makes yer sick it does!"

Miss Frayle glanced round, but the two men, they appeared to be studio workmen, had moved off. She glanced at Doctor Morelle to see if he might also have heard perhaps and been amused by the scrap of conversation. But his face was as disinterested as ever. She turned to the scene before her again. It seemed to be about to end.

Presently Keller returned, bringing with him the director of the film, another American named Al Palmer.

"Now I'll leave you two together to figure out this poison business," smiled Keller benevolently, after he had introduced them. "I got a conference to attend at twelve." He glanced at his wrist-watch. "See you later, Doctor."

In spite of the director's loud attire, Doctor Morelle found Palmer quite a reasonable individual, who fired a series of questions at him while a stenographer took down the Doctor's replies.

"All right," said Palmer presently, "we'll shoot the poison scene.

"The poison scene!" yelled somebody, and the cry was taken up by a number of other voices.

"First, before we start, Doctor Morelle," said Palmer, "I want you to meet Miss Lagrande." He turned and called quietly: "Lilli . . . Lilli . . . come on over and meet Doctor Morelle."

While Miss Frayle watched goggle-eyed, Lilli Lagrande came over and extended a slim beautiful hand to the Doctor. Introducing them, Palmer went on: "He's an expert in this Belladonna business, Lilli . . ."

"Ah, Doctor Morelle, I am so glad to see you. Now at last we will get this scene right. Already we have taken it five—six times, but each time something tells me it is wrong. Now, once and for all, we get it right, eh?" Her accent was most attractive, her voice throatily alluring, her smile brilliant, as she looked up at Doctor Morelle.

"I hope so, indeed," he replied. "My time is extremely valuable, and I have a consultation immediately after lunch."

She gave him a wide-eyed look and pouted. Then Palmer was edging her back to the set with final instructions before they began work on the important scene. After delays for various reasons the poison scene began.

But it seemed that the French star had been more than a little optimistic. She was herself mainly to blame. She had an irritating habit of forgetting all the actions and reactions drilled into her by Palmer, and devising touches of her own that were quite inaccurate when the scene was actually shot. As time wore on, tempers became more frayed, and even Miss Frayle decided Lilli Lagrande really was not over-gifted with intelligence. The Doctor was frankly bored, and took little pains to conceal it.

When a bell outside the building rang shrilly to announce to everyone's relief it was lunch-time, the poison sequence still had a long way to go.

"What can you do with a woman like that?" Palmer said in disgust to the Doctor, as the workmen tramped noisily out of the building. "No wonder she drove Hollywood crackers! That fellow Bell may get under your skin with his conceit, but he does remember what you tell him. You'll have lunch with me Doctor?"

Doctor Morelle shook his head. "I must return to town at once. I have an important appointment. If you will kindly direct me to Mr. Keller's office, I will explain to him."

"Too bad you have to go," said Palmer, and he gave Miss Frayle a friendly grin. "Hope we'll be seeing you again."

"I think that is hardly likely," said the Doctor firmly.

"Well, anyway, we've got all the technical details fixed now," said Palmer. "Thanks to you. And Lilli won't be able to say it isn't the real thing, knowing as she does you were here on the spot to give us the correct reaction stuff and all that. Thanks a lot. You can't imagine what a headache it's been."

"I rather imagine I *can!*" murmured the Doctor with a thin smile.

The other gave him a quick look and then laughed outright. "I guess you can, too!" He shook hands genially with them both and then directed the Doctor and Miss Frayle to Keller's office.

They made their way through the same heavy, sound-proof door by which they had entered the stage, and found themselves in the main corridor. Doctor Morelle and Miss Frayle set off in the direction Al Palmer had given them.

It was Miss Frayle who saw the scrap of white against the wall where it had been kicked aside. She picked it up. It was a tiny handkerchief, perfumed and initialled in one corner: "L.L."

"Must be Miss Lagrande's," she said to Doctor Morelle.

"Quite the little Sherlock Holmes!" was his only comment.

She looked round for someone to whom she might hand it over. But there was nobody near. Clutching the handkerchief in her hand, she followed Doctor Morelle hesitantly. They came to a point where another corridor cut across the one along which they were proceeding. They turned left as instructed by Palmer.

Some few yards along Miss Frayle's eye caught sight of a door with a silver star painted on it. Beneath the star was the name: LILLI LAGRANDE. She halted, looking at the handkerchief.

"Do you think I might take it in to her?" she asked Doctor Morelle.

"I have no doubt she will be delighted to receive it from you," he said sarcastically. "Though whether such a moronic creature will recognise the initials as her own is a debatable point."

She stood indecisively outside the star-marked door.

"Do not stand there like someone in a trance, perform your errand as quickly as possible and rejoin me in Keller's office," the Doctor snapped irritably and strode off. So rapidly did he proceed that he bumped into a large, moon-faced young woman who was hurrying down the corridor. Complaining bitterly about the inability of people to watch where they were proceeding, he went off with long raking strides. The young woman stared after him, her mouth open with fright.

This incident inspired Miss Frayle into action, and with a sympathetic smile towards the large young woman, she knocked at the door. As she stood waiting, glancing at the crushed morsel of linen and lace she held, a voice which sounded as if it might be the film-star's told her to come in. Lilli Lagrande lay upon a large pink sofa, and was wrapped so far as Miss Frayle could judge in a great cloud of pink feathers. She was alone in the dressing-room and surveyed her with great round and very blue eyes over a small parcel which she was in the act of undoing.

"Oo are you? What do you want? "

Miss Frayle stammered and held out the handkerchief. "Er—excuse me, Miss Lagrande—" She wondered desperately if she should not have addressed her as "Mademoiselle," after all she was French "—er—but I found this out there—".

"You find what out where? "

"Your handkerchief, I think."

She extended her small soft white hand and took it from her. "It is mine, yes," she nodded. "Thank you very much for bringing it to me."

Miss Frayle wriggled with nervous excitement. And then she wondered how she could take her leave.

Lilli Lagrande gave her a bewitching smile. "Perhaps you could untie this parcel for me, pliz? My maid she has gone to lunch . . . It is such a nuisance . . ."

"Why, of course," and Miss Frayle took the parcel and proceeded quickly and deftly to untie the string.

"That is so kind of you." And the smile became more brilliant as the wrapping was removed to reveal a cardboard box of attractive design. She took it from Miss Frayle with a gurgle of delight, negligently throwing the visiting-card which accompanied it on the floor, after a perfunctory glance at it.

"It is lovely perfume he give me," she exclaimed, opening the box and taking out a luxurious-looking, beautifully cut bottle and glancing at the gilt label. "'Serenade in the Night' it is call—I have never tried any of this sort before." She took out the stopper. "Ahh—! " she breathed ecstatically.

Miss Frayle's nostrils quivered as the clingingly heavy exotic scent was wafted in her direction. She thought it was a decidedly sickly odour. But she said: "Very nice," politely. She wondered what Doctor Morelle's reactions would be if he caught her using such an exotic perfume.

"You must have some," said Lilli Lagrande generously, at that very moment. To her dismay, Miss Frayle realised she could not possibly refuse without offending her. "Oh, it is *merveilleuse !* " cried the other, liberally dabbing her neck and behind her ears with the contents of the bottle, and shaking some drops on to a handkerchief. "Give me your handkerchief," she said.

Apprehensively she did so, and Lilli Lagrande sprinkled it generously with the scent. The air in the dressing-room was now heavy with the powerful aroma, and Miss Frayle was thankful when the

film-star relaxed languidly on her cloud of feathers and waved a hand in dismissal.
"You have to go? " she pouted. " Such a peety. Good-bye. Shut the door gently please, I have a headache."
Miss Frayle went out quietly, and took a deep breath of comparatively fresh air. She made her way somewhat unsteadily along the corridor in the direction of Mr. Keller's office. There, she found the Doctor fuming, as he paced up and down. It seemed that the great producer had not returned from his conference, though secretaries continually looked in to inform Doctor Morelle: " Mr. Keller is expected any minute."
"Where have you been all this time, Miss Frayle?" he demanded. "You have had ample opportunity to return lost handkerchiefs of the entire personnel of the studios! "
"I'm sorry, Doctor—Miss Lagrande—er—detained me— "
He raised his thin aquiline nose and sniffed.
"What a disgustingly heavy perfume there is in here! " He suddenly turned a piercing gaze on her. " I hope," he said with a sardonic expression indicating he was already aware she *was* responsible, " you can in no way be connected with this peculiarly oriental aroma? "
"It was a present to Miss Lagrande from one of her admirers," explained Miss Frayle desperately. " She made me take some."
"And of course you lacked the moral courage to refuse? You will kindly remain at a reasonable distance so long as that clinging and revoltingly penetrative odour persists."
"Yes, Doctor Morelle," said Miss Frayle miserably, and humbly removing herself to a distant corner of the room. At that moment Sam Keller hurried in. He waved aside the Doctor's protests with an apologetic smile.
"Now, now Doctor, I haven't forgotten you have a consultation this afternoon. You'll be in plenty of time—I've arranged for the studio car to take you wherever you want to go—and we've a chanc·ᴉ to eat in here before you start. I've ordered it to be sent in right away."
Almost as soon as he had spoken, the door opened to admit a waitress carrying a large tray.
Keller beckoned to Miss Frayle.
"Come on over here, Miss Frayle, don't sulk in the corner! " he grinned. " Help set the table."
He sniffed appreciatively. "That's nice perfume you're using," he declared. " You must tell me the name, I'll buy my wife some."
Miss Frayle gave him a shy little smile of gratitude.
When they were sitting around a most appetising lunch, Keller turned to Doctor Morelle and asked:

"Well, how did you get on with Lilli? "

"I regret to say I consider her to be a somewhat cretinous creature," declared Doctor Morelle acidly.

Keller laughed. "I've been having a word with Palmer—he says you've got the whole business straightened now anyway. He can go right ahead now he knows the layout. He'll worry Lilli till she delivers the goods."

"That I feel sure should prove very gratifying! "

Keller pushed his hat back on his head, and sighed.

"If you knew the worry I have over that woman. We've been getting threatening letters for weeks. One came just now demanding five thousand pounds by this morning or she would disappear! "

"You—you mean a threat to kidnap her? " gulped Miss Frayle.

"That's the idea, and then where would my picture be? "

"I should think it might show a considerable improvement! " commented Doctor Morelle.

Keller shook his head. "You don't know this business, Doctor. Lilli Lagrande's got the goods. We know it. She knows it."

"Is the—er—lady concerned aware of these letters being sent? " asked the Doctor disinterestedly.

"No. I decided it wouldn't help at all. She'd get in a state of jitters."

"I could prescribe a course of extreme physical exertion," mused Doctor Morelle, "that would doubtless rid her of some of her temperamental excesses . . ."

The film-producer shook his head. "It's her temperament we want. It's what the public wants, too. So long as we can keep it within limits. I've been handling stars like her for years—it's not too tough when you know how. Keep a tight rein, but not too tight. Know when to tick 'em off, when to encourage 'em, when to— "

The loud speaker telephone on his desk clicked.

He pressed down a switch.

"What is it? "

"Mr. Keller—Miss Lagrande . . . " The voice was urgent, almost incoherent.

"Well? "

"She's disappeared," came the voice from the instrument. "Her maid went to get her some lunch. When she came back Miss Lagrande had vanished."

Miss Frayle choked.

"My God! " exclaimed Keller. He stood up for a moment nonplussed, then pressed the switch again.

"Tell Collins to come here right away—and Palmer. And keep your mouth shut," he snapped.

THE CASE OF THE VANISHING FILM-STAR

"Yes, Mr. Keller."

Collins, who was Keller's right-hand man, proved to be a tall, alert individual in the early thirties. He arrived with Palmer in less than five minutes. As they came in, Doctor Morelle was just intimating that he was about to take his leave. The harassed producer waved him back.

"No, no, Doctor, can't you wait a moment? Maybe you could help us on this? I've heard how you solved the Disappearing Admiral Case, long after the police had given up.* I'm against yelling for the police unless it's absolutely necessary—maybe you could solve this case *before* we call 'em in!

Collins and Palmer looked at Doctor Morelle anxiously. Palmer said, not very hopefully: "Maybe it's a false alarm—maybe she's only taking a walk in the park."

"She hardly looks the type of person who would go for a country walk," said the Doctor. "However, perhaps you would be good enough to inform me who knew about these threatening letters."

"Just the three of us," replied Keller decisively. The other two men nodded.

"Who first made the discovery Miss Lagrande was missing?"

"I did," replied Collins. "I went along to her dressing-room to see her about one or two matters, and found only her maid there. She said she'd brought Miss Lagrande's lunch, and it was getting cold. She'd no idea where Lilli was. I got into touch with one or two likely people, but they hadn't seen her. Then I remembered about those letters, so I thought I'd better tell Mr. Keller's secretary to get through here."

The producer nodded approvingly. He turned to Doctor Morelle. "Any other questions you want to ask, Doctor?"

The Doctor shook his head negatively, and, warned to say nothing about what had occurred, Collins returned to his own department.

Keller said to Palmer:

"Now, Al, tell us what you know about this—"

He was interrupted by the door opening suddenly to admit Anthony Bell, his wavy hair somewhat awry, and a peculiar expression on his made-up features.

"I've been threatened!" he announced in a voice a shade too high-pitched. He waved a letter.

"What—you as well?" Keller snapped at him.

The young actor's handsome face took on a puzzled look.

"Why?" he began, "has somebody else—?"

* The details of the "Disappearing Admiral Case" are, of course, known to the public—at least almost all of them are. There is one vital fact, however, which is in the nature of a Naval secret and was never disclosed. For this reason this case cannot be included in these memoirs at present.

75

"Lagrande's disappeared," said Keller. "Kidnapped, we think. But for God's sake, keep it to yourself. What's this letter of yours? " He took the letter from Bell, then unlocked and opened a drawer in his desk and offered several others for Doctor Morelle's inspection.

"Where did you find your communication? " the Doctor asked the young actor.

"On my dressing-room table. It was there when I came off the set. I expect it's a joke of some sort really . . . " He smiled as if to dismiss it after all as a matter of little importance.

Doctor Morelle lighted a Le Sphinx. He said through a cloud of cigarette smoke: " Are you suggesting now that this is perhaps not so important after all? "

Anthony Bell seemed to grow even more uncomfortable. He looked at the door as if undecided whether to stay or go. Miss Frayle, who had remained in the background during the discussion between the Doctor, the producer and the others, decided the young man's face was really somewhat displeasing when viewed at close quarters. She recalled the conversation she had overheard between the two cockney workmen, and agreed to herself they had been right about the actor. His face was full of conceit, and there seemed to be something more evident in his expression now, she decided. There seemed to be a shadow of fear across it. He was answering Doctor Morelle with ill-assumed composure.

"Well—er—no, I shouldn't think so—after all I get dozens of odd sorts of letters— "

He spread his hands expansively as if to indicate the volume of his fan-mail. Doctor Morelle mentally reached the conclusion the young man was, at any rate, a singularly indifferent actor out of his professional environment however adequate a performer he might be in it.

"Such a letter might result in some quite advantageous publicity," he murmured in a quiet, insinuating tone. There was a silence for a few moments. Then Bell coughed and grinned sheepishly.

"Well, I expect you'll be busy with this other job," he murmured.

"Did you see anything of Miss Lagrande when you came off the set? " asked Keller.

"Good heavens, no! My dressing-room's in the opposite block. Besides, off the set we're not speaking."

Keller could not refrain from exchanging a grin with Palmer, as Anthony Bell made a comparatively unobtrusive exit.

"Well, what d'you make of that? " asked Keller.

"It rather looks as if Mr. Bell, unaware of an apparently real danger threatening Miss Lagrande, was seeking rather more than his fair share of publicity," said Doctor Morelle.

"Just the kinda trick he'd go for," declared Palmer contemptuously. "The swollen-headed dummy!"

"He's got a nerve!" chuckled Keller, glancing again at the note Bell had left behind. "Fancy putting his price at ten thousand. Does he really imagine we'd pay that to save having him kidnapped?"

"Your guess is as good as mine, Mr. Keller," grinned Palmer.

"Maybe I should have a serious talk to that guy," murmured Keller. "Now, Al, what d'you know about this Lagrande business?" Palmer shook his head.

"Not a thing—but I hope she turns up pretty soon. We're two days behind schedule. And I'm due back on that set right now." Keller looked across at Doctor Morelle who nodded.

"All right, Al," the producer said. "We know where to find you. Better shoot one or two of those scenes which don't include Lilli." He spent a few moments indicating the nature of the work Palmer could proceed with during the film-actress's absence.

When he had gone, Keller lowered himself into his revolving chair with a sigh.

"As if I haven't had enough worries with this so-and-so picture! Trouble with the story, trouble with the title, the cast, the sets, and now Lilli has to go and get herself kidnapped!" He gave his hat a vicious tug that pulled it over one eye.

Miss Frayle smiled at him sympathetically.

"Try not to worry, Mr. Keller," she said. "I'm sure we'll get her back for you safely—that is, if Miss Lagrande really has got lost."

"Thanks, Miss Frayle," smiled the American somewhat wanly.

"Might we not take a look at Miss Lagrande's dressing-room?" suggested Doctor Morelle. "It would be as well if you remained here, Mr. Keller, in the event of any fresh news materialising."

Keller nodded, his face brightening a little.

"I'll get my secretary to take you along."

He pressed a button, and a stalwart, moon-faced young woman entered. Miss Frayle and Doctor Morelle recalled simultaneously that she was the young woman he had bumped into in the corridor a little earlier.

"Take Doctor Morelle and Miss Frayle to Miss Lagrande's room," Keller instructed her.

"Yes, Mr. Keller," she answered in a colourless voice.

As they were going, Keller recalled her and handed over a sheaf of papers. "On your way back, call in and give these production schedules to Mr. Collins, and ask him to check with all departments."

"Yes, Mr. Keller."

77

She led Doctor Morelle and Miss Frayle out into the corridor, and eventually they came once more to the dressing room of the missing film-star.

"There are only four other rooms in this corridor," noted Doctor Morelle, eyeing the secretary. "Could you inform me who occupies these rooms?"

"Well . . ," the girl thought for a moment, "next to Miss Lagrande is—". She mentioned the name of a well-known character actress, and rattled off the names of two other actresses who used the dressing-rooms. One of them was not at the studio that day, she added.

"And the fourth room?"

"Empty just now." The secretary opened the door of Miss Lagrande's room. They were greeted by an overwhelming waft of the inevitable perfume. Morelle turned to the young woman. "There is no need for you to wait," he said.

The secretary muttered something and hurried back along the corridor towards Keller's offices.

When the door closed, Doctor Morelle began a careful examination of the room. There were some signs of a struggle. Two pots of vanishing cream had been overturned. Cosmetic bottles had been swept to the floor; so had the ornate bottle containing the perfume, "Serenade in the Night."

The Doctor picked up this bottle and sniffed at it thoughtfully and with considerable repugnance.

"Miss Frayle, you were probably the last person to see Miss Lagrande before she was abducted. I feel certain you have a number of helpful theories to put forward regarding the matter?"

Miss Frayle ignored the sardonic tone of his voice and looked completely bewildered.

"I—I can't understand it," she stammered. "I—I—don't know what to think. It—It's all so strange."

He smiled frostily. "You surprise and disappoint me," he murmured. "I had hoped for sensational revelations," and he sighed elaborately. Then he said: "The person who perpetrated this abduction is still at large and on the premises. That much I have ascertained."

Miss Frayle's eyes widened in alarm behind her spectacles.

The Doctor chuckled at her expression of apprehension.

"Do not distress yourself, Miss Frayle. Let us proceed to investigate the adjoining dressing-rooms."

She followed him out and along to the next dressing-room. He tried the door and looked inside. It was a room similar to Lilli Lagrande's, though very much less ornately and expensively furnished, and not so large. The same applied to the other dressing-

78

rooms. Then they came to the end room, which the secretary had described as unused. The door was locked. Doctor Morelle paused and eyed the door reflectively.

" Shall I get the key, Doctor? "

" No, Miss Frayle. You remain here. I will obtain it myself. No doubt the secretary who conducted us here will have some idea as to its whereabouts."

He made his way back along the corridor.

The moon-faced young woman's office proved to be a small room, crowded with files. The girl was typing rapidly, amidst stacks of papers and documents of every description on her desk. The walls were smothered with photographs of film-actresses.

" I wish to have the key of the end dressing-room, which you described to me as empty," he said to her. She looked surprised for a moment, then recovered.

" Oh yes, I forgot to mention it's usually kept locked. There should be a key somewhere, in the commissionaire's office I expect."

" You have no duplicates? "

She appeared to ponder his question for a moment, then opened a drawer and produced a small bunch of keys. Each was labelled, and she finally selected one.

" I think you will find that's it."

He thanked her and returned to Miss Frayle.

The empty dressing-room was dusty, and contained little of interest. It was very much like the other rooms except that it had an emergency exit which led out to the back of that part of the studio. Doctor Morelle looked round and then suddenly stepped forward and picked up a large piece of curtain, old and faded, which had been carelessly thrown on top of a large locker. He pulled it off and threw it on to the floor. Miss Frayle saw his eyes narrow as he bent and sniffed. She noticed four large holes in the lid of the locker, which was fastened with a small padlock. Doctor Morelle looked round quickly and indicated a large chisel lying on a table by the door. It had obviously been left behind by a forgetful workman. Miss Frayle handed it to him. Inserting it under the lid, the Doctor managed to burst it open without much difficulty.

Within lay Lilli Lagrande, gagged, bound and unconscious.

" Miss Lagrande! " gasped Miss Frayle, goggling.

" Brandy quickly! " snapped Doctor Morelle, quickly unfastening the cords which bound the film-star. Miss Frayle rushed out of the room and almost collided with Keller's secretary.

" Brandy—for Miss Lagrande," gasped Miss Frayle.

The young woman stared at her in amazement. Then she pulled herself together.

" I'll get it—come with me— " she said.

79

By the time Miss Frayle had returned, Lilli Lagrande was moaning and seemed to be recovering consciousness.

"Did you happen to see Mr. Keller's secretary?" was Doctor Morelle's first question as he took the brandy and held it to the actress's lips.

"Mr. Keller's secretary? I—I don't know—I think she went back to her office. It was she who got the brandy for me," explained Miss Frayle.

"Then go and find Mr. Keller immediately and advise him to detain the young woman!" Doctor Morelle snapped.

Miss Frayle stared at him in blank amazement.

"Det—detain her?" she gulped. "But what for? Why—?"

"If you would restrain yourself from asking futile questions and carry out my instructions at once I should be better pleased."

"Yes, Doctor Morelle, of course." And, completely in a daze, Miss Frayle hurried off in search of the film-producer.

A little while later, Doctor Morelle was saying to Keller:

"Your secretary's idea was to keep Miss Lagrande in that locker until to-night. Then, under cover of darkness, bundle her into her little two-seater car, via the emergency exit which leads from that dressing-room, and take her to her bungalow where she lives alone."

Keller pushed his hat on to the back of his head with a groan. "But what beats me," he said, "is why she should do all this. Threatening letters! . . . Kidnapping! . . . It's fantastic!"

Doctor Morelle smiled sardonically.

"It may not occur to you, but the world in which she works is somewhat fantastic! Undoubtedly it finally affected her mind. The young woman is obviously unbalanced. Witnessing these—er—strange creatures around her incessantly gave her a craving for fame, or notoriety. Being a secretary offered her practically no opportunity to fulfil this ambition, therefore she was forced to evolve some plan by which she could achieve the desire for publicity."

Keller nodded thoughtfully.

"So that's how it was? Well, we were damned lucky she didn't suffocate Lilli in that locker."

"Yes, that would have been even more unpleasant for both the young woman and Miss Lagrande," said Doctor Morelle.

"Not only that—my film would have been ruined!" declared Keller emphatically.

On the way back to London in the luxurious car, Miss Frayle remained deep in thought until they reached the outer suburbs.

"I still can't see how you came to suspect that girl, Doctor Morelle," she said at last.

Doctor Morelle lit a Le Sphinx.

"What was the name given to that perfume used by that moronic creature, the aroma of which still pervades the atmosphere about you?"

"You mean 'Serenade in the Night'?"

He received the information in silence. Then he mused: "Yes . . . Quite the most pungent aroma I have encountered for a considerable time. However— " he smiled thinly as he went on, " —it's an ill wind that blows nobody any good! But for that scent I might have taken longer to suspect the secretary of being concerned in the abduction."

Miss Frayle stared at him, not grasping the significance of what he was saying. He went on smoothly:

"When first she came into Mr. Keller's office, I imagined I received a fresh waft of the perfume, but could not be positive you were not still responsible for it. When, however, I visited her later in her own office, the matter was placed beyond any doubt. I argued, therefore, the young woman must have followed you into Miss Lagrande's dressing-room, for I had already collided with her in the corridor just after you left me to visit Miss Lagrande. At that time she was certainly free of the perfume, or I should have noticed it. It was during her struggle with Miss Lagrande that the bottle was overturned and some of the scent precipitated on to her attire."

"So that was it," murmured Miss Frayle, reconstructing the events in her mind.

"As you so succinctly phrase it, my dear Miss Frayle, 'that was it'. A perfectly simple matter of ratiocination which you, no doubt, confidently feel *anyone* could elucidate! After all, it needs only shrewd perception, a gift—one might almost say, genius—for collating the facts as they present themselves to the observer . . ."

Miss Frayle sighed as Doctor Morelle launched into one of his moods of self-commiseration. She closed her eyes. The speeding car hummed onwards and the sardonic voice in her ear became a blurred sound that gradually drifted further and further away.

When Doctor Morelle paused in his tirade to demand of her why she made no answer, he observed that she was asleep, her spectacles half-way down her nose, a little smile touching her lips.

"What a careless young woman!" he murmured in a tone of exasperation. "If they were to break she would be unable to perform her work—doubtless she has omitted to provide herself with a spare pair." Leaning forward, he gently replaced her spectacles to their proper position on Miss Frayle's nose.

CHAPTER VI

THE CASE OF THE ANONYMOUS POSTCARDS

Doctor Morelle regards the strange happenings at Bleakcliff as perhaps the most unique of all the cases he has investigated. True, he is not accustomed to understatement in his description of the mysteries he has solved, any more than he is inclined to underestimate his own peculiar powers of deduction and ratiocination.

One reason, however, for his high estimation of this particular case as a *tour de force* among his catalogue of criminological successes is admittedly justifiable. It is the fact that an outstanding feature of the case was the complete absence, in any material sense, of any clue.

Nevertheless the Doctor's elucidation of the mystery was achieved by his extraordinary aptitude to grasp the essential facts, logically to arrange them so that they presented a true picture of the actualities. Added to these undeniable gifts was his shrewd and penetrating insight into the human mind. To him, it seemed, all the processes however secret, however twisted and subterranean, of the human intellect were laid bare for his dissection at his will.

Bleakcliff has always steadfastly refused to be classified as a holiday resort, though it occupies a pleasant position on the edge of the Thames Estuary. Little more than a village with perhaps a dozen shops in its narrow High Street, it is well off the beaten track between London and the East Coast popular resorts so favoured by the holiday making multitudes. Bleakcliff offers no attractions apart from its bracing air, its well-ordered countryside, surprisingly unsullied in the immediate vicinity by petrol pumps or cheap building enterprises. In fact, there are very few new houses in the district, chiefly owing to the fact that local authority frowns in no uncertain manner upon anything which might in any way endanger the quiet, rural attractive atmosphere. Faced with such a backward and unimaginative attitude, the two local building contractors have long since transferred their activities to more go-ahead and remunerative fields.

Doctor Morelle had recommended the tonic qualities of Bleakcliff to Arthur Hall, when he was treating him for after-effects of a motor accident, which had exacted a heavy toll on his nervous system. His case had proved responsive to the Doctor's treatment. After only a few visits to the charming house his patient had been fortunate enough to secure at Bleakcliff, Doctor Morelle considered the man had adjusted himself satisfactorily to a new life and his services were required no longer.

Hall and his wife settled down to become highly respected residents, living a staid, unexciting life. The neuroses which had affected Hall as a result of his accident gradually faded into the background of his mind like the remnants of half-forgotten evil dreams. He could not imagine that he had ever endured such sufferings of the mind and spirit, so far removed were they now, so dim and hazy were their memory. Life had become a gentle flow of incident and interest as unruffled and unhurried as a slow, quiet stream. And then evil disturbed the peace and contentment, not only of Hall's placid life but the lives and uneventful happiness of other residents of Bleakcliff.

Doctor Morelle had, not unnaturally, in the course of his subsequent busy career almost forgotten Hall's existence. He was somewhat surprised one morning to receive a letter from the husband stating that his wife was very ill, and that he would take it as a great favour if the Doctor would pay them a visit as soon as possible.

As it happened, Doctor Morelle had just concluded a spell of intensive laboratory experiments, and the two hours' drive by car to Bleakcliff appealed to him as a very welcome break. Miss Frayle was even more eager and delighted at the prospect of a drive to the coast. She had spent the last few days in the laboratory taking copious notes of names she found difficulty in spelling, and endeavouring to simulate an interest in a series of chemical processes which appeared to her singularly intricate and difficult to comprehend.

They found Bleakcliff very little altered from the Doctor's memory of his last visit some years previously. The stately Victorian houses still edged the High Street. The little shops still dressed their windows in a style which had long gone out of fashion in the chromium-plated shops of the sophisticated large towns.

" It would be rather nice to retire and live here, wouldn't it, Doctor? " suggested Miss Frayle brightly, as they drove up the short drive in front of the Hall's house.

" So far as I am concerned, retirement suggests two provisos—failing physical health and decaying brain tissue," he replied acidly " At the moment, I possess neither one nor the other! "

He brought the car to a standstill. As he did so the front door opened and Arthur Hall came running down the front steps to greet them.

" I'm so glad you could get here, Doctor," and there was relief and hope shining plainly in his eyes.

" This is my assistant, Miss Frayle, who occasionally assists me in my work," said Doctor Morelle, sardonically ambiguous. Hall ushered them into a cheerful sitting-room, and ordered tea to be brought in at once. While it was being served he gave a description of the illness which had struck at his wife. When he had finished his story the Doctor asked to see Mrs. Hall right away.

"I'm afraid she's very upset, Doctor. She may not answer your questions." He went on, his face worried and puzzled: "You remember what a cheerful sort of person she used to be? "

Doctor Morelle nodded: "Her good spirits were of great assistance in effecting a cure in your own case."

"That's true . . . well I'm afraid you'll find she's changed. Since she went to bed four days ago, she's refused to get up. Hardly speaks to anyone. As I've told you, she thinks she's being spied upon— "

"A common hallucination in such cases," the Doctor informed him as they went into the hall, leaving Miss Frayle to continue her tea. They were away nearly half-an-hour, and when they returned Doctor Morelle appeared thoughtful. He took a Le Sphinx from his case and lit it. Hall, his eyes dark with anxiety, filled an old pipe.

"There would seem to be a somewhat obscure reason for Mrs. Hall's illness," murmured Doctor Morelle. He turned to the other: "Have you no clue as to what may have been responsible for her suddenly retiring to bed suffering apparently from nervous collapse? "

Hall was silent for a moment, then slowly took a wallet from his inside pocket and extracted a postcard. "I didn't mention it at first," he said. "I didn't quite know whether you ought to be told, or the police. I—I felt perhaps I ought not to worry you with it, that it hadn't really got anything to do with my wife being ill like this—"

Miss Frayle saw Doctor Morelle take the postcard will ill-concealed impatience.

Hall went on: "It arrived the morning my wife collapsed. She saw it before I could intercept it. That card is the cause of all the trouble, I feel it in my bones, but I—I don't know . . . you may think it's nothing—just a practical joke or something . . ." his voice trailed off.

Doctor Morelle read:

"YOUR CONSCIENCE MUST BE AROUSED. EXPIATE YOUR CRIME OR THE POLICE WILL BE INFORMED. THE VOICE OF YOUR GUILT WILL NOT BE SILENCED."

It was written by hand in neat block capitals, and addressed to Mrs. Hall.

"Obviously," he snapped, "this is a contributary cause of your wife's breakdown."

"It must have been dropped through the letter-box either late at night or early in the morning."

"I had already assumed that it was not delivered through the post."

"Why? " asked Miss Frayle, somewhat unthinkingly.

"Because," said Doctor Morelle, "I had observed the absence of any postage stamp! " Hall seemed about to speak, then hesitated.

"You have no idea who might be the perpetrator of this hardly innocent little missive? " the Doctor asked.

The other shook his head.

"All I know is that several others in Bleakcliff have received these poison-pen cards."

"Indeed? " The Doctor gave him a narrowed look.

"What a beastly thing to do! " exclaimed Miss Frayle.

"I don't know if the police are trying to trace the writer," added Hall.

"They would have a somewhat difficult task," was Doctor Morelle's comment. "However, with my assistance they should in this case succeed."

Hall looked at him quickly, a surprised expression momentarily creasing the worried frown:

"I had no idea, Doctor, that you interested yourself in—? " he broke off.

"Criminal investigation? " the Doctor smiled a smile of somewhat over-elaborate deprecation.

"Didn't you read his evidence in the Mayfair Poisoning Case? "* asked Miss Frayle. "Oh, it was most interesting! "

"Thank you, Miss Frayle! " murmured the Doctor sardonically.

"I—er—I'm afraid I don't read court cases," Hall admitted, obviously embarrassed at his ignorance of Doctor Morelle's eminence in criminological matters.

"Indeed? " The Doctor regarded him with an interest somewhat similar to that he might have shown on encountering for the first time a sample of bacteriological evidence hitherto unknown to him. He gave a slight cough. "However, no doubt you are familiar with the whereabouts of the local Police Station? "

"Why yes. It's at the other end of the village—opposite the Post Office."

"Are we going there, Doctor? " asked Miss Frayle with a little anxious frown, noting him pick up his hat and gloves. He turned to her with the merest flicker of a smile.

* Doctor Morelle's evidence on this occasion was delivered to a packed court. In the form of a learned thesis on toxins and biochemical reactions, largely over the heads of the listeners, it affected the trial in no unsensational way.

" Be not afraid, my dear Miss Frayle, they won't need *your* fingerprints— " and added as if as an afterthought: " *Yet!* "

" Would you like me to come with you? " suggested Hall rather helpfully. " Perhaps I could—er—explain—who you are— " he broke off vaguely.

" That will not be necessary," the Doctor reassured him " I imagine my name might be familiar even to a village constable—no doubt they have access to the daily newspapers here! Come, Miss Frayle, let us call upon the rural constabulary . . . "

" I believe one of the officers is named Preedy—er—Sergeant Preedy," Hall said to him as they went into the hall. Leaving the car outside the house, he made his way, followed by Miss Frayle towards the village. It was early evening, drowsy after a long, fine summer's day, and there were few signs of activity. One or two cars passed them ; in them middle-aged ladies who appeared as if they might be on their way to pay calls upon their fellow residents. The atmosphere of the High Street was rather reminiscent of a miniature edition of Bath or Cheltenham.

They had no difficulty in finding the Police Station. It was a fairly large Victorian building with an imposing front entrance marred somewhat by its notice board, overflowing with a varied collection of announcements. Most of them appeared to be concerned more with agricultural than criminal matters.

Sergeant Preedy himself answered the Doctor's ring. Upon learning his visitors' identities he welcomed the Doctor and Miss Frayle with eager interest. He very rarely saw a new face in the district, let alone visitors from London—and the arrival of such distinguished personalities as he was now entertaining was an event of unprecedented importance! Preedy, despite his bucolic countenance, was by no means the yokel policeman so often burlesqued on screen and stage.

He ushered them into a large room which had been converted to the purpose of an office. The walls were generously plastered with the same posters and notices which were exhibited outside. Two policemen's helmets hung behind the door. He said with suitable deference :

" Well, Doctor Morelle, what can I do for you? What's the trouble? "

" I imagine it is conceivably your trouble, too, Sergeant," the Doctor replied smoothly. " Briefly, it concerns these anonymous postcards, a number of which I understand have been delivered in the village." A worried look immediately appeared on Sergeant Preedy's pleasant face. He pulled open a drawer in a big desk by the window.

" Like this? " he asked.

Doctor Morelle took the postcard the other handed to him and examined it. It was an exact duplicate of that addressed to Mrs. Hall, but was in this case addressed to a Mr. Barwell.

" Nothing to go on, you see," said Preedy. " Nothing. And that's the trouble."

Miss Frayle glanced at his troubled expression and back to the Doctor who said:

" Merely these postcards, each with precisely the same message? And delivered in a like manner? "

" Seven of 'em in all."

" Eight, including Mrs. Hall," murmured the Doctor.

Sergeant Preedy stared at him. " Mrs. Hall—is she another one? "

The Doctor nodded.

" Poor woman, it's upset her terribly," put in Miss Frayle, " How can people be so cruel? "

" How did you know about it? " asked the other, scratching his grey head in perplexity.

" Mr. Hall happens to have been a patient of mine," explained Doctor Morelle. " When his wife received this postcard the shock affected her and she is now on the verge of a nervous collapse."

" I see."

He glanced at the postcard the Doctor had returned to him and rubbed his chin thoughtfully.

" I wish the people who get these wouldn't take 'em so seriously," he ruminated. " It's just what the person who sent 'em wants! "

" The recipients are prominent persons locally it would seem? "

" Oh yes, bigwigs of the neighbourhood. Think a lot o' themselves they do! " He grinned tolerantly at Miss Frayle. " Come and tell me all about it in a proper fluster that anybody should dare to insinuate they were mixed up in anything not quite above-board." He chuckled reminiscently. " I've told one or two of 'em that a man who's never broken the law in some way or other must have spent his life in a monastery or something like it! Be surprised how that makes 'em stop and think."

Miss Frayle gave him a little smile conveying approval.

" All the same," he continued, " it's a worrying business. Especially with rumours beginning to get about. You know how these people are, Doctor Morelle. When they're up against something a bit out of the ordinary. Lot of scared hens! "

Doctor Morelle nodded. He offered no comment.

" Had a couple of silly old spinsters in here this morning. Insisted, if you please, I should go and arrest Miss Lang up at Bleak Priory."

" Miss Lang? "

Sergeant Preedy rubbed his chin again. " Queer old girl who lives at Bleak Priory. Been here years, writing a book on the

87

locality—that's why they say she knows everything about everybody."

"She sounds as if she might, don't you think?" put in Miss Frayle tentatively.

Preedy shrugged non-committally. "Anyone, for that matter, who's been in Bleakcliff any length of time, can find out all there is to find out about the other inhabitants. Yes. Got nothing else to do but gossip and tittle-tattle."

"Nevertheless, I should care to converse with this Miss Lang."

"If she'll let you, Doctor Morelle!" the other returned.

"You feel she may object?"

"Try her and see!" Sergeant Preedy's attitude implied the Doctor would be wasting his time.

"That is exactly what I propose to do!" Doctor Morelle ignored the implication. "Bleak Priory, did you say is her place of residence?"

"That's right, Doctor. Stands on the hill at the back here." He pointed through the window. "You can't miss it. Turn left at the cross-roads. They say monks lived there about five hundred years ago, and it's undermined with secret passages. Cosy little corner—I *don't* think!"

However, this somewhat sinister description was entirely wasted upon the Doctor. Informing the Sergeant he would advise him in the event of his discovering anything, he set off in the direction indicated at a brisk pace. Miss Frayle hurried along after him, being forced to make strenuous efforts to keep up with his long strides. The sky had suddenly become overcast and clouded. A chilly north-east wind was whistling through the trees as they came into sight of the Priory. It was a gaunt and black-looking building, standing on the side of a hill, as Sergeant Preedy had told them. As they approached it, however, it became evident that it was in an uninhabitable condition. They paused for a moment to survey the place.

"Do you think this *can* be the place, Doctor?" asked Miss Frayle doubtfully.

"According to Sergeant Preedy's directions, it would appear so."

"But it's an old ruin."

And indeed, most of the walls were crumbling, and several of them had been reduced to nothing more than heaps of stones. Masses of dark ivy crawled over the derelict mass.

"The fading light obscures one's vision, but the building does present a somewhat derelict appearance," conceded the Doctor, as they drew slowly nearer. "Possibly, however, there are habitable quarters in the regions at the back."

They walked through towering entrance-gates which swung rusted and creaking on massive pillars. The moss-patched and weedy gravel path crunched under their feet as they approached the wide porch. The wind whistled dismally through the broken windows and crevices in the stonework. Bats fluttered silently over their heads. Somewhere an owl hooted.

Miss Frayle could not suppress a shiver as the wind moaned more loudly round a corner.

"Just listen to the wind!" She spoke in a whisper, as if in danger of being overheard.

"Miss Lang would obviously appear to be a devotee of the fresh air cult!" was Doctor Morelle's comment.

Miss Frayle suddenly clutched his arm. "Listen!"

They listened intently. Very faintly, came the sound of a stick tapping upon worn flagstones. In a moment the heavy door before them creaked open and a strange figure presented itself in the doorway. A long grey cloak was thrown over her shoulders ; her white hair fluttered in the gusts of wind.

"Go away!" the apparition screeched. "Go away!"

"Miss Lang!" breathed Miss Frayle.

"No doubt she would answer Sergeant Preedy's description!" murmured Doctor Morelle.

Apprehensively she clutched his arm more desperately than ever. Miss Lang came nearer and waved a thick, heavy stick threateningly. Her eyes were hidden by tinted spectacles which gave her an even more forbidding appearance.

"Oh Doctor—she's terrifying—those dark glasses—!" Miss Frayle gulped.

"I know what you've come to find out, but I won't answer," called Miss Lang hysterically. "Go away—I won't answer!"

Although Miss Frayle was dragging at his arm, urging him to move, the Doctor stood his ground. The advancing woman halted a few feet away.

"You've no reason to suspect me any more than the others in Bleakcliff," she shrilled.

"Why, Miss Lang?" asked Doctor Morelle, calmly and quietly formidable.

Miss Frayle imagined she saw the eyes flash behind the dark glasses.

"Because there are no secrets in this village! Everyone spies on their neighbours!"

"Have they discovered the particular skeleton that rattles in your cupboard?" the Doctor queried in an insinuating voice. The thrust seemed to find its mark.

"Go away!" Miss Lang was advancing on them again, her voice discordant and cracked with fury. She waved her stick with increasing menace. "Strangers aren't welcome here! Away!"

89

"She'll attack us!" cried Miss Frayle, now thoroughly frightened. The wrath seemed to be about to burst over them. It was too much for her. Letting go the Doctor's arm, she ran for dear life the way she had come.

Miss Lang came almost within striking distance of Doctor Morelle, her stick raised threateningly.

"Be advised and follow her—go!"

He shrugged resignedly.

"Since there would seem little to be gained by remaining, I will accept your advice." Turning abruptly on his heel, he murmured, elaborately polite: "Good evening, Miss Lang!"

"Good riddance!" she flung after him. He heard the tapping of her stick retreating back the way she had come until it was caught in the howling of the wind.

He made his way unhurriedly through the gates. Outside he stood for a few moments to turn back and survey the desolate scene in the growing dusk. The woman had disappeared into the crumbling mass of stone and ivy. Suddenly, he imagined he heard a muffled cry for help. It appeared to come from somewhere down the road. He walked quickly in the direction from which it came, and on the other side of a low hedge a sorry spectacle met his gaze.

Miss Frayle had fallen into a pond, half hidden by weed and grass. It seemed to be filled to a depth of about three feet, for she was up to well above her waist in muddy, stagnant water, and was floundering about in an attempt to negotiate the steep bank. So far poor Miss Frayle had failed.

Doctor Morelle looked down at her with a sardonic smile at the corners of his mouth.

"Whatever are you doing there, Miss Frayle? Do you suddenly imagine yourself to be a newt?"

"I—I fell in," she informed him unnecessarily. "I thought this might be a short cut, and was looking back to see if you were coming—" She forced the words through chattering teeth.

"How long do you propose to continue your ablutions?" he queried as she splashed about in a vain attempt to pull herself out.

"Instead of asking silly questions, couldn't you help me?" she said miserably, half crying with mortification.

Suddenly from behind them came the sound of rapid footsteps, and a voice approaching called out:

"Someone in trouble there?"

A well-built, middle-aged man appeared out of the gloom. He stopped on seeing them. "Oh, hello," he said, and then coming forward again offered in a friendly voice: "Can I help?"

"Good evening," replied Doctor Morelle calmly. "Merely my assistant investigating pond life."

The newcomer seemed rather mystified by the Doctor's explanation. He gave him a sharp look, then glanced at the shivering Miss Frayle.

" Better give her a hand, hadn't we? " he suggested.

" I was about to do so."

" Come on then, I'll help. Catch hold, young lady, and we'll have you out in a jiffy." And he extended his hand. Miss Frayle thankfully grasped it.

" Heave ho! " the man exclaimed heartily, and in a second she was standing on the bank, gasping for breath.

" My word, you're wet all right!." he said, looking at her dripping clothes, muddy and weed-bedraggled.

" Ye—yes—the water's terribly cold," she replied through chattering teeth.

" You'd better come along to my place at once," the man went on briskly. " Cottage just across the field—you can dry your clothes and knock back a warm drink."

" You're very kind," chattered Miss Frayle gratefully. She adjusted her spectacles which had fallen awry during her misadventure, and made a wan attempt to smile her gratitude at him through the mud and water-bespattered lenses.

" What d'you say, sir? " The stranger turned to Doctor Morelle, who had stood there silent, surveying Miss Frayle and her rescuer with a saturnine expression.

" Yes," he murmured condescendingly. " I feel somewhat chilly myself. A little stimulant would prove very acceptable."

" Come along then, let's hurry—we'll be there in five minutes . . . " As he moved off he added : " By the way, my name's Archer—Gilbert Archer." Doctor Morelle made the necessary introductions for himself and Miss Frayle. The man led the way and they followed, Miss Frayle flapping her arms to restore the circulation.

The cottage proved to be a substantial, half-timbered low building, with attractive lounge, in which the Doctor and the man who had introduced himself as Gilbert Archer sat before their drinks. Before them blazed a cheerful log fire. Presently, they were joined by Miss Frayle, clad in a huge dressing-gown, the property of her host, who insisted on lending it to her while her clothes dried over a clothes-horse in front of a great stove in the kitchen.

Archer was a man of obviously cultured tastes, and an agreeable hour was passed before Miss Frayle was attired once more in her own clothes. She and Doctor Morelle rose to go, and he turned to thank the man.

" Well, Mr. Archer . . . Rest assured Miss Frayle and I are greatly indebted to you for your hospitality."

91

"Yes," added Miss Frayle gratefully, and suppressing a sneeze, "you have been most kind."

"Not a bit," he answered genially. "Afraid you're in for a cold, Miss Frayle . . . I've been only too glad of your company. You see, I've been in Bleakcliff only a few weeks, and are people here sticky to know! "

"The natives appear to be somewhat unfriendly?" queried Doctor Morelle with an expressive lift of the eyebrows.

"Rotten, miserable lot of snobs, that's what they are! " burst out Archer viciously, knocking out the ash from an old pipe. He realised that he must have appeared rather vehement, and with an apologetic smile he subsided.

"Sorry, I didn't mean to let fly like that! But I *am* a little bitter about 'em. Downright unpleasant, they've been. Give you an example: Only this evening, just before I saw you, I met a fellow named Carpenter, who lives at the big house along the way. My nearest neighbour. We met point-blank in the lane—not another soul in sight. D'you think he'd wish me ' Good evening '? Not on your life! That's the sort of people they are. Because they live in a bigger house, or have been here forty years, or happen to be second cousin to a bishop—! "

He broke off with a shrug. "There—I'm at it again."

"What a shame! " sympathised Miss Frayle in slightly muffled voice. "I'm so sorry, Mr. Archer."

Doctor Morelle, however, shook his head, his expression censorious:

"I feel your attitude indicates a somewhat scanty understanding of human behaviour," he pronounced. He paused, then said through a puff of cigarette-smoke: "Somewhat incomprehensible, Mr. Archer, in one who would seem to be a student of psychology." He indicated the large bookcases round the walls, where there was row upon row of formidable volumes.

"Oh, you've noticed my little library? " said Archer. "Yes, I've studied the subject deeply, and still read everything on it I can."

Doctor Morelle crossed over to a bookshelf and thoughtfully scanned its contents.

"Um . . . Freud . . . Jung . . . Adler . . . and the other school, I see . . . Watson . . . Pavlov . . ." He turned to the other with a curious little smile. "You *have* delved deeply into the subconscious! "

At this point Miss Frayle found it humanly impossible any longer to suppress a gigantic sneeze.

"Almost as deeply as Miss Frayle delved into the pond," the Doctor added, with a sardonic glance in her direction.

"It's a fascinating subject," Archer said with enthusiasm.

92

" The investigation of any mystery is fascinating," Doctor Morelle said absently, moving away from the bookshelf and thoughtfully tapping the ash off his Le Sphinx.   " Especially when one sees its elucidation near."

If Miss Frayle had not been too preoccupied with her cold, she might have detected an implication in his words.   But they seemed to have fallen on empty air.

Soon afterwards, Doctor Morelle and Miss Frayle wished Gilbert Archer good-night, and hurried on their way back to Arthur Hall's house.   They arrived there without any further mishap.   Their host would not hear of their returning to London that night ; it was by now dark and the night uninviting for travelling. He had already prepared their rooms for them, he assured them, and Miss Frayle was thankful to retire with a hot water bottle and a glass of hot milk.

" I should like to use your telephone before I partake of some supper," Doctor Morelle said to the other after Miss Frayle had gone upstairs.

Hall looked at him interrogatively, but the Doctor gave no explanation for his request.

" Yes . . . yes. Of course! " Hall suddenly realised he had not answered him.   " Can I help you find the number? "

" That will not be necessary," the Doctor suavely assured him. " I merely wish to telephone the Police Station."

Doctor Morelle, Miss Frayle—little the worse for her experience of the previous evening—and Hall, were finishing breakfast the next morning, when they heard a sound in the drive outside. Miss Frayle recognised Sergeant Preedy, his face glowing with exertion and excitement, pedal energetically up to the front door. He had rung the bell and been admitted into the room almost before she had announced that it was he.

" We got him, Doctor—we got him! " He gasped for breath, mopping his brow.   " Caught him red-handed right outside Major Carpenter's front door. Just like you said! " He grinned in open admiration at the Doctor.   " Though how you found him out is a mystery! A quiet feller like that . . . Last person I'd suspect . . . " He went burbling on excitedly.

A cryptic smile flickered for a moment across Doctor Morelle's saturnine features.   " It's rather too long a story, Sergeant Preedy," he said quietly.   " And I have to go up in a moment to see my patient, Mrs. Hall.   Then I must return to Town without delay." And he went out of the room, leaving the Sergeant scratching his head in bewilderment and Miss Frayle goggling at Hall blankly.

Later, Sergeant Preedy had departed, and Arthur Hall was saying to the Doctor with a puzzled air:

93

"And you really mean to say that this man Archer sent those poison-pen cards?"

"Undoubtedly."

"But—but we hardly know the man."

"That was a contributary cause of the trouble." With that enigmatic utterance Doctor Morelle seemed to dismiss the matter from his mind, and went on to reassure the other that his wife's recovery was merely a matter of a week or two's rest. The shadow that had suddenly darkened her life was as suddenly swept away.

On the return journey, Miss Frayle was silent for some time. Presently, however, she turned to him, her face puzzled. "I still can't see how you found out about Mr. Archer," she said.

He bestowed a condescending smile on her. He said:

"It was merely a question of taking each piece of the jig-saw and fitting them together until one outstanding factor emerged. This was that the writer of the postcards was in each case unaware whether or not the recipients actually had a guilty secret. Otherwise the nature of the crime would obviously have been stated in order to achieve the maximum effect of fear in the intended victim. All the postcards, however, referred to 'your crime' and nothing more."

Keeping one hand on the steering wheel, he contrived dexterously to take out his cigarette case, extract a Le Sphinx and light it.

"The writer was obviously a person of some education," he went on through a cloud of cigarette smoke, "which narrowed the list of suspects. The motive was not of a mercenary nature, nor with intent to discredit the recipient with the outside world. Each card, you may recall, was delivered, not through the post, but privately. It would appear, therefore, the poison-pen writer was a person who, without knowing them very intimately, bore a grudge against a number of Bleakcliff's most prominent inhabitants, and out of revenge merely aimed at frightening them. That person, moreover, was a student of the human mind; someone who realised that almost without exception every one of us suffers from a latent sense of guilt—the universal guilt complex which lurks in the subconscious."

"And of course Mr. Archer *was* a student of human nature," she remembered. "All those books he had on psychology and all that."

"Precisely, my dear Miss Frayle."

There followed a short silence. She seemed to be wrestling with some intricate problem. Then:

"Of course, you were right, Doctor Morelle—I know— "

"Thank you!"

"But— " she went on determinedly, " —but we don't *all* have these 'guilt complexes' you speak about— "

94

" No? " He gave her a sardonic look.
" No," she said firmly. " I mean— "
He interrupted her. " That reminds me," he said in an off-hand tone. " Scotland Yard telephoned this morning before we left for London." He went on, with a sinister emphasis : " *They asked for you—!* "
" Scotland Yard? " she exclaimed.
" I decided I would not mention it to you at the time— "
She went pale. " But why—? What have I done— "
And then she realised his face was twisted with repressed saturnine amusement. " My dear Miss Frayle! " he chuckled, " how white you have gone! Can it be that even you have a guilty secret? "
Indignantly she said : " No, no! Of course not—! "
" Nevertheless," he mocked her, " your subconscious guilt would seem to be working at full pressure! As indeed it does with everyone . . . "
Miss Frayle glared at him through her spectacles. Still chuckling delightedly at the manner in which he had succeeded in making an example of her to prove his argument, Doctor Morelle pressed his foot on the accelerator and the car sped onwards towards London.

CHAPTER VII

THE CASE OF THE MYSTERIOUS MAHARANEE*

Doctor Morelle stepped on to the lecture-platform and surveyed his audience. There were several hundred people present ; young intense-looking medical students armed with notebooks ; a gratifying number of men who were distinguished members of his own profession. There was also the usual sprinkling of women. These he regarded with his usual somewhat over-elaborate disinterest—until his gaze rested on one whose presence he registered, with an inward feeling of self-satisfaction.
The Maharanee was sitting in her usual place near the door. She had so far attended every lecture in the series, and her continued attendance had intrigued even his curiosity, which was not of the most pressingly obvious kind. Her perfectly chiselled features, jet black hair and colourful Eastern robes added a distinctive touch to the proceedings. She had, moreover, maintained a mysterious aloofness, never uttering a word even during question time.

* This is another case in which it has been felt wiser to omit the full name of one of the chief protagonists.

Miss Frayle had, of course, been greatly intrigued by the presence of the Maharanee. She had a somewhat old-fashioned notion that all Indian women led a secluded life. She imagined that scientific research would have been quite outside their sphere of activities. The Maharanee, however, and to Miss Frayle's continued interest, seemed to absorb every word Doctor Morelle spoke. She always stayed to the end of the lecture, and seemed to take her leave at the end with some reluctance. She gave the impression on several occasions that she would like to have remained behind to speak to the Doctor.

It was a medical student who happened to sit next to Miss Frayle at one of the lectures who informed her that the woman was a Maharanee. The young man also added that it was rumoured she was in London on some mysterious mission which neither she nor any member of her retinue would divulge. This latter information made her appear even more intriguing in Miss Frayle's eyes, though the Doctor, when she told him what she had heard, discounted the "mysterious mission" in his usual sardonic way. But then, as she reminded herself, he *would!* She continued to weave her own idea of the Maharanee's reason for coming to London. She had to admit, nevertheless, that it was difficult to associate anything particularly strange about her regular attendances at the Doctor's lectures. She could only surmise that his own rather odd and mesmeric personality in some way attracted her. To-night, as Doctor Morelle glanced at his notes preparatory to beginning his lecture she had a seat in the audience from which she could observe the Maharanee closely. She gazed at her now and then through her spectacles, her mind full of conjectures about her.

The Doctor began to speak, and dutifully Miss Frayle forced her gaze and thoughts upon him and his words.

". . . This evening I propose to deal with some of the rather more obscure poisons of Eastern origin," he was saying. "Many of them date back thousands of years, their origins lost in the mists of antiquity, and consequently little is known of them in this country. It is, of course, to be hoped—even perhaps assumed—that it is merely a question of time before our research chemists discover all the true facts concerning all these drugs in question. In the meantime, let us commence with the narcotic group . . ."

Miss Frayle, whose attention had again wandered towards the Maharanee, noticed she had leaned forward slightly in her seat. She seemed particularly attentive to what the Doctor was saying. The intense interest manifest in her grave features, very lovely in their utter repose, did not leave her throughout the time Doctor Morelle was speaking.

When at length he had quitted the platform to the usual demonstration of enthusiastic admiration which he found secretly so gratifying, he retired to a room set aside for that purpose. He was arranging his notes and references in his brief-case, when Miss Frayle appeared. She was very excited and rather breathless. He glanced at her shrewdly.

"While I am aware that my lecture—unique as it undoubtedly was—received a worthily enthusiastic reception," he commented sardonically, "I had no idea it would reduce *you* to this state of extreme agitation!"

Then he noticed she was clutching a folded slip of paper.

"You appear to be the bearer of a communication of some nature," he said.

"It's for you—from the Maharanee," she panted. "It's most mysterious—she gave it to me, very quickly, as she was going out. She didn't say anything—"

He took the note.

"What does it mean?" She goggled at him.

"Apparently an appeal for assistance," he murmured, without raising his eyes from the message. "'Please come to my help'" he read half to himself. "'I am in great danger. Trust no one. I am surrounded by enemies'."

"Gracious!" gasped Miss Frayle, clutching at her spectacles agitatedly. "And she's so young and lovely, too!" She went on breathlessly: "I found out where she lives—it's just off Park Lane. I believe she's tremendously rich and—"

"What prompted you to learn her address?" He interrupted her with a quizzical look.

"Well—er—" Miss Frayle hesitated. "I thought you might want to see her and find out all about this." She indicated the note he was holding with a vague wave of the hand.

"Why should you assume I might be interested?"

She stammered hesitantly. Then she blurted out:

"Because she's—well, she *is* very charming—and it's rather romantic."

"My dear Miss Frayle, are you not becoming somewhat too adult to indulge in dream-fancies usually associated with children's picture books and fairy-tales?"

"But she never took her eyes off you the whole time you were lecturing," she persisted.

"Ah, yes," he murmured in an irritatingly smug tone of self-satisfaction. "I thought I spoke exceptionally well to-night. And, of course, a great part of my lecture referred to that part of the world with which she must be familiar." He lit a cigarette. "After what you have informed me, Miss Frayle, I feel I can hardly disappoint you! Let us therefore proceed towards Park Lane."

"We can walk—it's a nice evening," she said, noticeably excited at the prospect of learning something about the mysterious message and its equally mysterious sender. "It's not very far."

"As you wish . . . Ah, yes, I have my walking-stick . . ."

They were walking without undue haste through the streets in the vicinity of Curzon Street towards the address Miss Frayle had ascertained, when the Doctor suddenly laid a warning hand on her arm.

"I am distinctly under the impression we are being followed," he announced in a matter-of-fact tone.

"Oh! " gasped Miss Frayle. "Followed? But who would it be? "

"I imagine we may ascertain our shadower's identity by slipping into this doorway we are now approaching. Come, Miss Frayle! . . . Quickly and quietly! "

He pulled her into the narrow entrance to a small block of flats. "Remain motionless," he ordered in a peremptory whisper. "In a moment, our curiosity should be satisfied."

For a few moments all she could hear was the sound of a radio in one of the flats, a dance-band playing a popular tune. Then suddenly she heard very soft footsteps purposefully approaching. She caught her breath as the stealthy tread grew nearer. Then she glimpsed a fleeting picture of the lithe, turbanned figure. Their shadower was almost past them when the Doctor called out:

"Good evening! Were you seeking someone? "

The man stopped dead, turned, and slowly retraced his steps. For a moment he stood watching them warily, his eyes gleaming in his dusky face. Then he spoke:

"You are Doctor Morelle? " he queried in a sing-song tone. "I have a message for you from the Maharanee."

"How are you aware of my identity? "

The man appeared not to understand. "The Maharanee says for me to tell you to forget what she wrote to-night," he gabbled. "The Maharanee says for me to tell you all is well now. If you visit her, it would cause trouble for her." The man bowed and stood as if awaiting a reply.

"Suppose," said Doctor Morelle after a pause, "I am not convinced of the authenticity of your message."

The man's attitude grew tense, and Miss Frayle, watching his eyes, felt a chill run down her spine.

"I have spoken! " he announced in a menacing tone. "If you choose to ignore my warning, you may well pay for it with your life! "

"Oh! " gasped Miss Frayle, now beginning to feel thoroughly frightened.

"You understand, Doctor Morelle . . .?"
"I understand perfectly." And the Doctor turned to Miss Frayle. "Miss Frayle," he said conversationally, "You observe that police-officer at the street corner? Would you hasten and bring him here at once?"

The man gave a quick exclamation: "Police!" and muttering unintelligibly, he darted off into the darkness. Doctor Morelle watched him go unperturbed.

"I imagined that might scare you," he chuckled, as the man vanished into the heavy shadows of some tall buildings along the street.

"There he goes!" cried Miss Frayle, as the speeding figure passed under the light from a street lamp. "Shall I tell the policeman to go after him?".

"What policeman, my dear Miss Frayle?"

She blinked up at him in owl-like fashion through her spectacles. "Why—the one you said—the one at the corner." She turned and scanned the street before them and realised there was no one in sight. She said, puzzled: "But there isn't a policeman at all—"

He chuckled sardonically. "Precisely!"

"And—and, there wasn't one?" she stammered.

"The rapidity with which your cerebral tissues operate is positively phenomenal!" he murmured. Then, as if explaining to a child: "Merely a subterfuge on my part in order to precipitate our native friend's departure."

"But if you spoke to him in the first place, why did you want to get rid of him?" she asked, still with an air of bewilderment.

He sighed with an expression of long-suffering patience. "Because I had discovered all he had to tell me," he said. "And I did not wish to lose any more time." He glanced up the street. "We had better engage this taxi approaching at once. Otherwise I fear I may arrive at our destination too late."

He hailed the approaching taxi-cab which drew up alongside them. He motioned her to step in while he directed the driver.

"Doctor, you don't think anything's happened to the Maharanee, do you?" she asked him anxiously, as they drove off.

"I fear there may be some malignant scheme afoot," he answered. "I would hardly describe our recent acquaintance as a *friendly* native!"

Thirteen was the number of the house outside which the taxi pulled up. It stood in a typical Mayfair thoroughfare, with other large four-storey houses on either side, and was fronted by elaborate ornamental iron railings.

"I hope it won't be unlucky thirteen," said Miss Frayle in a low voice, catching sight of the number on the door as she followed the Doctor up the front steps. She had hardly spoken when the front door began to open silently, as if operated by a hidden hand.

" Oh! " she gasped. " It's as if we're expected! "

" No doubt the writer of the missive had some confidence that I should answer it in person," murmured Doctor Morelle. He paused for a moment, Miss Frayle peering short-sightedly from behind him. The door swung back silently wider. No one appeared to be within. The hall was dimly lit and quiet. An atmosphere of expectancy seemed to grip the house.

" How does the door open by itself? " Miss Frayle breathed in a puzzled whisper. He made no answer to her question, but moved forward with the remark :

" The invitation extended us to enter could not be more apparent. Follow me, Miss Frayle—and pray do not dig your nails into my arm! " he snapped, as she clutched him in apprehension.

As they stood inside, she looked round to see the door silently closely behind them. With a startled gasp she drew the Doctor's attention to this ; he murmured impatiently :

" Merely a mechanical device operated by remote control."

In the dimly lit hall they could discern the outlines of large old-fashioned pieces of furniture. The rugs on which they stepped were thick and luxurious. There was a wide archway with a heavily beaded curtain of Eastern design facing them, and as they were approaching it a gong boomed somewhere beyond it. The gong boomed again reverberatingly. They stood till the last eerie echo had died away.

" Possibly the dinner gong! " suggested the Doctor with sardonic humour.

" What a heavy scent! " commented Miss Frayle, sniffing. " It's like incense." The perfume seemed more overwhelming as they moved forward.

They had almost reached the archway when the curtain was thrust aside with a discordant rattle. An Indian woman appeared with such startling abruptness that for a frightening moment Miss Frayle felt she must have materialised, genii-like, out of the heavy incense that seemed now to engulf them. The woman wore striking Indian robes, and there was the light musical clinking of bangles as she stood there barring their path aggressively.

" Who are you and whom do you seek? " she demanded menacingly. She spoke English with only a slight accent.

" I am Doctor Morelle— " the Doctor began in level tones, and then turned on Miss Frayle to snap : " Your fingers are like claws! " Hurriedly, and with an apologetic murmur she withdrew her terrified grasp on his arm.

"I wish to speak to the Maharanee," he pursued, addressing the woman.

She shook her head deliberately.

"What you ask is impossible."

"I refuse to believe anything to be impossible," he answered.

The woman stared at him slowly, her eyes glowing. After a moment's level scrutiny, she spoke and there was a hint of sarcasm in her voice.

"You are no doubt a being of great resourcefulness, great skill, Doctor Morelle— "

He made a deprecating movement.

"But even you," she went on steadily, "may not speak to my mistress."

"May I enquire what is to prevent me? "

"She is dead! "

"Dead! " echoed Miss Frayle in shocked tones.

"She passed away a few minutes ago."

For a moment no one spoke. Then: "And the cause of her demise? " asked Doctor Morelle.

"An overdose of Atropine. When the Maharanee returned here she was suffering from a severe headache. She had heard of Atropine for the alleviation of pain, and begged of me to get her some at once from a chemist nearby."

"And you obeyed her request? "

"No." Her lips moved as if she was struggling to check her grief. "Had I done so, this tragedy might not have occurred."

"What happened? "

"I—I sent one of the servants. When he brought the tablets, I took them to the Maharanee." She paused. Again it seemed she was overcome with grief and was summoning up all her will-power to prevent her from breaking down completely. "I—I was called away," she went on in a low voice. "When I returned she was dying."

She wrung her hands in despair.

"Oh, if only she had seen a doctor," she cried. "But she never would! She must have taken too much of the drug— "

"Poor woman," said Miss Frayle in a low voice.

"It would not have been difficult for her to have administered to herself an overdose of the drug," the Doctor mused. "The appropriate dose of Atropine is one two-hundredth or one hundredth of a grain. One grain might easily prove fatal."

"Had I been there it would never have happened! " The woman seemed to be able to control her emotion no longer and buried her face in her hands while sobs racked her.

"Doctor, how terrible! " whispered Miss Frayle.

101

"If you are alluding to her histrionic performance, on the contrary!" he observed shortly. "She is quite a consummate actress!"

"Doctor Morelle, what do you mean—?"

The woman had ceased sobbing and was staring at the Doctor with a baffled expression. He interrupted Miss Frayle's surprised questioning to address the other:

"If the Maharanee never consulted a doctor in her lifetime, as you have stated," he snapped grimly, "it will be necessary for a member of the medical profession to see her now! That is, in the event of your desiring to comply with the demands of the law."

He paused, his eyes narrowed as he regarded her. Then he said peremptorily: "Show me to her room without delay."

"No! No!" She stepped quickly back, stretching her arms across the archway, as if she would forbid him to pass.

"Very well." Doctor Morelle's tone was calm and deliberate. "In which case there will be no alternative but to summon the police."

He glanced round purposefully in search of a telephone. The woman who had been hesitating now suddenly seemed to make up her mind.

She stood aside, holding the curtains apart, and said over her shoulder: "Follow me."

She led the way up a wide staircase, and showed them into a room at the front of the house. It was dimly lit, the atmosphere oppressive. Miss Frayle noticed the Doctor's nostrils quiver suspiciously once or twice as he went across to the bed where the Maharanee lay. Her eyes were closed. An expression of profound repose was upon the finely chiselled features.

Miss Frayle watched him breathlessly as he raised a slender wrist and felt the pulse. Then he bent over the inert form and lifted one of the eyelids. The pupils were contracted. Slowly he rose to his feet.

"Miss Frayle," he said, without taking his eyes off the figure before him. "Telephone at once!" He snapped out a number. "Request them to send an ambulance immediately." He turned and indicated the telephone at the bedside. Miss Frayle moved forward with alacrity to obey.

"No! No!" cried the woman, stepping forward as if to prevent her reaching the telephone. "The Maharanee must not leave this house!"

Doctor Morelle turned his level penetrating gaze on her.

Then his voice seemed to crack like a whip-lash. "Those are my orders," he replied imperturbably. "You are aware as well as I that the Maharanee is not dead!—She is merely under the influence

102

THE CASE OF THE MYSTERIOUS MAHARANEE

of an obscure narcotic of Indian origin known as—." He mentioned the drug by name.

The woman's whole attitude seemed to sag as the blow struck home.

" Miss Frayle—the telephone! "

The other now suddenly gathered herself and darted forward as Miss Frayle picked up the receiver. Before she could achieve her object she found herself confronted by Doctor Morelle's tall and dominating figure.

" Remain where you are! " he charged her, his eyes boring into hers. " My will compels you! "

The woman halted in her stride.

" My will forces you to obey . . ." his voice was terrifying in its intensity. " Make no sound, remain quite, quite still! "

She sank into a chair, and remained motionless while Miss Frayle, in a rather unsteady voice, completed the telephone call. Nor did she move again until the ambulance had arrived and the inert form of the Maharanee was borne away upon a stretcher.

" What made you suspicious about that native woman in the first place? " asked Miss Frayle some time later. The Doctor had just returned from the hospital to which the Maharanee had been conveyed with the news that the antidote to the drug had proved effective. The Maharanee was slowly recovering.

He gave her a thin smile. " I should have thought even you, Miss Frayle, would have realised that the woman's account of how the Atropine was administered was an entire fabrication. No chemist in this country would supply Atropine or any other drug of a poisonous nature without a written prescription from a medical man. The fact that the woman gave no such prescription to the servant who was supposed to have obtained the drug was confirmed later by her statement that the Maharanee had no medical attention."

He paused to light an inevitable Le Sphinx.

" My suspicions were aroused, however, even before she launched upon that highly fabricated description," he went on smoothly. " I happen to know the nearest all-night chemist is situated a mile distant. Even if the servant entrusted with the errand had taken a taxi, it is highly improbable the drug in question would have taken effect so completely within the brief time between the servant's return and our arrival on the scene. Furthermore, when I examined the Maharanee the contracted condition of the pupils of the eyes was palpable." He paused theatrically. " In point of fact, a delirient such as Atropine would *enlarge* the pupils! "

* Doctor Morelle has directed that under no circumstances should the name of the drug be specified.

" You knew she was alive then? "

He shook his head negatively.

" I was not certain. It was very probable that an injection of the drug used by the woman induced a trance of a death-like appearance." He shrugged his shoulders. " However, I summoned the ambulance in the hope that this supposition might be correct. Fortunately for the Maharanee, my somewhat speculative diagnosis was proved to be a fact."

" But—but what was behind it all? "

He puffed a cloud of smoke non-committally ceiling-wards. " I prefer to confine my interest in such matters to the purely scientific."

" I'm afraid I don't much care for the mystic East either," Miss Frayle agreed.

" Mystic East my pedal extremity! " was his emphatic reply. " I could produce all the manifestations you witnessed to-night in my own house now! "

She goggled at him doubtfully. " Oh, Doctor," she said, " I don't think you could! " His face assumed an expression more saturnine than ever.

" Would you care for demonstrative proof? " he said between his teeth, drawing menacingly closer.

She gasped, terrified by his demeanour.

" Oh, no, no! I believe you," she stammered hurriedly. And added: " After all, you *did* mesmerise that Indian woman in some magical way! "

" Precisely! " he snapped. " That incident alone establishes my claim that all so-called magic, Eastern or Occidental *is* explicable. Let us briefly return to that incident which you were pleased to describe as mesmerism. When you were telephoning, Miss Frayle, you may recall that your back was turned to the lady in question."

" I was so frightened and terrified I wouldn't get the number in time I expect I *was* preoccupied," she admitted.

" Your back was towards her," he snapped with finality. " But my *dear* Miss Frayle, had you displayed a trifle more curiosity, you might have observed that she was kept at bay not by my mesmeric powers, but by a thin blade of cold steel! "

" Your sword-stick! " she gasped. " Oh—! "

" And whatever magic powers that woman may have possessed they were of no match for the persuasive powers of my sword-stick! "

And he smiled triumphantly at her and tapped the ash off his cigarette.

CHAPTER VIII

THE CASE OF THE KIDNAPPED CHILD

Doctor Morelle first attended Mrs. Carter as the result of an urgent and agitated telephone call one morning in the very early hours from her husband. Accompanied by Miss Frayle, he arrived at the Carters' house situated in an exclusive square off Park Lane. Miss Frayle rang the bell and after a few moments the door was opened by a butler of such repulsive aspect that she drew back with a gasp of apprehension.

"Wot yer ringing for? " the man demanded.

"Presumably with the object of attracting your attention," murmured the Doctor, eyeing him with abstract interest. He was conjecturing what Lombroso* might have made of the physiognomy before him.

"You Morelle? "

"I am Doctor Morelle."

The butler glowered at him for a moment then turned his menacing gaze upon Miss Frayle, who shrank back behind the Doctor. Then he growled reluctantly: "Uh! . . . Come in both you . . ."

Doctor Morelle, followed by Miss Frayle, who could not refrain from goggling at the man in morbid fascination, entered. The door closed behind them.

"Wait in here," was the grunted instruction, and they found themselves in a luxuriously appointed library.

"I'll tell him," the butler growled, and left them abruptly. As the door closed after him Miss Frayle exclaimed:

"What a horrible man! "

The Doctor lit a cigarette.

"A noteworthy subject for the anthropologist," he mused. "Quite remarkably Simian characteristics and abnormally long arms."

"Like a gorilla, d'you mean? "

He bestowed upon her a supercilious smile: "Precisely, Miss Frayle! "

At that moment the door opened and a plump, middle-aged man came in. His face appeared harassed. His voice, as he came towards them, was quiet with undertones of anxiety in it.

"Doctor Morelle? I'm Carter."

The Doctor nodded. "This is my assistant, Miss Frayle," he said, Carter gave her a wan smile.

* Doctor Morelle has given several lectures on Lombroso's " L'Uomo Delinquente," disposing of its theories and supporting the later views of Dr. Goring (" The English Convict," 1913).

"It's an unearthly hour," he apologised, "and I'm afraid you'll think it's the—well—" he hesitated, and then went on quickly "—the police—I should really have sent for."

"Police?" Miss Frayle blinked at him behind her spectacles.

The Doctor raised his eyebrows slightly. He surveyed the tip of his cigarette attentively. "You intimated over the telephone," he murmured, "that your wife was in a state of collapse?"

"Yes . . . You see—" again the hesitation and words blurted out "—our little girl has disappeared—she's been kidnapped!"

"Kidnapped?" breathed Miss Frayle.

"When did this occur?" Doctor Morelle queried.

"About an hour ago. My wife went to the nursery to see if she was asleep, and she'd vanished."

"Why *didn't* you send for the police?"

There was a perceptible pause. He considered the Doctor, as if weighing him up. Then he seemed to come to a decision. He squared his shoulders and said slowly: "Doctor Morelle . . . I must explain . . . My wife is not a happy woman." He passed his hand across his brow with a gesture of anxiety and doubt. With a muttered apology he beckoned them to sit down. The Doctor remained standing, however, and waited expectantly for Carter to continue. After a moment he began, leaning forward in his chair, and talking quickly and earnestly. His story was one that was not unfamiliar to the Doctor's ears.

Bella Carter was thirty-four when he had married her, and they had not considered the possibility of having children. When, however, a child, Sally, was born a change began to manifest itself in the Carter household, imperceptible at first and slow in development, but growing in intensity. She had suffered considerable nervous strain during the birth of the child, and her convalescence was prolonged. During this time she actually saw very little of Sally, pleading that the baby's crying tried her nerves.

So the child's early years were spent chiefly in the company of nurse-maids and that of her father. He had been delighted at her arrival, and began to spend more and more time with her as she reached an interesting age. Sally held an increasing fascination for him. On arriving back from the City, his first visit would be to the nursery. Nevertheless, and in spite of the breach that was growing palpably wider between them, he remained affectionate in his relationship with his wife.

Bella began to nurse a grievance. She had more time to brood now that her husband's business prospered and he became wealthier and correspondingly generous to her. She had all that she wanted in a material sense. Servants, clothes, her own car, an attractive town house and a lovely rambling old place in Sussex. And yet all

106

the time she was weaving the pattern of her life into a highly tragic melodrama, with herself in the leading rôle of the wronged and neglected wife and mother.

Not unnaturally her attitude became responsible for her husband focusing his attention and affection increasingly upon his daughter. This in turn heightened Bella's 'persecution complex'. More and more she imagined herself the innocent victim of almost every sort of malicious action. And so the vicious circle was tragically completed. It was not in her nature to suppress her highly-coloured imaginings. All her life Bella had dramatised every passing fancy that flitted through her somewhat shallow mind. It had always given her considerable satisfaction. Moreover, such flights of histrionics had, in the early days of his marriage, never failed to achieve their object where her husband was concerned. Lately, as her dark imaginings became almost continuous, he was becoming somewhat innured to them and inclined to discount her extravagant assertions. Like a drug addict increasing the dose, she became more violent and outrageous ; her actions became more eccentric in her frantic bid to steal the limelight from her daughter, now an attractive child.

"How old is your daughter? " the Doctor asked him as Carter came to the end of his story.

"Just five."

"Poor little thing! " sympathised Miss Frayle.

"An only child," continued Carter. "I'm passionately devoted to her, but I was determined she should not be spoilt. That was the origin of the estrangement between my wife and me— "

He was about to go on, when Doctor Morelle suddenly raised his hand for silence, and moved swiftly across to the door. Noiselessly, he grasped the knob and turned it, flinging the door open with the same movement.

The huge figure of the butler jerked up from what was palpably a listening attitude. Miss Frayle was unable to suppress a tiny scream.

"I thought my intuition was not without foundation," the Doctor murmured, eyeing the man with a sardonic smile.

"Riley! What d'you want? " demanded Carter sharply.

"I—er—I was—just— "

"Indulging in a little eavesdropping, possibly? " suggested Doctor Morelle, helpfully.

"I dunno what yer mean! "

Carter dismissed him with an impatient wave of his hand.

"I'll ring when I need you," he said curtly. When the man-servant had gone on his way muttering to himself, Carter turned to Doctor Morelle.

107

"I must apologise, Doctor. Riley's rather unconventional."

"Quite!"

"I'd get rid of him, but Mrs. Carter won't hear of it." He sighed heavily. "This house seems to become more complicated every day!"

"Perhaps I might see your wife now?" queried the Doctor.

"Of course! Er—she'll be in her bedroom." He paused. "I know you are accustomed to somewhat strange cases, Doctor, but perhaps I ought to warn you—you may find my wife's room somewhat—er—unusual. Dark draperies . . . burning incense . . . and —er—well a coffin for a bed."

"A coffin?" echoed Miss Frayle wonderingly.

"She insists on it—won't sleep anywhere else," said the other with a shrug as if apologising for his wife's unaccountable behaviour.

The Doctor gave him a shrewd look, an interested expression in his narrow eyes.

"H'm . . . doubtless some inhibition connected with some obscure fixation complex."

"If you'll follow me," said Carter. He moved to the door with some reluctance. This time there was no eavesdropping figure in the doorway.

"Thank goodness that man's gone," whispered Miss Frayle.

"Not for goodness I should imagine!" came back Doctor Morelle's swift retort.

"This way," called Carter, turning and beckoning them up a fine oak staircase. "My wife's room is on the other side of the house."

He led the way along a wide corridor with polished floors. Presently they came to a room which seemed to stand on its own in a corner of the house. For a second he paused outside the door, as if nerving himself to face an ordeal. Then he knocked gently and called:

"Bella! Bella! Doctor Morelle's here . . ."

There was no reply, but the Doctor thought he detected the sound of a swift movement inside the room.

"We'll go in," said Carter softly. He opened the door.

If he had not forewarned them, the room might have indeed proved startling, with its heavy black and purple drapings, subdued light and unusual furniture. Everywhere the oppressive smell of incense.

But the Doctor's attention was rapidly directed to the fact that the huge manservant was standing at the foot of the coffin in which a woman was languidly reclining. His attitude could only be described as aggressive.

"Riley, send them away—I don't want to see any doctor!" complained the voice from the coffin.

"Yes, madam!" growled the butler, directing a dark look towards the Doctor and Miss Frayle.

"Now, now, my dear . . ." began Carter persuasively, moving towards her.

"Go away, all of you!" cried Mrs. Carter, her voice high-pitched and melodramatic. "Leave me in my grief!"

"Perhaps I might help," suggested Doctor Morelle, stepping forward, and concentrating his gaze upon her. As he did so the butler stood between them, his shoulders hunched, his jaw jutting forward threateningly. Miss Frayle gasped in fearful anticipation of what might occur.

"You heard what she said," the huge man grunted. "Yer not wanted!"

The Doctor surveyed him calmly. "I was not aware I was addressing you," he murmured.

"But I'm addressin' you! Get out, afore I—!"

"Riley!" cut in Mr. Carter, moving towards them, while Miss Frayle hovered uncertainly in the background, goggling nervously from behind her spectacles.

"You do as I say, Riley," ordered the woman. "Clear them off!"

"Yes, madam," Riley squared up to Doctor Morelle. "Now then, you want me to throw you out?"

"Oh, Doctor!" cried Miss Frayle.

"Calm yourself, Miss Frayle," the Doctor reassured her. "There is not the slightest danger."

The butler advanced a step, shoving his face close. "So yer *do* want to be thrown out?" he rasped.

The Doctor regarded him levelly, his eyes narrowed and piercing. While Miss Frayle watched with bated breath as the man's arm which had been raised threateningly, sank helplessly to his side. Doctor Morelle was speaking slowly in a deadly quiet monotone.

"Riley, your brute strength cannot prevail over my will! As my eyes hold yours . . . So . . . You are experiencing a unique sensation such as you have never felt before . . . Are you not Riley?"

The voice held an extraordinary quality. To Miss Frayle watching open-mouthed, there seemed to be something compelling, mesmeric, about it. The big man's muscles sagged.

"I—I—what's happening?" he mouthed, trying feebly to avoid the steady gaze.

"Riley—what's the matter?" gasped Mrs. Carter, sitting bolt upright, staring at him incredulously.

Doctor Morelle went on in the same monotone while the other stood rooted to the floor. "Your strength is ebbing away, Riley. You are as weak as a child . . . completely dominated by my will. Are you not?"

109

"I—I can't move! " he choked in baffled fear. "Let me go—let me go! "

Doctor Morelle stood with arms folded.

"You may go! " he said, after a moment.

The power of movement seemed to return to the man, and he backed hurriedly towards the door.

"Do not hurry," the Doctor murmured. "And close the door behind you, quietly."

His face a mask of amazement and almost pitiful terror, Riley vanished.

No one spoke for a long time. And then:

"Well, I'll be damned! " said Carter softly to himself. Although he had, of course, heard a certain amount about hypnotism and its wider use by the medical profession, this was the first occasion upon which he had witnessed its powers actually being put into operation.

The woman, sitting up in the coffin, however, was by far the most visibly impressed. The amazing episode appealed to her sense of the melodramatic more than anything she had known for a long time. She eyed the Doctor with awesome respect.

"Who are you? " she asked.

"I am Doctor Morelle," was the studiously simple reply. "And this is my assistant, Miss Frayle."

"How—how did you scare him off like that? " she asked.

"Quite simple. So simple I fear it would be far beyond the scope of your comprehension! " He turned abruptly to the husband.

"Mr. Carter, would you be good enough to absent yourself for a brief while? I wish to talk to your wife."

"Certainly," agreed Carter willingly. "I'll be downstairs when you want me." And with a quizzical glance at his wife he went out. Doctor Morelle drew a chair up to the coffin and waved a hand vaguely to Miss Frayle. "Sit down, Miss Frayle," he said.

"Er—there's nowhere for me to sit," she answered with a look at the chair he was occupying. It was the only one available.

"Then place a cushion on the edge of the coffin," snapped the Doctor.

She gave a shiver and shook her head. She said:

"I think I'll stand! "

Doctor Morelle turned, clicked his tongue impatiently, and then surveyed the woman in the coffin. He observed she still bore some traces of make-up. Her features, which had once been strikingly handsome, now wore a pudgy, unhealthy appearance. The pupils of her eyes were appreciably dilated.

"Now, Mrs. Carter," he began firmly, "tell me, at what time did you learn your child had disappeared? "

110

At once, her voice reached a hysterical note. "I was just going to bed—I went to the nursery—and there I found—"

"Answer each question I ask you in as few words as possible," he interrupted her sharply. The effect was salutary. She became much calmer. "Now . . ."

"Twelve o'clock," she told him. "I heard it striking as I went into the nursery."

"Have you no nursemaid?"

"She went yesterday morning."

"You dismissed her?"

"Yes. I didn't like her. I—I felt she wasn't good for the child."

"Do you suspect her of being involved in the kidnapping?"

"I don't know. She didn't write the note."

"Note?" the Doctor queried, with a lift of the eyebrows.

"It was left on the pillow. This is it."

She passed him a sheet of notepaper, on which was typed a message in capital letters. It had been folded across the middle.

"Any envelope?"

She shook her head. He looked at her keenly, then without a word slowly perused the note. He folded it, tapped it against his fingers, an abstract expression on his face. Then he passed it to Miss Frayle.

Somewhat surprised that he should have noticed she was in the vicinity, she took it. She read:

YORE LITTLE GIRL IS SAFE AS LONG AS YOU DON'T TELL THE POLICE. WE WANT £1,000 FOR HER AND WILL TELEPHONE TO-DAY AND TELL YOU WERE TO SEND THE CASH. IF YOU VALUE YORE CHILD'S LIFE KEEP QUIET AND DO WHAT WE SAY.—X.

"Do you observe anything significant about this missive?" the Doctor asked as she handed it back to him.

"Yes, Doctor Morelle," she answered promptly, pleased that he had asked her a question to which she could give an immediate reply. "Although two or three of the words are mis-spelt, the actual typing is neat and expert."

"You fill me with amazement, my dear Miss Frayle! Your powers of observation would appear to be reaching a stage that might be described as almost adolescent!" He went on in an exaggerated tone:

"Do sit on the coffin. You will find it quite comfortable with a cushion on the edge."

"Very well," agreed Miss Frayle, gingerly placing a cushion at the extreme foot of the coffin. The Doctor had turned to Mrs. Carter once more.

111

" You say the nursemaid did not write this? "

" Well, she wasn't illiterate," she explained.

" I see . . . And you last saw your child, when? "

" At ten o'clock. I looked in the nursery to see if she was asleep."

" She was sleeping? "

" Yes."

He nodded thoughtfully.

" Two hours later, however, when you next went to see her, she had gone." He spoke almost as if to himself. " So that between the hours of ten and midnight the child was removed. And a note left by the kidnappers . . . "

" Yes! Yes! I was demented! " she cried. " I didn't know what to do! "

" Quite," he said.

" The shock was terrible. Terrible! " she moaned.

" How awful for you," sympathised Miss Frayle.

Doctor Morelle said: " Your affection for the child is very deep, no doubt? "

" She's all I have in the world! "

" You have your husband," he gently reminded her.

" Him! " she curled her lips scornfully. " What does he care for me? "

" That, I feel certain, is a matter for you to decide between yourselves," he murmured. " What interests me at the moment is the reason why you prevented him from communicating with me until over an hour after you had discovered the child had gone."

" I tell you I was out of my mind," she said desperately. Then added: " And Riley said I was to leave it to him."

" I understand," nodded the Doctor, rising to his feet. " We must set his and your husband's mind at rest forthwith."

" What do you mean? " she asked in an astonished voice.

Doctor Morelle regarded her with an air of reassurance.

" Your child is quite safe, Mrs. Carter," he informed her quietly. " Furthermore," he went on smoothly, " I am confident I shall very shortly be able to ascertain her whereabouts."

There was a gasp from Miss Frayle, followed by an exclamation of alarm. In her utter amazement at his astonishing statement, she had overbalanced, clutched vainly at thin air for a second, and then subsided into the coffin.

Downstairs, they found Carter restlessly pacing the library.

" That fellow Riley's gone—left no word— " he greeted them.

" You are well rid of the creature," said Doctor Morelle.

He nodded. " I know. The only thing that worries me is whether he may have anything to do with this kidnapping."

112

"I very much doubt if he had the intelligence," said the Doctor. "No, the person you must seek out if you wish to find the child is the nursemaid your wife discharged yesterday. Rest assured she will not be very far away." He lit a Le Sphinx and spoke through the cigarette-smoke: "In fact, I should not be greatly surprised if your wife is not aware of her address."

The other's jaw sagged. "What—? What—?" he gasped. "You don't mean Bella engineered the kidnapping of her own child?"

The Doctor eyed him keenly.

"Knowing her these past few years as you have done," he said quietly, "would that greatly astonish you?"

"I—I—" Carter was at a loss for words. Then shrugged his shoulders helplessly. "Perhaps you are right, Doctor. She's behaved very strangely lately." He set his jaw determinedly. "I'd better go and have a talk with her."

Doctor Morelle said: "That might be advisable at the appropriate moment." As he and Miss Frayle presently took their leave, he said: "If you will keep in touch me, I may be able to advise you as to the precise course of action to pursue."

Early the following morning Carter was on the telephone asking for the Doctor. Miss Frayle stood by expectantly as he took the call, but his comments in reply to whatever it was Carter was saying were characteristically enigmatic. When he had replaced the receiver she asked: "They've found the little girl?"

"Precisely as I anticipated," he affirmed. "Mrs. Carter had purposely dismissed the nursemaid, bribing her to lend her aid in contriving the bogus kidnapping as a revenge upon her unfortunate husband for some imagined grievance. Mrs. Carter, however, gave away the plot when she committed a minute but damning error in the note which purported to have been left by the kidnappers, but which she had, in fact, concocted herself."

Miss Frayle appeared suitably intrigued, and asked the expectedly appropriate question: "How was that, Doctor?"

"You may recall Mrs. Carter assured me the kidnapping had occurred between the hours of ten p.m. and midnight. Yet the note contained the sentence: 'We will telephone you to-day and tell you were to send the cash.' Had real kidnappers taken the child, they must have written the note sometime before midnight, and would therefore have used the word 'to-morrow' and not 'to-day.' Therefore, the implication was that the note had been typed and placed on the pillow *after* midnight. The logical conclusion to be drawn then was that she was lying, which subsequently proved to be the case."

"And what's going to happen now, Doctor Morelle?"

"It merely remains for Mrs. Carter to place herself under my treatment. Need I add that in due course her neuroses will be eliminated and she and her husband reunited and the welfare of their child assured? "

"Oh, I *am* glad you're going to get her right," Miss Frayle said brightly. Then she smiled: "But of course you couldn't have allowed her to go on sleeping in that awful coffin! "

His reaction to her remark that was intended to be slightly humorous was typical. He took her perfectly seriously.

"My dear Miss Frayle," he snapped. "Why must you pick on a mere side-issue of the case? "

"I'm sorry," she began, "I didn't really mean— "

But her apology was too late to repair the damage.

"Will you cease chattering," he cut in. "Do you not realise that what Mrs. Carter is suffering from and what I am about to dispose of is a mass of psychological complexes deep-seated in the sub-conscious, and that all outward manifestations . . . "

Miss Frayle sighed, and nerved herself to listen to another profound and lengthy discourse that might have been poured into her ears in the language of Ancient Baghdad for all the sense she could make of it.

CHAPTER IX

THE CASE OF THE FINAL CURTAIN

Slowly the man backed across the room, horror and entreaty in his face, his eyes wide and staring. Still the woman advanced, the sinister black revolver pointed at him, her attitude grim and purposeful.

"No, no you wouldn't! " the man sobbed. "You *can't* shoot! "

"D'you think I haven't the courage to kill you? "

"No! No! Put away that gun! I beg you—let—let's talk this over calmly— "

"The time for talking is finished! "

"Listen to me . . . " But she cut him short. Brutally and deliberately she said:

"You're going to die."

"Listen! Please listen—! "

He was on his knees now, grovelling at her feet. She shot him as he held out his hands towards her in a last appeal. He stared at her, his jaw sagging as if in surprise, and then he fell forward on his face. There followed a moment's breathless silence . . .

114

And then—as the curtain slowly fell—a thunderous wave of applause surged on to the stage from the packed theatre. Miss Frayle sniffed her smelling-salts clasped tightly in her hand for the nth time. Doctor Morelle shifted impatiently in his seat, and his supercilious glance swept the applauding audience around him. He turned to observe Miss Frayle as she fumbled with the stopper of her smelling-salts, sniffing convulsively as she did so.

"My dear Miss Frayle," he murmured viciously in her ear, "if you must use stimulants so often, could you not contrive to do so with a little less sound accompaniment?"

"I—I can't help it," she gulped. "You—you shouldn't have made me c-come to this aw-awful play!" And she gave a long and shuddering sniff.

He bestowed a look of disgust and displeasure on her.

"Hysterical nonsense!" he snapped.

Doctor Morelle had but little taste for theatre entertainment, but the play he had decided to witness this particular evening was one which had appealed to him purely from a scientific aspect. It was, in fact, a play of a somewhat macabre nature. It had captured the interest and purse of the public, and was one of the most phenomenal successes the London Theatre had known for a long time.

It had occurred to the Doctor that the effects of vicarious horrifics viewed at close quarters upon the human mind might be worthy of some study. Accordingly, he had cast about for a subject whom he might put to the test. He had failed to hit upon the person whom he felt would most suitably react to the experiment—until he realised with some sudden sardonic satisfaction that none other than Miss Frayle would be ideal for the purpose.

He had, of course, discreetly omitted to acquaint her of the fact he had chosen her because of his considered opinion that she might be of some value to him in the rôle of a human "guinea-pig," and had prevailed upon her to accompany him to a performance. As the close of Act II approached he was seriously beginning to regret his choice, for Miss Frayle seemed to have had recourse to her smelling-salts more frequntly than he could have imagined possible. Her continued sniffing allied to the, to him, appalling credulity of the audience who were lapping up as puerile a farrago of futile nonsense as he had ever encountered grated upon him with increasing irritation. His lip curling with open distaste, he once more surveyed the people about him who were still applauding with almost hysterical vigour the end of the second act. He was about to raise a hand to stifle a deliberately ostentatious yawn, when suddenly the applause faltered and subsided.

Miss Frayle was tugging at his elbow.

115

"Doctor Morelle!" she whispered. "Who—who's the man who's just come in front of the curtain?"

He glanced up as a man with greying hair and in evening dress stood before the purple stage curtain and held up a hand for silence. His face was troubled and grave.

"Ladies and gentlemen," he said. The auditorium was now deathly silent. "Ladies and gentlemen . . . Your attention, please. If there is a doctor present would he please come round immediately? I—I regret to state there has been an accident . . ."

"Doctor Morelle!" gasped Miss Frayle.

He drew his lips together in a thin line of displeasure.

"There is almost sure to be another member of the medical profession present," he murmured, glancing round. But if there was another doctor in the theatre he apparently preferred to remain anonymous. After a short pause, Doctor Morelle rose irritably to his feet and moved towards the end of the row of stalls where he and Miss Frayle had their seats. Hundreds of faces watched them as Miss Frayle followed him.

The Doctor appeared oblivious of the intense interest in him as, without condescending to apologise, he made his way quickly through the audience. Miss Frayle blundered short-sightedly in his wake, tripping over feet and ankles and apologising profusely as she tried to keep up with him. They were directed through a small door at the side, up a short flight of steps and through another door on to the side of the stage. The man who had appeared before the curtain greeted Doctor Morelle with undisguised agitation.

"It's Gerald Winters!" he said.

"That's the actor who was shot in the play?" asked Miss Frayle.

The man, who had introduced himself as the stage-director, was leading them through a door that opened off the stage on to a short passage.

"Yes," he nodded. Then to the Doctor: "He's in here."

He pushed open the dressing-room door. Doctor Morelle crossed over to a narrow couch on which the inert figure of the actor lay. His make-up was incongruous and ghastly on a face that was grey beneath. Miss Frayle shuddered and looked away. Doctor Morelle was bent over the figure on the couch.

"Bullet in the heart," he murmured. "Death must have been instantaneous."

Miss Frayle was looking at an attractive young woman who had edged into a corner of the dressing-room as they entered. The stage-manager had spoken to her solicitously, and Miss Frayle had recognised her as the actress who had fired the revolver. She was staring at the Doctor with a face that was distraught. Obviously

tears had played havoc with her make-up. Miss Frayle noticed tiny black daubs around her eyes where the mascara had run.
"It's terrible . . . terrible! " she sobbed.
"Please, Miss Carson . . . Please."
The stage-director moved over to her and patted her shoulders clumsily. The young woman sank into a chair and sobbed into a handkerchief. The other looked at her in blank helplessness, then crossed over to the Doctor.
"What—what are we going to do? " he muttered hopelessly.
Doctor Morelle glanced up with a saturnine expression.
"No doubt a solution to the problem will present itself," he murmured enigmatically. Miss Frayle gave him a quick look, and was about to speculate on the meaning that lay behind his remark, when a tall, heavily-built man wearing an evening tail-coat came bustling into the room. He wore a gardenia in his button-hole, and also an air of great importance. He glanced at the stage-director who indicated the Doctor. The new comer went over, to recoil with a gasp as he glimpsed at the dead actor.
"My God! " he exclaimed.
Doctor Morelle eyed him quizzically.
"I'm Pemberton," the man said, fingering his white tie. "Maurice Pemberton. I'm the manager of the theatre." He paused, and then, as the Doctor merely made a grave inclination of the head, went on: "This is a shocking business! What's—er—what's to be done about it? "
"I should imagine your first step would be to inform the audience that the performance cannot continue."
The other nodded. "In view of all this . . . Yes, I agree." He spoke crisply. He glanced at the stage-manager, then at the actress who was quieter now. "Yes," he said decisively, "I'd better go and tell them . . ." He turned abruptly on his heel and went quickly towards the door.
Doctor Morelle murmured: "You are, of course, aware that the police must be notified? " Pemberton stopped as if he had been struck, and stared at him. The actress looked up with a startled face.
"Police! " she gasped. "They won't think I did it? I didn't know it was really loaded . . ."
Pemberton went over to her.
"Now, now, my dear Mary, pull yourself together! " He turned to the stage-manager. "I think you'd better see Miss Carson to her own dressing-room."
"Let me take care of her." It was Miss Frayle who came quickly forward and took the young woman's arm. "Take a sniff at these smelling salts," she coaxed her, and led her out of the room. Mary

117

Carson had started to cry again, and as the sounds of sobbing receded the stage-manager carefully closed the door.

Pemberton stood in a thoughtful attitude. He appeared to be considering Doctor Morelle's last remark.

"I suppose we've no alternative but to 'phone the police," he muttered dubiously. "Nasty business. Damned unpleasant publicity." The Doctor, eyeing him shrewdly, found no difficulty in discerning he was weighing up the affair almost entirely from the angle of the effect it might have upon the receipts at the box-office of his theatre.

"Will you wait here, Doctor, while I go and make that announcement? " he said. "Then we'll 'phone the police from my office in the front of the house."

"Very well."

With a nod the other went out briskly. The Doctor took an inevitable Le Sphinx from his cigarette-case and flicked his lighter. The stage-manager, who remained behind, looked at him uncertainly. Then he took down a sheet which was used to protect the actor's clothes hanging on the wall from face-powder dust, and covered the dead man with it. Doctor Morelle watched him in silence. The man said, after a moment:

"Shocking thing for Miss Carson. I think she was, well—rather keen on him."

"Indeed! "

"Yes," the other mused. "Take her a bit of time to get over it, I'm afraid. Firing the revolver and everything. Terrible for her."

Doctor Morelle blew a puff of cigarette smoke towards the ceiling. He watched it spread and disintegrate into the atmosphere with an abstracted gaze.

"Poor old Gerald Winters, too! " the other was saying. "Final curtain for him all right." He sighed heavily.

"That is a remarkably fine glass eye you have," Doctor Morelle observed suddenly.

The other gaped at him in surprise.

"Why yes," he stammered. "You—er—you're one of the few people who've noticed it."

"My powers of observation are not unexceptional! " The Doctor gave him a complacent smile. There was a moment's silence. Then he went on: "So you are the—ah—stage-manager, did you not say? "

"That's right."

"You've no doubt examined the firearm Miss Carson used to-night? "

"Certainly. Grabbed it and had a look at it soon as I knew something had gone wrong." A thought struck him, and he pulled

118

a revolver from his pocket. Doctor Morelle noticed it was carefully wrapped in a silk handkerchief.

"This is the gun."

The Doctor took the revolver and, holding it carefully, snapped open the breech.

"It would appear that a live cartridge has been substituted for a blank," he said at length.

The other nodded.

"I've seen nobody else has touched it." Then he added: "In case the police want to test it for finger prints."

Doctor Morelle inclined his head in approval. He re-wrapped the gun in the handkerchief and returned it to the man.

"As the stage-manager, you would be responsible for this?"

"Yes, I take charge of it—see it's okay before the curtain goes up, then pass it on to Miss Carson. After the second act, she gives it back to me, and I load it up again, ready for the next show."

"You keep a container of blank cartridges specially for the purpose?"

"That's right. In a box."

"You always load the firearm in a good light? There would be no chance of a live cartridge, providing one had in some manner found its way into the container, escaping your notice?"

The other shook his head emphatically.

"Not a chance!"

Their conversation was interrupted by the return of Maurice Pemberton.

"Well, that's that," he declared as he shut the door after him. "Now I suppose we get the police."

The Doctor tapped the ash off his cigarette.

"I would like a word with Miss Carson before you do that," he suggested.

"Certainly." He turned to the stage-manager. "Better wait around, Denning," he said, "just in case."

"Right."

Mary Carson's dressing-room was two doors along the corridor. They found she had recovered her composure to the extent of removing her stage make-up. She was in the process of putting on her ordinary make-up, and was chatting to Miss Frayle when they entered. Pemberton took her hand and patted it sympathetically.

"We all know how you feel, dear," he told her. "Try to bear up. There'll be no more show for to-night, so just you get home and make an effort to get some sleep. Doctor Morelle here wants to ask you a question or two." He added: "No doubt if you feel you'll need it, he'll give you something to make you sleep."

"I think Miss Carson's feeling better," put in Miss Frayle.

119

Doctor Morelle chose a chair which had the strong lights of the mirror as much as possible behind him.

"Concerning the firearm used by you, Miss Carson," he began smoothly. "I understand it is brought to you every evening? "

"Yes," she said slowly. "Jim Denning always brings it along to my dressing-room himself. I leave it here on the dressing-table, ready for my entrance just before the shooting scene."

"I understand. I assume you are out of your dressing-room from time to time? "

"Of course."

"During the time between it being left with you and your taking it with you on to the stage, could anyone else have access to it? "

She thought for a moment. She said:

"It would be very difficult for anyone to tamper with it without being seen."

"You would appear to be somewhat positive on that point."

"Well, you see," she explained, "until the end of the second act, Gerald and I never meet in the play. As he makes his exit, I go on—and vice versa."

"I remember noticing that," corroborated Miss Frayle. Doctor Morelle directed a look of irritation at her, and she subsided.

"When I'm on the stage, and Gerald's in his dressing-room, he always kept his door open, so's he could hear me and judge his cue. He never relied on the call-boy."

"Your suggestion is, then, that no one could have entered this room in your absence without being observed by the deceased?"

"Nobody . . ." Her voice broke and she choked: "Oh, poor Gerald! "

"Need you ask her any more questions? " put in Miss Frayle with an anxious look at Mary Carson. The Doctor turned on her, his eyes narrowed ill-temperedly.

"Why, do you mind? " he queried with excessive solicitude.

"Well, don't you think that perhaps Miss Carson— " She broke off under his baleful stare.

Pemberton, with a look at the actress, who seemed distressed and about to break down once more, said hurriedly: "I think Doctor, perhaps she *isn't* quite up to answering a lot of questions— "

He was interrupted by the door opening. A man stood there looking at them uncertainly. He was a slim young man and Mary Carson turned to him with a cry.

"Oh, my dear—! "

"Can I come in? " And the newcomer came in, pushing the door closed. He spoke in quick, clipped phrases.

"How ghastly about Gerald! "

Mary Carson turned to the Doctor and Miss Frayle.

120

"This is my brother . . ." She introduced them.

He gave them both a quick look. Then: "You're the doctor, are you?"

"Good evening," Doctor Morelle replied suavely.

"Always thought that gun was dangerous!" he rattled on. To Pemberton: "Remember? On the first night, I said to you: 'Bet you'll have an accident with that damned gun!' Remember? Too realistic!"

He turned to his sister: "You poor darling! How frightful for you."

Pemberton said: "Mary's suffering from shock, Mr. Carson."

"I can't believe it's happened." She drew a hand across her face and shuddered.

Carson blurted out: "Suppose it sounds rottenly callous and all that—but, well—it's a bit of a blow to me, too." He hesitated as if deciding whether he should continue, then went on: "Gerald owed me five hundred—"

"Oh, please—!" Mary Carson looked up at him appealingly.

"Sorry, old thing," he apologised. "But he was up to the neck in debt all round." No one spoke. Doctor Morelle's thoughts seemed far away. Carson mumbled: "Ah, well . . . poor chap."

The atmosphere of embarrassment he had caused as a result of his talkativeness was relieved by the entrance of the stage-director.

"I've told no one to leave the theatre, Mr. Pemberton," he said, "until the police have given them permission. Is that right?"

The other nodded. "Right, Denning—By Jove! I'd better get on to them, too," he exclaimed. "Doctor Morelle, perhaps you'd care to come along with me to my office while I telephone Scotland Yard?"

"As you wish. Miss Frayle, you will remain here."

"Yes, Doctor."

Mary Carson whispered brokenly: "Will they want to question me?"

"I'm afraid so," murmured Doctor Morelle.

"Oh . . . Oh! I can't bear it—"

"Please try and keep calm," Miss Frayle said quietly. "It'll be all right."

"It—it's like a nightmare—!" the young woman choked.

Her brother patted her shoulder ineffectually. "I say, try and take it easy, old dear."

Doctor Morelle said to Miss Frayle from the door: "This, Miss Frayle, should provide you with an opportunity to observe police procedure—when the authorities arrive—at close quarters. A unique experience!" And with a saturnine glance at her, he went out.

A few minutes later in Pemberton's office, he lit a Le Sphinx and observed as the manager picked up the telephone:

" It would considerably facilitate matters if you asked to speak personally to Detective-Inspector Hood. That is, in the event of that officer being there at this hour."

Pemberton looked at him somewhat questioningly.

" I have some acquaintance with the Detective-Inspector," he condescended to explain through a cloud of cigarette smoke.*
" Merely mention my name and he will react with appropriate despatch."

The other spoke into the telephone. As it happened he was able to catch the Detective-Inspector just as he was leaving for his home. Pemberton gave him the message as he had been instructed by the Doctor, and Hood promised to come along to the theatre immediately. Replacing the receiver, Pemberton regarded Doctor Morelle with an expression of new and profound respect, which was accepted with a typically self-satisfied and bleakly humorous smile.

" While we are awaiting the arrival of the Scotland Yard representative," he murmured to the theatre manager, " you might supply me with the answers to one or two questions I should like to ask."

" Certainly—if you think I can," replied Pemberton, pinching the end off a cigar and carefully lighting it.

" I am under the distinct impression," said Doctor Morelle smoothly, " that those who have so far vouchsafed any information concerning the unfortunate incident to-night have contrived to remain suspiciously reticent."

The other's cigar was halted abruptly half way to his mouth.
" You mean, you think that—? "

" If we might confine ourselves to *facts* and omit attempts at surmise in terms of generalities," the Doctor interrupted him with an imperious wave of his hand. " Tell me," he went on suavely, examining the tip of his cigarette with elaborate interest, " are you aware that the deceased had incurred the enmity of any person? "

The other seemed puzzled.

" Well, I don't know," he said slowly. " Gerald Winters was a pretty decent chap. I liked him. There may have been one or two who didn't—professional jealousy, perhaps, and all that. But—"

" But no one was, to your knowledge, sufficiently antagonistic towards him to perform an act of homicide? "

" Oh, no, I'm quite sure not."

There was a brief silence. Then Doctor Morelle observed

---

* Detective-Inspector Hood was in charge of the curious affair dubbed by the newspapers as " The Gardenia Case." The Doctor had written him a letter pointing out certain features of the crime, as a result of which the detective opened up a new line of investigation and solved the case.

casually: "It will be wiser for you to let me have all the information—however, irrelevant it may seem to you—concerning either Miss Carson or Gerald Winters." He added significantly: "*Or both.*"

Pemberton shot him a wary glance. He hesitated a moment, shrugged his shoulders and pulled at his cigar thoughtfully.

"You might as well know . . ." he said slowly. "The first point is that a year or two ago, Gerald Winters and the Carson girl had a pretty hectic love affair." He paused. Doctor Morelle made no comment.

"Well," the other went on, "you've seen her to-night. Daresay gathered she's a superficial sort of creature. Rather like her acting, I suppose, effective within a certain range, but lacking in depth of character. So it may not be much of a surprise to you to know—it certainly didn't surprise their friends!—that she began to get tired of Winters. And the man to whom she transferred her attentions was another actor as he then was, named Jim Denning."

"Denning?" The Doctor's eyebrows shot up.

"Yes—the stage-director you met to-night. Well, Gerald Winters was fiercely possessive about Mary Carson, not unnaturally, and it so happened that at the time he and Denning were both attending the same fencing school—lots of actors go in for it in case they might appear in a costume play—and rumour has it that one day they fought a sort of unofficial duel over Miss Carson. Anyhow, that's how Denning lost an eye. Perhaps you didn't notice he wears a glass eye."

Doctor Morelle chose to ignore the last remark with the contempt he considered it deserved. Pemberton went on:

"The whole business was hushed up, Denning himself swore it was an accident. But that wasn't the end of it. Anyway, Mary Carson went back to Winters—for a time. She chucked him altogether after a few months."

"Do you think Denning might harbour malice?" asked Doctor Morelle. "Men of his type—the quiet, introspective mentality—sometimes do. It would appear that to substitute a live cartridge in the revolver would be a comparatively easy matter for him."

The theatre manager surveyed the glowing tip of his cigar, with a thoughtful air.

"I must say I *had* viewed the matter in that light," he confessed. "There may be something in what you say. Though, personally, I'd never have considered Denning a vindictive chap. After all, he was decent and generous enough over the duel. Losing an eye is no laughing matter for an actor . . . In his case he felt he couldn't continue in the theatre—except on the technical side."

Doctor Morelle said:

"Did Winters marry someone else in due course?"

"Yes, two years ago. I believe they've been very happy. I don't think Mary Carson's ever married. And that's about all I can tell you of their private lives. Sure you won't have a drink?"

Doctor Morelle shook his head. The other poured himself a generous whisky and soda.

"I suppose it was risky to have had them in the same play together," he said as he took a drink. "Never trust women when they come up against old flames! Eh, Doctor Morelle—? His expression changed. "That reminds me," he said suddenly. He appeared to be trying to recall something from the depths of his memory.

The Doctor eyed him narrowly.

"It was this afternoon," Pemberton said slowly. "After the matinee I happened to be back-stage, and heard a dressing-room door open—either Gerald Winters' or hers—and I got the tail-end of a conversation. It sounded like a bit of a quarrel—the voices were loud—I couldn't help hearing him say something about: 'I tell you I can't do it—I'm up to my eyes in debt, thanks to you.' Yes, that was it . . . Then she said: 'I'll give you till to-morrow!' Then the door slammed, one of them must have come out. It didn't occur to me to see who it was. I was pretty busy at the time, didn't think very much about it. I supposed one of them had probably been lending the other money or something, and—" He broke off with a shrug.

"What you have told me opens up an interesting avenue for speculation," Doctor Morelle murmured.

"In a way, though, it clears Mary Carson," the other pointed out. "That is, if there was any suspicion against her. I mean, she gave him till to-morrow to repay this money, or whatever it was, so she'd hardly have wanted to kill him to-night!"

The Doctor gave him a non-committal glance. He said:

"Alternatively it postulates the possibility of another and rather more subtle crime."

Maurice Pemberton was appreciably startled.

"Good God! This is getting a bit involved!" He hesitated, then asked: "Will it be necessary for the police to go into all this?"

"You may rely upon me to offer Detective-Inspector Hood just as much of the information I have elicited as I deem expedient for the purpose of accelerating the wheels of justice," Doctor Morelle replied with enigmatic suaveness. The theatre-manager looked at him sharply. He was taking a hurried gulp of whisky when there was a rap on the door. With a nervous glance at the Doctor, he called out: "Come in!"

It was Detective-Inspector Hood who stood in the doorway.

At the house in Harley Street some two or three hours later, Detective-Inspector Hood was being served coffee by Miss Frayle. They were in the study, and he was saying to the Doctor who was leaning casually against his desk: "Never like dealing with these artistic people. Always try to make you, and themselves for that matter, believe they're what they're not." He shook his head. "Perhaps it's all in the nature of their work, as you might say!"

He sipped his coffee.

"However . . ." he went on cheerfully, and thrust a hand into a pocket to produce a tiny object which he held out for the Doctor's inspection. Miss Frayle watched Doctor Morelle gaze at it through a cloud of cigarette smoke with interest.

Hood was saying: "I made a pretty thorough search of the dressing-rooms. Found that behind the dressing-table mirror in Miss Carson's room."

Miss Frayle goggled at the small unexploded blank cartridge which lay in the palm of the Doctor's hand. He returned it to the detective.

"Too small to register a clear fingerprint," he murmured.

"Yes."

"Then I don't quite see how it can help very much," put in Miss Frayle.

Doctor Morelle eyed her superciliously.

"You amaze me, my dear Miss Frayle!" He turned to Hood and went on: "It merely confirms my theory, however, that the person responsible entered Miss Carson's dressing-room during her absence on the stage, and substituted a live cartridge for this blank."

"Unless, of course, she did it herself," Hood said over his cup of coffee.

The Doctor regarded him with a saturnine smile. "If you can supply a convincing reason why Miss Carson should choose to murder Winters before a theatre full of people your suggestion might be worthy of consideration."

The Detective-Inspector thought for a moment.

"That is a bit of a poser," he admitted heavily. "Of course, she's tough enough. Got plenty of guts. Might have thought she could get away with it—"

"But the motive?" Doctor Morelle persisted.

"Yes, why should she do that—?" began Miss Frayle, but he waved her into silence.

"You've got me there, Doctor. According to Pemberton, they'd had a bit of an argument in the afternoon. About money or something. But these actors are always going up in the air over something!"

"I would make the suggestion that you interviewed the one non-

125

artistic person involved in the case. I refer to Mrs. Winters, the deceased's wife."

The other nodded. "Seeing her first thing in the morning." He put down his empty cup and produced a pipe. "Well, I'll be getting back to the theatre, I suppose. Still got plenty of routine stuff to check."

At the front door he said:

"You like to talk to Mrs. Winters with me, Doctor? "

Doctor Morelle said with studied disinterest: "If you wish."

Hood grinned at him. He knew the Doctor would have harboured it as a grievance against him for ever had he omitted to invite him along.

"Fine! Collect you nineish . . . Good-night . . . Good-night, Miss Frayle! "

Mrs. Winters proved to be a sturdily good-looking young woman with a firm grip on herself, and obviously determined not to break down under the stress of the tragedy which had befallen her.

She said, in answer to one of the Detective-Inspector's questions:

"He always said that if ever anything happened to him I was to go to the Central Bank—the branch office nearby—and see the manager. I haven't had time to give it a thought yet."

Hood nodded sympathetically.

"You haven't been to the bank? " It was Doctor Morelle who sought a definite statement.

"No, not yet."

The detective's skilful questioning, together with one or two shrewd queries from Doctor Morelle had elicited the following:

Gerald Winters had been leading a comfortable life, happily married to all appearances, and, it seemed, just about to achieve success of a more outstanding nature in the theatre. He owned an expensive car, and his wife had only recently returned from a holiday at a fashionable resort. She wore expensive-looking clothes of excellent taste. On the surface there appeared to be nothing which could be associated with a reason for his death.

Doctor Morelle suggested to his companion that he had sensed, however, an indefinable feeling of insecurity and instability about the atmosphere of the Winters' home. They were quitting the opulently architectured building in which the flat they had been visiting was situated as the Doctor made this observation.

"I agree," said Hood. "Something wrong there, though you can't put your finger on it." He sighed heavily. "Well . . . what next? "

"Might we not pay a visit to the Central Bank, while we are in the vicinity? " insinuated Doctor Morelle. On the Scotland Yard official producing his authority, they were ushered into the bank manager's office. The manager was a plump little individual with an ingratiating manner. He seemed more anxious to chat to them on generalities than he was to reveal anything concerning his client's account. Detective-Inspector Hood was very firm, however.

"I merely want a little advance information on a matter which will have to be revealed to Somerset House in due course," he said. "Of course, if you prefer it, my Chief can get into touch with your Chairman . . ."

The plump little man seemed to make up his mind at last. He coughed delicately, glanced quickly at the detective and then at Doctor Morelle.

"Very well, Inspector, what exactly did you want to know? " he said.

"First of all, is Gerald Winters' account overdrawn? "

"It most certainly is," was the straightforward answer. "I telephoned him the other day, as a matter of fact, to advise him that his account was in a condition such as could no longer be permitted to continue."

"Had you no security? " queried Doctor Morelle quietly.

The man smiled slightly. "It is not the practice of the bank to advance loans without security. Mr. Winters deposited with us a life policy. Quite a large policy—a matter of seven thousand pounds in the event of his death."

"Might I peruse the policy in question? "

The manager looked inquiringly at the Doctor, then quizzed Hood, who nodded his confirmation of the request. The other spoke into his private telephone. In a few moments the policy was brought in. While the manager chatted agreeably with the Inspector, Doctor Morelle read the document through, clause by clause. Presently, with a smirk of self-satisfaction, he returned it.

The manager said, placing the document in his desk:

"I'd had a talk previously with Mr. Winters in this office only a few weeks ago. He wanted me to increase his limit. He'd been borrowing from friends, it appeared, and wished to repay them. I fear I gave him quite a lecture—in a friendly way, of course! " He spread his plump hands expressively. "These artistic people seem to have no sense of proportion where money is concerned! D'you know I believe they regard it simply as something to spend . . ."

In the police car which was dropping Doctor Morelle at Harley Street before proceeding on to Scotland Yard, Detective-Inspector Hood sucked a cold pipe and grumbled:

"Well . . . Been a pretty wasted morning, I must say! "

The Doctor made no reply. His eyes were closed. Hood glanced at him, wondering if he had not fallen asleep. His eye lids flickered

127

open momentarily and then closed again. The detective said:
"I don't see how anything we've discovered helps us an inch further."

"On the contrary," murmured Doctor Morelle in an almost somnolent tone, "it has furnished us with precisely the information we seek."

Hood stared at him.

"How d'you mean? " he asked with a puzzled frown.

"I refer to the missing motive," the Doctor said as he took a Le Sphinx from his case and lit it. "If you would care to stop at my residence for a brief while, I will amplify my statement accordingly. You will then be able to proceed directly to Scotland Yard with a complete report upon this somewhat unusual case."

The detective laughed admiringly.

"All right, Doctor, I have to hand it to you! " And he gave the policeman at the wheel appropriate instructions.

A little while later Doctor Morelle, in his most condescending mood was sitting back in his chair listening to the sound of his own voice with ill-concealed self-satisfaction.

"Motive," he was saying, his gaze flickering from Detective-Inspector Hood to Miss Frayle and back again, both of whom were hanging on his words with suitably awe-inspired expressions. "That was the key to the mystery of Gerald Winters' mysterious demise."

He paused, flicked the ash off his cigarette and went on in the same pompous and yet curiously fascinating tone which held his listeners' attention.

"It was Miss Carson's brother who first suggested to me—inadvertently, needless to say—that *motive* might be the vital clue which would lead to the elucidation of the problem. You may recall the remark the young man passed to the effect that the deceased owed him money and was in fact deeply in debt? That remark prompted me to consider a theory which—ah— " he smiled indulgently " —had so far escaped attention."

He blew a cloud of cigarette-smoke through his finely chiselled nostrils. He said:

"That theory was based on an obvious if not immediately apparent fact: The one person who could benefit by the tragedy was the chief actor in it. In other words, Winters himself! "

He paused dramatically. Miss Frayle obligingly filled in the gap of silence with a gasp of admiring amazement. He rewarded her with a patronising smile.

"His demise," he went on, "covered—as was subsequently revealed to be the case—as it was by an insurance policy, would relieve him in every sense from financial difficulties and leave his dependants, his wife in particular, secure."

128

Hood interjected: " But why go to all that trouble? Slipping into Mary Carson's dressing-room, substituting the cartridge, and all that? "

" Because," Doctor Morelle almost stifled a yawn at what he regarded as the other's dullness, " the insurance policy in question contained a clause. A clause which declared the policy void in the event of the holder committing *felo-de-se*. Winters' problem, therefore, was to stage his death in such a way that it would not appear self-inflicted. He hit upon the ingenious plan of having himself shot as the result of an ' accident '."

" You mean he really committed suicide? " Miss Frayle goggled at him through her spectacles.

" Precisely, my *dear* Miss Frayle! " the Doctor said with heavy sarcasm.

The detective scratched his head. " Beats me where people get their ideas from! " he said at length.

Doctor Morelle regarded him thoughtfully for a moment.

" I am constrained to wonder that myself," he murmured softly, " on occasion! "

And with this ambiguous observation he stubbed out his cigarette with an air which conveyed that for him, at any rate, the case he had elucidated so simply could now be considered closed.

CHAPTER X

THE CASE OF THE FLOATING HERMIT

They caught the 6.22 from Waterloo to Parkham Creek, and found, as the train steamed out, they had the compartment to themselves. Miss Frayle sat in a corner-seat and watched the suburbs of Greater London slip past. The streets, blocks of flats and factories were bathed in a golden haze of fading evening sunlight, lending to their begrimed, unprepossessing exteriors a fleeting appearance of brightness and glowing colour.

Presently, her eyes a little dazzled by the shining vista slipping swiftly past, Miss Frayle blinked and turned from the window. She adjusted her spectacles, picked up the evening paper and then paused to bestow a glance at Doctor Morelle opposite her. He was reading a book with what appeared to be avid interest. She was about to look at her paper when she caught the title of the book and the author's name, and she gave a little sigh.

He did not raise his eyes from the page, but, tapping the ash off his cigarette, observed: " Finding the journey tedious already, my dear Miss Frayle? "

129

She started, and laughed with a little embarrassment. "Why, what made you think that, Doctor?"

"I was under the impression you had given a yawn of ennui."

"No. I—er—just sighed, that's all."

"In a somewhat melancholy mood, perhaps?"

He continued reading and she wriggled with annoyance. Why did he always pounce on her with a question to which she could give no ready answer? "I didn't know I had sighed, as a matter of fact—" she began, then bit her lip as she realised she had only a moment before admitted she had.

"To prevaricate successfully, a retentive memory is essential," he murmured. "And yours would seem to be woefully short!" He flashed her a glance, narrow-eyed and searching. "However, if you have some secret which you prefer to withhold from me, I have, of course, no desire to drag it from you." He compressed his lips and returned to his book.

Oh, dear! groaned Miss Frayle inwardly. She had looked forward to the journey all day, and it had only just begun and she had unwittingly annoyed him. She fiddled with her spectacles, looked out of the window again and then stared at her newspaper unseeingly. If only she could have thought of something to say! Not the truth, of course, that would have made him more sardonically irritable than her silly little lie. No, she couldn't reveal her sigh had been actuated by the fact the book he was reading was one he had written himself. She couldn't admit she had sighed with wonder at the blatant conceit that had prompted him to bring the book with him in the hope other passengers would notice it and the name of its author! It was a large volume, conspicuously bound. And there he was, pretending to be absorbed in it as if he was reading it for the first time.*

He raised his head suddenly and, through a cloud of cigarette smoke, said: "I hope you do not imagine I have brought this volume with me for any ulterior motive? I think I may say I am not *quite* so vainglorious as to wish to flaunt my works before the public at large!"

She could only goggle at him in stupid amazement. It was moments like these when she felt convinced he was not human, but possessed of some extraordinary power which she hazily associated with Cagliostro, voodooism, high priests of the occult and the ability to see through a woman. For this was when she was certain he could read her innermost thoughts, could see into the limitless future. This was Doctor Morelle at his most frightening!

The train roared into a tunnel. The compartment was plunged

* "A Study of the Criminal Subconscious" (Manning & Hopper) London, (Karter) New York.

into inky blackness before the electric lights tardily came on, and when she looked next at him his saturnine face was bent once more over his book. She might have imagined he was as deeply engrossed in its pages as before—but for the sardonic smile which she could discern flickering at the corners of his mouth.

Doctor Morelle had accepted an invitation to spend the week-end at the country house of Henry Myers, the founder of the famous firm of manufacturing chemists. A Northerner of the self-made industrial type, he was also a man intensely interested in scientific research. He had contributed a large part of his fortune for the furtherance of work in this sphere. He had chanced to hear one of the Doctor's lectures on a particular aspect of biochemistry relating to industrial workers and had introduced himself. The Doctor had been favourably impressed by his good-humoured, simple and straightforward personality ; and, incidentally, flattered not a little by the man's respectful thirst for knowledge on scientific subjects. Hence the acceptance of Myers' invitation to visit him. Miss Frayle had also been included in the invitation.

The train was now running through open country. Miss Frayle, who had been glancing idly through her paper, looked up with a sudden exclamation: " Parkham Creek? Isn't that where we're going, Doctor? "

" To the best of my knowledge, yes. Have you any reason— apart from idle curiosity—for asking? "

She indicated an item in the newspaper with some excitement. " In to-night's paper! It says— "

" Do you feel that what, as you so vaguely put it, ' it says,' can be of sufficient interest to me that I should interrupt reading my book? "

She stammered under the rebuke. " I—I thought you might like to see. It's this paragraph here." She read aloud:

" ' Mysterious Hermit Drowned. Body Not Yet Recovered . . . Early this morning—' " Miss Frayle went on

" '—the body of a man was seen by two farm labourers being carried out to sea. The men hurried to the beach and a fisherman took them out in a rowing-boat in the hope of overtaking the body. By that time, however, it had disappeared from sight and the men failed to locate it. Returning to shore they informed the police, and subsequent inquiries revealed that a local character known as Old Charlie the Hermit was missing from the hut where he lived. It is believed it is his body that was seen floating out to sea . . . ' "

Miss Frayle paused for breath. Doctor Morelle said: " Most

131

interesting. *Most* interesting! And now, I hope, my dear Miss Frayle, I may be permitted to return to my book? Thank you! "

" But didn't you hear? " she squeaked, " it was at Parkham Creek! "

He looked up sharply. " Why, we are proceeding there! Why did you not mention that fact before? "

She ignored his unjust accusation. She rushed on, unable to resist an anticipated moment of triumph. " And if you'd let me finish reading," she said, " I would have told you that the two farm labourers are employed by Mr. Myers."

" Perhaps if you would be good enough to hand me the journal so that I may peruse it myself? . . . Thank you . . . Now I may at last obtain a coherent account of the incident to which you have mumblingly referred! " He read the account quickly and returned the paper to her without any comment. He picked up his book and it was not until some moments later that he murmured, half to himself: " One would imagine it to be a case of *felo-de-se*. People who pursue a solitary existence tend to abnormalities of thought and behaviour." And he puffed at his cigarette as if to dismiss the matter as one of little importance.

Some time later the train drew into a typical branch-line station, and a porter was calling out in a country burr: " Parkham Creek! Parkham Creek Station . . . ! " Doctor Morelle and Miss Frayle alighted and dumped their suitcases on the platform. Miss Frayle sniffed the fresh, sea-laden air.

" Ooh! What lovely air! I'm going to enjoy this week-end! "

" It seems we might expect somewhat recalcitrant weather," the Doctor said, eyeing a distant mass of dark, heavy cloud. But even he could not dampen her sudden wave of high spirits, and she laughed irrepressibly. He contemplated her with raised eyebrows and a somewhat disagreeable expression but said nothing. A man in a chauffeur's uniform approached them and touched his cap.

" Doctor Morelle? Miss Frayle—? "

" Good evening," she smiled at him.

He grinned back. " 'Evening, miss. Good evening, sir. I'm from Mr. Myers," he said in a pleasant sounding burr. He stood there a little indecisive and the Doctor indicated the suitcases. " Would you take them? " he said sharply.

The man started and picked them up. " Sorry sir! I—I was wandering a bit." He marched off sturdily towards the station exit. They followed, giving up their ticket-halves to the friendly porter-cum-ticket-collector-cum-stationmaster, who wished them a cheery " Good-night." The chauffeur had the car door open for them and was stacking the suitcases into the seat beside him.

As Doctor Morelle followed Miss Frayle into the car the man

132

said: "This suicide has upset us a bit round here and I wasn't thinking properly." He was evidently explaining his absent-mindedness on the platform. The Doctor lit a Le Sphinx, and glanced at the lowering sky. "The inclement weather I prophesied should make itself felt unpleasantly soon! " he murmured.

"Aye," agreed the chauffeur, cocking an eye out of the window and starting the car. As they drove off, Miss Frayle was wearing a preoccupied frown. "Poor man," she said, half to herself, "how awful, committing suicide." The man in front darted a quick look back at her. He had caught her words referring to his explanatory remarks—the window separating the driving-seat from the back of the car was down—and he nodded with a lower lip glumly protruding. "Ah . . ." he said, and gave his attention to the road again.

Doctor Morelle blew out a cloud of cigarette smoke. "Has it been established it is a case of *felo-de-se*? "

"Beg pardon, sir? " said the chauffeur over his shoulder.

"Self-inflicted homicide."

The man still didn't get it. "Ah—er—that is—ah, er— " he mumbled.

"Doctor Morelle means is it certain the poor man took his own life? " Miss Frayle explained.

"Thank you, Miss Frayle! " said the Doctor mockingly.

"Oh . . ." said the chauffeur. "Oh, yes, he didn't fall into the Creek accidental—But you seem to know a bit about it yourselves."

"It was in to-night's paper."

"Was it, Miss? Well now . . .! " He clicked his teeth and shook his head in wonderment. "The news don't half get round quick—especially if it's bad news! "

Miss Frayle laughed. The other went on: "No, Old Charlie was too careful for it to've bin an accident. And he hadn't got no enemies—hardly spoke to anyone—so nobody did it purposely, nor nothing like that."

"Do they know why he committed suicide? "

The chauffeur shook his head.

"They do say he had a tidy bit o' cash stowed away," he volunteered, "so it couldn't have been money trouble."

They rounded a bend and came in sight of an estuary flowing swiftly seawards and dominated on either side by ragged cliffs.

"That's Old Charlie's hut, across the field yonder," said the chauffeur, indicating a small, derelict-looking bungalow with a single chimney. It had a deserted and solitary appearance in the fading light. A stile and a narrow footpath marked the approach to it.

"You might pull up for a moment," said Doctor Morelle, and the car was brought obediently to a standstill near the stile.

"I was afraid of this! " sighed Miss Frayle.

The Doctor paid no attention to her remark, if indeed he heard it ; he sat thoughtfully contemplating the landscape.

"Isn't it getting rather dark to go for a walk? " she went on insinuatingly.

"You are anticipating my thoughts, Miss Frayle," he said.

"Oh," she said in a tone of relief, misunderstanding his response, "I thought you were going to have a look at the hermit's hut."

"That is precisely what I propose to do! " he murmured. And he quickly opened the door and got out. "If you are in the least apprehensive, however, by all means remain in the car. The chauffeur and I will not be long, I feel certain."

"I—I think I'd rather come with you," she hurriedly decided. She was not particularly enamoured with the prospect of remaining alone on the deserted road in the gathering dusk.

"If you will lead the way," Doctor Morelle murmured to the chauffeur.

The man first extracted a torch from one of the side pockets of the car. Presently they stood at the door of the hut. The door was unlocked. As Doctor Morelle pushed it open and entered, there was a slight sound of scuffling from a corner. Miss Frayle, following close behind drew back with a startled cry.

"Oh! What's that? "

"Calm yourself " chuckled the Doctor mirthlessly. "They are merely small rodents of the *genus Mus.*"

"Mice! " gasped Miss Frayle, horrified. She rushed to jump on an old chair that stood by the table.

"S'orl right, Miss " the chauffeur reassured her. "They've 'opped it."

"I wonder what attracted them," pondered the Doctor, looking round the room. His gaze fell upon a table in the centre of the room. As he approached it he observed a small piece of cheese on a plate, beside which was a knife and other obvious indications of a meal. The cheese was almost entirely covered with mildew.

"Ah yes, the deceased's last meal which, if you will have the courage to approach more closely, might be worthy of inspection." Miss Frayle followed him to the table. "Observe the minute fungi known as mildew, Miss Frayle. One might almost describe it as fur-coated, so heavy is the fungus! " No one smiled at his somewhat heavy attempt at humour. He sighed. "Never mind! Let us return to the car."

"I'm sure Mr. Myers will be wondering what's happened to us," said Miss Frayle, welcoming the opportunity to leave the desolate hut.

"He may possibly be interested in my explanation of our delay," said Doctor Morelle, as they made their way back to the road.

134

Shortly afterwards—just before a heavy downpour of rain began—they had reached their destination, and their host was conducting them into a comfortable lounge hall, where a huge log fire blazed cheerily. Miss Frayle began to feel her drooping spirits revive.

" Yes . . . I was beginning to think ye'd missed train or something," said Myers in a marked Yorkshire burr.

" I fear it was sheer inquisitiveness on my part which is responsible for our belated arrival," admitted Doctor Morelle.

" I was afraid you'd think we'd got lost," Miss Frayle smiled.

" Well, you've got here and that's the main thing—and before you got caught in the storm! " and the other handed a sherry to Miss Frayle. He observed to Doctor Morelle: " They say every real scientist is inquisitive. I'm a bit of a busybody myself." And he chuckled good-naturedly.

" I paused en route to investigate the mystery of the hermit's murder."

" Murder? " repeated Miss Frayle in a startled tone, goggling at the Doctor, who seemed blandly unconscious of the significance of his remark.

" Murder! " laughed Myers. " You mean suicide . . . Poor Old Charlie— It was two of my men spotted his body floating on the tide. They rushed and got a boat to try and get him, but he must have gone well out to sea—they couldn't find any trace of him. The police have been up here checking their story, I know."

" The body has not so far been recovered? "

" No, but it was him all right. The men recognised his long hair and beard he wore—eccentric old boy he was. And anyway he's disappeared from his hut."

They heard the front door-bell ring.

" That'll be Harvey, my agent," explained Myers. " He'll tell you all about the suicide, Doctor. I believe he was the last to see the old chap alive."

Harvey proved to be a man in the middle thirties, with dark eyes and a genial, brisk manner. He laid what appeared to be a number of business papers and account books on a side table. Myers introduced him to his guests.

" The Doctor seems to have an idea that old Charlie was murdered—t'wasn't suicide," he said as he poured the newcomer a drink.

Harvey laughed easily.

" Oh yes? The police would be glad to know about that I'm sure," he chuckled, taking the glass the other handed him. He went on confidently: " They happen to have discovered exactly how the whole accident occurred."

Myers looked at him sharply.

135

"Accident? " he queried. "But I thought it was— "

"I'm afraid we were all wrong, Mr. Myers," the agent confessed.

"That makes the—ah—incident even more intriguing," declared Doctor Morelle, lighting one of his inevitable cigarettes.

"Well, let's hear the latest news about it, anyway," Myers said.

Harvey glanced at them. His manner suggested that he was inclined to enjoy occupying the centre of attention.

"Well . . ." he began, taking a drink. "It was I who saw the old chap this morning—about five o'clock. I was getting up, and happened to catch sight of him through my bedroom window. He was making for the wooden bridge over the narrow part of the creek—coming from the direction of Long Oak field where he has his hut."

"Did you see him actually in transit over the bridge? " asked the Doctor.

The man shook his head.

"I wish I had," he said regretfully, "because I might have saved him. But I just called out to him through my open window, and he waved back. Then I went straight down to breakfast."

Myers said: "Go on . . ."

"It seems the bridge-rail must have been rotten in the middle, and as old Charlie leaned on it, it must have snapped— "

"Why should he lean on the rail as heavily as all that? " murmured Doctor Morelle shrewdly. "Surely a handrail would be a light affair—merely a precautionary safeguard? "

Myers shot the Doctor a look appreciative of a point he had raised.

"I've seen Old Charlie lean on that rail many a time," Harvey explained readily. "He used to rest there for a few minutes and look down into the water. You know how people do when they stand on a bridge."

"Yes, that's true enough," conceded Myers.

"Yes, I like to myself," said Miss Frayle. "So long as it doesn't make me feel giddy! "

"The police examined the rail a little while ago," the other went on. "It was pretty rotten."

The Doctor looked at his host.

"What time did your men see the body floating out to sea? "

"Er—seven o'clock, that was."

"That's right," nodded Harvey. "The police say two hours is about the time it would take from the bridge to reach the point where your men saw it, the tide running as it does."

The Doctor carefully examined the tip of his Le Sphinx.

"How extremely fortuitous," he observed in a silk-like tone, "that the tide should be on the turn when the—ah—accident occurred! "

136

THE CASE OF THE FLOATING HERMIT

"How d'you mean, Doctor?" It was Myers who asked the question.

Doctor Morelle smiled frostily. In a manner suggesting he was explaining an obviously simple fact, he murmured: "Merely that had the rail collapsed when the tide was *coming in,* the corpse would have been washed ashore to provide evidence."

Harvey's face widened in an expansive grin of toleration.

"You still seem pretty sure it was murder, Doctor Morelle!"

"The term 'pretty sure' is in this case an understatement!" He paused melodramatically, and Miss Frayle goggled at him through her spectacles as he said quietly: "I can place my hands on the murderer now . . ."

"Well, well," said Myers in an indulgent tone. "I'm sure we'd like to hear more of your theories, Doctor."

Harvey nodded genially, although there was a sting behind his words as he said:

"Yes . . . We don't always get the chance to hear an expert's views on this sort of thing . . ."

Doctor Morelle merely smiled thinly through a puff of cigarette-smoke.

"I doubt if this is quite the correct moment to make any such disclosures," he said with a judicious air. "But I will give one or two indications as to why the suicide theory is obviously in error. First of all, on visiting the deceased's hut, I discovered a piece of cheese somewhat heavily mildewed on the table. This was incompatible with the suggestion it had formed part of a meal of which he had partaken this morning. That mildew would have taken more than one day to form."

"H'm, something in that," said Myers.

"Yes," conceded the other man. "But hardly conclusive evidence, though. You mean it indicates that he was killed some days ago?"

Doctor Morelle nodded. He said: "Furthermore, the body of a drowned human being does not rise to the surface for several days." He glanced at Myers. "Yet your employees witnessed it floating out to sea this morning."

Myers appeared obviously impressed.

"You're right there," he said slowly. He turned towards Harvey about to say something and stopped short. The agent's face war contorted with murderous fury.

"Don't move—any of you—don't move—!"

Miss Frayle gave a sharp gasping scream as a black automatic pistol appeared in his hand. His eyes darted from one face to another, as he weighed up his chance of escape.

There came a sudden ring at the front door. Doctor Morelle, who had remained unmoved by Harvey's reaction to his words, now

137

glanced at his host. With an elaborately simulated apology in his voice, he murmured:

"I fear I forgot to mention the fact that on my way here I paused at the telephone-box at the cross-roads to request the local police authorities to visit me at their earliest convenience. That will, no doubt, be them."

Harvey stared at the Doctor like a trapped animal. He took two rapid steps backwards towards the door, his gun still menacing them, and then suddenly appeared to stumble. Before he could regain his balance, Myers had thrown himself at him. Doctor Morelle promptly gained possession of the revolver as it was jerked out of the man's grasp. Harvey's resistance collapsed as Miss Frayle rushed to admit the local police-sergeant and a constable.

Later the Doctor addressed Miss Frayle in a censorious tone:

"I really must reprimand you about the habit of sprawling your feet half-way across the room!"

"But, Doctor Morelle——" she protested, "I tripped him up deliberately!"

He permitted himself a thin smile of scepticism. "Were you not too occupied in drawing a deep breath preparatory to screaming for help?" he retorted.

She ignored the remark to ask:

"Did—did he confess?"

"Certainly. He bludgeoned the old man to death some days ago."

"But why?"

"He had embezzled a sum of Myers' money, and was anxious to replace it before the yearly audit. As it transpired, his crime was fruitless, for his victim had, in fact, no secret hoard whatever."

"Did he break the bridge hand-rail?"

He nodded: "Harvey broke it deliberately in order to lend colour to his entirely fabricated story."

"Well," said Miss Frayle, "I must say if I were going to murder anybody for their money, I should jolly well make sure it was there first!"

Doctor Morelle clicked his tongue in mock disapproval.

"Tck! Tck! Can this cold and calculating tone be that of my prim and meek Miss Frayle!" He went on, his saturnine face bent close to hers. "Have you, by any chance, made certain of the whereabouts of *my* secret hoard of gold?"

She smiled at him disarmingly.

"Oh, I should never dream of murdering *you*, Doctor Morelle!"

He eyed her narrowly.

"Thank you! I'm deeply touched," he said. Then, with deepen-

138

ing suspicion, " Is there any particular reason for this charitable feeling you harbour towards me? "

She regarded him blandly from behind her spectacles.

" Only that you'd be bound to pop up afterwards to jeer at me and point out the incriminating mistake I'd made! " she said.

CHAPTER XI

THE CASE OF THE INTERRUPTED TELEPHONE CALL

Miss Frayle said, as she came into the study:

" What have you been saying to poor Inspector Hood? He looked quite upset as he went out."

She blinked interrogatively at the Doctor who had settled himself again at his desk and was scanning a file of papers. He made no reply to her question, but went on reading as if oblivious of her presence. She gave him a reproachful glance and busied herself checking the last few pages of a voluminous note-book. Silence fell on the study, except for the occasional rustle of a paper or document. From outside came the muffled hum of the evening traffic passing up and down Harley Street.

It was several weeks after Doctor Morelle had solved the strange mystery of Gerald Winters' tragic death during the performance of London's most popular horror-play. The Doctor had almost forgotten Detective-Inspector Hood's existence, though he had been reminded of him on occasion when passing the theatre at which the tragedy had occurred. For he had observed with sardonic mirth which, in his case, passed for humour, that the horror-play, with another actor in the rôle Gerald Winters had so tragically vacated, was playing to packed audiences. Maurice Pemberton, manager of the theatre, had calculatingly taken full advantage of the publicity the play had attracted as a result of the dramatic circumstances surrounding Winters' death.

It was somewhat of a surprise to him, therefore, when Miss Frayle had earlier that evening informed him Detective-Inspector Hood was on the telephone asking for an appointment as soon as possible. Having a comparatively free half-hour at that time, the Doctor had invited the detective along whenever he wished, and the latter had left his office at once. The ensuing interview occupied only a few minutes and the sturdy Detective-Inspector had taken his leave, sucking his pipe noisily and with only the barest glimmer of a smile for Miss Frayle as he left.

Miss Frayle looked up from her note-book as Doctor Morelle

139

gave a little murmur that might have indicated puzzlement. It was the sort of murmur she found difficult to associate with him. He glanced at her through narrowed lids and rose to his feet. He took a cigarette from the skull cigarette-box and lit it thoughtfully. He gave a little cough and cleared his throat. She looked at him expectantly. Satisfied she was all attention, he spoke:

"I have always been at a loss to comprehend," he said in slightly pained tones, "how anyone could at any time be actuated by a feeling of dislike towards me."

Miss Frayle goggled at him.

He paused and regarded her as if expecting an immediate answer. She strove heroically to think of something to say.

"Why, Doctor, *has* anyone ever told you they disliked you?" was all she could hit on. And then added judiciously: "I wonder why?"

He said with calm seriousness:

"I could only conclude it was merely a matter of their jealous envy of my obvious talents."

She was by now, of course, more than used to his moods of overbearing egotism and merely said:

"You mean people who didn't like you *really* wished they could be as you were?" (For a horrified moment she wondered if she had not even for him laid it on a bit too thick. But he appeared to accept her question as being completely in the nature of things. There was no doubt, the thought flashed through her mind, when at a loss, just tell him he's wonderful!)

He was answering her spoken query.

"Precisely. A psychological trait not uncommon in characters of lesser quality—" Suddenly he broke off to observe in a dangerously level tone: "Did I detect, my *dear* Miss Frayle, a suggestion in your question of derisive sarcasm?"

She caught her breath, gulped and only just managed to blurt out: "Oh no, Doctor Morelle, of course not! You have *all* my sympathy."

He stared at her through the smoke of his Le Sphinx. Then he said: "H'm . . . I feel a little less sympathy and more application to your work would make a greater appeal to me!" And he returned to his desk. She could not restrain a feeling of some amusement at the way she had been congratulating herself upon her cleverness, only to learn as she always did that he was never on any occasion to be deceived.

"And kindly remove that irritating simper from your face!" he snapped at her across the room.

She was about to sigh when the telephone rang. She answered it. "This is Doctor Morelle's house," she said.

She could plainly hear over the wire heavy, distressed breathing. As if the caller was terribly agitated and in great haste.
"The Doctor! " a man's voice gasped. "I must speak to him! It's a matter of life and death! Quick—I must speak to him! "
"Who are you, please? "
"Never mind who I am—! Get me the Doctor—I must speak—!"
"Who is it, Miss Frayle? What do they want? "
Doctor Morelle had snapped the query without looking up from his desk. She glanced at him helplessly.
"It's some man, Doctor," she stammered. "I don't know who he is—he won't say— "
With an exclamation of impatience he was beside her.
"This is Doctor Morelle," he snapped into the telephone. "Who are you? "
"Doctor—? " The voice seemed to give a sob of relief. Then it babbled on: "This is a friend. Listen! You're in danger. Jim Carver's out to do for you! " The voice rose higher. "*Don't go to Orient Wharf!* "
Doctor Morelle's eyebrows shot up in surprise.
"Orient Wharf? Carver? Who—? "
"You got his brother a stretch! " came the succinct explanation. The voice went on:
"I tell you Carver's going to trick you down to Bridge House, Orient Wharf, and— "
"From where are you telephoning? " the Doctor cut in.
"A call-box in River Street. You've got to believe me, Doctor! You've got to—! "
Suddenly the voice at the other end of the wire broke off. The man spoke now in a horrified whisper.
"He—he's coming along the street! He's seen me—! " Again the voice broke off. It rose again in what was almost a scream: "My God! He's got a gun—! Carver's got a gun—! "
There was the sound of a revolver shot, a tinkle of glass, a choking cough. Then silence.
Doctor Morelle depressed the receiver rest rapidly.
"Hello? Hello? . . . "
Miss Frayle was at his side, her spectacles slipping on her nose in excitement.
"Doctor Morelle! " she gasped breathlessly. "What happened? It sounded like a shot! "
"It *was* a shot! " he snapped, and replaced the receiver. He stubbed out his cigarette. He moved quickly to the door.
"Where are you going? "
He spoke over his shoulder. "To an urban thoroughfare known, I understand, as River Street. If you wish to accompany me you

141

had better accelerate your reflexes and at the same time restrain your spectacles from being precipitated to the floor! " And he was out of the room.

Grabbing her recalcitrant lenses just in time, Miss Frayle shot after him. In the taxi she asked him:

"Didn't you mention the name Carver over the telephone? Wasn't that the name of the man who was sent to prison for blackmail? "*

"The answer to both your questions is identical and in the affirmative," he informed her in a tone of mock gravity.

River Street, they discovered, was a branch off one of the innumerable byeways leading from the Limehouse Road. It was a *cul-de-sac* with the River Thames at one end, and already a thin curtain of evening mist was muffled round the gaunt warehouses and derricks which hemmed in the dark and somewhat forbidding-looking street. Miss Frayle shivered as Doctor Morelle instructed the driver to stop on the corner and she got out. He paid off the taxi and it disappeared into the gloom. She followed him, glancing apprehensively about her, as he moved briskly off.

"It—it's all rather sinister, don't you think? " she shuddered.

"You must take a grip on that imagination of yours, Miss Frayle," he snapped. "I am acutely aware this is not exactly a salubrious district, but there are doubtless many worse neighbourhoods."

"I find it hard to believe! " she said, quickening her pace to keep up with him.

"This that we are now approaching is, no doubt, the telephone-box I wish to investigate." He indicated a call-box which stood on the corner of an entrance to an alleyway between the buildings.

"Yes!—look—! " she cried. "The window's broken—that would be by the shot! "

She indicated a small hole drilled in the side of the box. It was about shoulder-high. Doctor Morelle produced a narrow torch and picked out several tiny splinters of glass on the pavement outside. He opened the call-box door and shone his torch inside.

"H'm the body would seem to have vanished! "

Miss Frayle glanced at him questioningly. He had spoken in a voice that betrayed no surprise. The telephone receiver had been replaced on its hook.

"What could have happened to him? " she asked.

He made no reply, but bent and examined the floor carefully. Straightening himself after a moment, he observed:

* It was directly as a result of Doctor Morelle's activities on behalf of one of his patients that a certain Richard Thornton Carver had received a term of penal servitude.

142

"Unfortunately, he failed signally to leave any clue behind . . . The floor is perfectly clean, as you will perceive." He gave the shelf which held the telephone a cursory look, and shook the directory. Nothing appeared to excite his interest.

"There's a funny smell, Doctor!" Miss Frayle was sniffing the atmosphere inside the box suspiciously. "It's like a strong cigar."

He permitted himself a mirthless smile.

"It would be a potent weed indeed which contained the ingredients producing *that* aroma!"

She looked at him sharply.

"What d'you mean?"

"Merely that it happens to be the odour of nitroglycerine plus nitrocellulose, explosive components of gunpowder."

"Oh," she said, with an expression of appropriate enlightenment, "I see . . ."

"On the contrary," he flashed back at her, "you are exercising your *olfactory* senses!"

Miss Frayle realised she was sniffing like an over-zealous retriever puppy and subsided. From the river a tug's syren hooted dismally. The mist swirled eerily about them. The Doctor seemed oblivious of his surroundings, however. Lighting a cigarette he stepped into the street, the door slamming behind. The flame of his lighter illuminated his saturnine features for a brief moment. His eyes were dark and speculative under the brim of his hat. Miss Frayle coughed as the fog caught her throat. With a shiver she hunched her shoulders into her coat.

"Do you think the man Carver's taken the—er—body to the place at Orient Wharf you said he mentioned on the telephone?"

He gave her a glance of studied admiration.

"Miss Frayle, your genius for perceiving the obvious positively overwhelms me!"

"Well, hadn't we better go there?" she suggested impatiently. "He may be only wounded, and we might save him."

"You possess a quixotically chivalrous nature," he murmured sardonically. But he made no move. He stood flashing his torch in the immediate vicinity of the box as if in search of something.

"Well then, let's go, shall we?"

"A moment, however, before we tilt at windmills!" Opening the door of the call-box again, he stepped inside.

"What are you doing?"

"Merely ascertaining whether or not this telephone is in working order," he said, operating the dial.

"Oh, but oughtn't we to hurry?"

"Hurry on, Donna Quixote!" he snapped. "I will overtake you and accompany you with all speed to our destination."

143

Goaded by his derisive tone, and feeling the necessity for some exercise to restore some warmth to her chilled limbs, she took him at his word. Slowly, however, and not without several backward glances, she proceeded along the street. Within a few moments his tall, gaunt figure loomed up out of the mist. She noticed his face wore a self-satisfied expression.

"Was it working? " she asked.

He glanced at her inquiringly.

"I beg your pardon? "

"The telephone. Was it in order? "

"Oh . . . Oh, yes! Eminently satisfactory," he murmured abstractedly. He was obviously thinking of something quite different.

Bridge House proved to be a decrepit, ricketty building which had, the Doctor deduced, at some time in the past been connected with one of the old bridges now demolished. It stood by itself on the edge of a wharf. Masses of decaying timbers blocked two sides of the building, and the back wall appeared to descend right into the river, where the gaunt outlines of a tramp steamer anchored not far distant loomed up black, its upper structure shrouded in the mist. The paint was peeling off the woodwork in the front of the place, and the windows were dirty and broken in places.

"Is—is this it? " Miss Frayle said dubiously.

"It would appear to be unoccupied," murmured the Doctor. He stood back to survey the front of the building. Then moved to a doorway in the centre.

"The door is open slightly," he said, " so let us enter."

The door squeaked complainingly as he pushed it back. He peered inside and looked round cautiously, allowing his eyes to grow accustomed to the gloom. Miss Frayle pressed close on his heels.

"Is—is it all right, Doctor? "

He turned and frowned at her obvious apprehension.

"Come, come, Miss Frayle, think of that poor suffering creature whom you are about to rescue! " he reminded her with heavy sarcasm.

He went in, his torch making a wandering pool of light on the walls. She followed him.

"It's very dark," she shivered. The door creaked back to its semi-closed position behind her.

"The building seems at one time to have been a store place," mused Doctor Morelle, noting several sacks in a corner and a number of empty crates. The light from his torch caught a ladder almost facing them. Evidently it led up to a loft.

"Would—would there be any rats? " came Miss Frayle's timid small voice.

"That we shall no doubt ascertain in due course!" he said, his sardonic tone giving her but cold comfort.

"Thank goodness you brought a torch—" she began, and stopped with a gasp. There was a sound of scuffling in the darkness.

"Oh! What was that?"

"Merely your imagination! Follow me. We will explore the upper regions."

The ladder proved to be an insecure affair, and Miss Frayle clutched it grimly as she ascended shakily after the Doctor. He stood looking down from the opening in the loft at her clicking his tongue impatiently.

"Come along, Miss Frayle!"

"You might give me a hand," she reproached him breathlessly, with a glance behind her. "I—I thought I heard someone down there behind us."

"Nonsense!" he snapped decisively. "The place is empty!"

As he spoke there came a metallic click from behind him and an electric lamp was switched on. Its glow revealed a heavily-built man with a soft hat pulled down over his left eye. A jagged scar showed disfiguringly at one corner of his mouth, thrown into relief by his high cheek-bones.

"Not exactly, Doctor Morelle!" the man jeered, coming forward menacingly.

"Oh, a man!" screamed Miss Frayle. "Hold me—I'm falling!"

She clutched wildly at the darkness and was in danger of falling backwards when Doctor Morelle reached down quickly. He gripped her shoulder and steadied her.

"You startled the young woman, appearing out of the shadows like that!" he observed coolly to the other.

The man laughed hoarsely: "I'll startle her more before I've finished! And you too! Move over there—both of you!"

As Miss Frayle scrambled up beside the Doctor the stranger placed himself so as to cut off any chance they might have of retreating the way they had come. A wicked-looking automatic gleamed at them.

"Oh Doctor, he's got a gun!" Miss Frayle gasped unnecessarily.

"And it's liable to go off!" The man grinned. He waved them over away from the opening. He stood there himself and glanced down the ladder. Then he looked at them malevolently.

"Tricked you here nicely, didn't we Doctor Smartie?" he laughed.

"Morelle is the name."

"I know who you are all right! . . . And perhaps you'd care to know my name?"

"No doubt you would be Carver," said the Doctor indifferently.

Miss Frayle caught her breath. The other stared at Doctor

145

Morelle, a faint look of surprise showing in his face. Then he said:
" Yes . . . I'm Jim Carver. You may have heard of my brother?"
he jeered ; then he rasped : " I swore I'd get you for what you did
to him, and here you are, all to myself . . . with my pal keeping a
look-out down below, so's we won't be interrupted ! "
" What—what are you going to do with us? " gasped Miss Frayle.
" All in good time . . . When the tide's a bit higher," and he
nodded significantly. He said, with a grim chuckle : " The river's
nice and deep round here at full tide."
Miss Frayle almost fainted with horror. She tried to tell herself
it wasn't true. She'd wake up in a moment from some terrible
nightmare. Doctor Morelle gave a little but somewhat ostentatious
yawn. Still with his automatic menacing them, Carver shouted
down the ladder :
" Everything okay down there, Eddie? "
" Oh, Doctor, we're caught! " Miss Frayle gulped. " What will
happen to us? " The Doctor did not even turn in her direction.
" Eddie! " Carver was calling again, a harsh note of impatience
in his voice. " Eddie—are you there? "
There was a sound of ascending footsteps on the ladder below.
" What are you coming up for? " snarled Carver. " I told you
to stay down there."
The footsteps halted imperceptibly, then continued their upward
journey. The man at the opening muttered, his expression puzzled.
Doctor Morelle said quietly :
" That, I regret to inform you, is Scotland Yard ascending the
step-ladder ! Your friend—er—Eddie down below, has no doubt
been quietly overpowered ! "
Carver shot a disbelieving look at him, then, convinced by something in the Doctor's face, swung round and held his automatic
pointed at the opening. As the footsteps came higher, Miss Frayle
gave a sudden scream.
" Oh look—there's someone coming through that window! "
She was staring into the shadows directly behind Carver. He
twisted his head to look.
The brisk voice of Detective-Inspector Hood hit him before he
realised his mistake.
" Drop that gun, Carver! I've got you covered ! " he warned
him, his head and a revolver alone showing above the opening.
Carver hesitated, his back to the detective.
" Drop it ! and don't look round or I fire! Just drop the gun."
The automatic clattered to the floor. Doctor Morelle stepped forward and retrieved it, while Hood clambered into the loft. He was
followed by three other determined-looking men who quickly took
charge of Carver and led him below.

146

"Thanks, Miss Frayle," the Detective-Inspector said gratefully. "Neat of you to distract his attention like that. Everything in order, Doctor?"

The Doctor nodded and handed the revolver.

"Our plan has worked with clock-work precision," he replied.

Miss Frayle gaped, first at the detective then at Doctor Morelle.

"Plan?" she echoed, completely mystified.

Detective-Inspector Hood chuckled at the expression on her face. He patted her arm and said: "I expect the Doctor'll explain every-thing to you presently, Miss Frayle . . ."

But she was goggling at Doctor Morelle.

"Do you mean," she said, "you knew all along we were going to walk into this trap? And—and the police would come to our rescue?"

"Precisely, my dear Miss Frayle," he smiled sardonically at the utter disbelief in her voice. He lit a cigarette and murmured with a sigh: "Ah, me . . . I fear I am beginning to possess a somewhat suspicious nature!"

And with this enigmatic observation he motioned her to descend the ladder. Gingerly, her face still wearing a bewildered look, Miss Frayle began the descent.

In the study of the house in Harley Street some time later:

"On arrival at the telephone-box, in which, according to his description over the telephone, the caller who purported to be warning me of my danger was shot from outside, I at once per-ceived the man had been lying."

Dutifully, Miss Frayle asked Doctor Morelle: "How?"

The glow from the desk-lamp added to the saturnine expression on his face as he went on with the air of addressing a small child.

"Because," Doctor Morelle said, "all the glass broken by the bullet had fallen on to the pavement. There was none on the floor *inside* the box. This, together with the presence within of gun-powder fumes was evidence that the revolver in-question must have been fired *inside* the telephone-cubicle, and not from without."

Miss Frayle nodded understandingly.

"And you mean," she said, "the whole business was arranged by that dreadful man Carver to—to lure you into a trap?"

"Precisely, Detective-Inspector Hood had warned me earlier that I was in some danger from the creature." He smiled thinly. "I fear I had not taken his warning seriously."

She thought for a moment, then said:

"You got on to Scotland Yard, I suppose, when you told me you were testing the telephone to see if it still worked?"

He smiled thinly.

147

"That was the object of my little subterfuge."

"Well . . . I think you might have warned *me* you were leading me into danger! " protested Miss Frayle.

He raised his eyebrows.

"My dear Miss Frayle! " he said suavely. "I wished merely to offer you an opportunity to display those remarkable gifts of resourcefulness, any evidence of which you had up till then been withholding from me! "

She chose to hear only the first part of his remark. She said with a shy, pleased smile: "You mean the way I made that awful man turn round so's he wouldn't shoot at Detective-Inspector Hood? " She made a deprecating movement with her hands. "Oh . . . that was nothing."

"Such a modest and unassuming young woman! " Doctor Morelle gave an ostentatious cough which made it palpably clear he was unconvinced. "I suppose," he said meaningly, "you did not for one moment imagine it really *was* someone climbing through the window behind Carver? "

Miss Frayle fidgetted uncomfortably.

Inexorably, that maddening sardonic voice insinuated:

"With your somewhat astigmatic vision, and in that shadowy light . . . "

Miss Frayle was blushing, and as he began to chuckle softly at her obvious discomfiture, tears of mortification blurred her spectacles. She blundered out of the study without pausing to say "Good-night."

Doctor Morelle's mocking laughter followed her as she stumbled upstairs to bed.

CHAPTER XII

THE CASE OF THE SUSPENDED FOREMAN

The letter arrived by the morning post. Miss Frayle handed it to the Doctor, together with the rest of the not inconsiderable mail. He glanced at the address with slightly raised eyebrows and then read:

"Dear Doctor Morelle:

I was particularly interested in your article in 'Industrial Science' for this month on the psychological reactions of industrial workers. Judging by your article, I imagine you have been engaged in considerable research upon this subject, and it occurred to me you might find it both profitable and

148

interesting to conduct some practical investigation into conditions at this Power Station.

"When I mention that during the past few months we have
suffered two deaths from ' misadventure,' you will, I think,
agree that there is considerable scope for an investigator of
your well-known capabilities, and my company will be pleased
to arrange for you to visit us at your earliest convenience. I
look forward to your acceptance of the invitation."

The letter was signed—" Julian Howard."

Miss Fràyle blinked at Doctor Morelle questioningly.

"Do you think you'll go, Doctor? "

He regarded the letter thoughtfully. Then, tapping it against a
thumb, gazed abstractedly over her head. He glanced again at the
heading on the notepaper.

"Kindly institute inquiries regarding the locomotive service to
Clayford," he murmured, "and make the necessary arrangements
for our journey to that destination accordingly."

"Oh, am I coming too? " said Miss Frayle with excitement.

He gazed at her with an expression of sarcastic admiration.

"Your powers of perception are growing more pronounced than
ever! Soon, no doubt, I shall be able to converse with you in
words of more than one syllable! "

They caught the two o'clock express to the North. They arrived
at Clayford just after six. It had started to snow, the station was
cavernous and draughty, and a heavy cloud, emanating presumably
from the huge chimneys of the power station, hung over the town.
Miss Frayle shivered miserably as they drove off in a taxi to the
hotel at which they had accommodation reserved for the night.

The hotel, however, gave promise of better things. It was comfortable in an old-fashioned, stolid way, and Doctor Morelle com-
manded speedy service from the porters, reception staff and waiters
with his usual effortless ease. Presently, they were enjoying a substantial dinner, in the middle of which they were interrupted by a
thick-set man, greying at the temples, who came over to them with
profuse apologies for not having met the Doctor at the station. He
was Julian Howard. Doctor Morelle introduced him to Miss Frayle,
who could not help noting that his suit bulged disgracefully as if
his pockets were crammed with blue prints and specifications. He
had a blunt, straightforward manner, and there was a vital look in
his expression. He seemed to be a man driven by enormous
enthusiasm for his work. The Doctor invited him to join them.

"I couldn't get to the station in time," he was saying, as the
waiter placed another chair for him. At the last minute there was
more trouble in the power-house."

149

Doctor Morelle gave a sympathetic murmur.

"Another turbine gone west," Howard went on, "Benson swears it's foul play, but we can't prove anything."

"Benson?"

"Our chief engineer. My right-hand man." He hesitated, then said: "Can't say I really like the fellow. Never took to him, somehow. Still, I have to, admit he knows his job inside out. If he only knew as much about handling men . . ."

The waiter approached and took his order.

Later they moved into the lounge and over coffee Howard unfolded the story he had to tell. Miss Frayle receded into the background and picked up a detective-novel she had been reading during the train journey.

According to Julian Howard the trouble had started about a year or so ago. An atmosphere of discontent had begun to pervade the Power Station. So unobtrusively that it was by no means easy to trace. Benson, it appeared, had not helped matters. His methods were fair but unsympathetic. Then there had been the first fatal accident. After this first death by electrocution, Benson had been heard to say openly on more than one occasion that the workman in question had only himself to blame for starting work on that particular section of cable without making quite certain the current was cut off. He had even declared that if he had been running the firm, the dead man's widow would have received no compensation.

"He's tough," said Howard, re-lighting his pipe which had gone cold. "But he's got the secret of these new American dynamos better than anybody. Got the knack of knowing just what to do when anything goes wrong."

"I understand there have so far been two fatal accidents?" Doctor Morelle reminded him.

The other bit on his pipe stem and sighed heavily.

"Yes, I'm afraid so. The second was of a more typical kind. One of the men was caught in a moving belt and dragged into the machinery. Sort of thing that happens somewhere every week." He paused, then added: "But there were again some unpleasant repercussions."

"Indeed?"

"Some of the dead man's fellow-workers dropped pretty strong hints that Benson had started up that particular belt before they were ready for it. Of course, it was part of their job to be ready— but they don't look at it that way."

Doctor Morelle eyed him over his Le Sphinx.

"Your chief engineer seems to be a contributary cause of a certain amount of friction," he remarked. "Have you ever considered—ah—dispensing with his services?"

150

"He has a three years' contract, of which there are about eighteen months to run. He gets big money, pulls his weight, and frankly we can't afford to let him go. We are continually getting new apparatus from America which he understands better than anybody. He was in the States several years." He shook his head. "Extraordinary chap! He has the most profound contempt for the working man I've ever come across. I've seen him get livid with rage because some poor devil hasn't quite followed his instructions. Well, of course, the men are apt to bear a grudge. They get their own back in little ways, and that makes Benson wilder than ever. There are times when I think the fellow is not quite right in his mind— but all the same he's A1 at his job."

The Doctor said:

"Is there any unusual feature concerning the home lives of your workmen?"

The other looked at him with some surprise. Then he said, after a moment's reflection:

"Well yes, now you come to mention it, I suppose there is. You see there's no other industry here. Clayford came into existence as a town when we started the Power-Station to take advantage of the Pennine streams six years ago. So in their leisure the men don't meet other workers to distract them from their own grievances. I've heard 'em at it, as a matter of fact." He smiled. "When they haven't known I've been there, of course!"

Doctor Morelle nodded as if to imply that the other had supplied a clue he had been hinting at.

"What is the gist of their grievances?" he queried.

"Oh, the usual sort of thing—petty interferences, nagging foremen, and so on."

"Do they refer to this man Benson?"

"Well—he isn't popular. Most of 'em seem to have suffered from his authority—or imagine they have. He's got a lashing tongue, and doesn't hesitate to use it. Some of our skilled electricians are the rather more sensitive type. Don't relish that sort of thing. Of course he can't be solely responsible for this atmosphere of unrest, I suppose. But there's no doubt an unpopular boss can stir up a lot of trouble."

"That has been my experience in my researches into the subject of the psychological aspect of industrial workers."

Howard nodded. He went on:

"There was some unpleasantness a couple of months back. Benson apparently took a dislike to a foreman named Gregory. Finally fired him for some petty neglect which resulted in a big transformer being burnt out. According to the men, this was merely an opportunity Benson had been waiting for. They argued

151

Gregory hadn't been responsible for the neglect—it was the duty of one of the under-foremen to check such things, which was true enough. However, we had to back up Benson."

"With what result? "

"The men staged a lightning strike! Came out for twenty-four hours. We were in a tough spot: our reserves ran right down, and in another couple of hours or so there'd have been no current leaving the station. Of course, under the grid system our load would have been taken over by somebody else, but there'd have been the devil of a fuss. Inquiries and all that. In the end, after a lot of argument, we had to re-instate Gregory."

He paused to light his pipe again.

"Of course," he continued, "we put Gregory on the night shift to keep him out of Benson's way."

Doctor Morelle smiled bleakly. "Benson is not responsible for the machines during the night hours? "

"Not officially. He occasionally drops in to see if everything is in order, particularly when there's any new machinery being installed."

"Your chief engineer seems remarkably interested in his work," murmured Doctor Morelle dryly.

It was approaching ten o'clock, and, tired after the journey Miss Frayle excused herself and went off to bed. The Doctor and Howard continued their conversation for another hour and then the latter got up to go, explaining with a smile that he made a practice of being in his office never later than eight-thirty each morning.

"Otherwise, I'd never get through half my work! Still, I don't expect *you* that early," he added. "Somewhere about ten-thirty would suit me fine, if that's all right for you? "

The Doctor assured him frigidly that he was himself habitually an early riser, and Howard took his departure.

The snow had ceased to fall, but the Clayford sky was still leaden when Miss Frayle looked through her window the following morning. She shivered and looked forward to their early return to Harley Street.

Over breakfast Doctor Morelle announced that they would walk to the Power Station. The exercise and fresh air would prove beneficial, he declared. Miss Frayle glanced down the dismal street and her heart sank. It couldn't have looked a more uninviting prospect, she thought.

Fortunately, however, a glimpse from the hotel entrance decided the Doctor that the roads were too thick with slush and melting snow, and he abandoned his plan to walk, sending Miss Frayle to order a taxi. They arrived promptly at the agreed time and found

Julian Howard busy at his desk. He occupied a very modern office with long steel-framed windows, steel filing cabinets, and an impressive-looking electric light and heat radiation system. He greeted them genially and pressed a button on his desk. His secretary appeared immediately.

" Ask Mr. Benson if he can come in."

He turned to Doctor Morelle. " I thought you might as well meet him right away." Then, with a grin: " We always used to reckon to start with the primary causes in the old days! "

From Howard's conversation which she had caught the previous evening, Miss Frayle had expected to see a somewhat large, aggressive individual enter, but Benson proved to be small, and dapper. He was spruce and well groomed with the sleekness of a cat.

" Benson, this is Miss Frayle and Doctor Morelle." Howard introduced them. " No doubt you have read some of his articles lately."

Benson bowed slightly. He smiled at the Doctor:

" Ah yes, the expert in creating happy workers! " And there was only the merest trace of sarcasm in his tone. Doctor Morelle did not permit it to pass unchallenged, however.

" Can it be that my theories have failed to impress you? " he queried suavely. Benson shrugged non-committally.

" My experiences have been pretty practical," he emphasised the word rather unnecessarily, Miss Frayle thought. " And I've always found the men most responsive to strong words and harsh treatment." He spread his hands. " Though I understand good results can be obtained by contrary methods. I believe the Maxwell Combine, for instance, have evolved some system: The men have to answer a specially prepared questionnaire amounting to four or five pages ; their work is based accordingly. Maxwell's claim it's increased their output twenty per cent. So there may be something in this psychology stuff, but I don't see it working here."

He glanced at Howard for corroboration. The latter made no comment. Benson showed fine, white teeth in a sceptical smile, and waited for the Doctor to speak. Doctor Morelle assumed an expression of disinterested impartiality which was disarming. It was meant to be.

Howard said: " Perhaps you'll take the Doctor and Miss Frayle round with you this morning? "

" Sure," agreed Benson pleasantly. He added, still smiling: " So long as you haven't got a four-page questionnaire to put to the workers! "

Doctor Morelle permitted himself a thin smile, but his eyes were narrowed and speculative as he and Miss Frayle followed the chief engineer.

153

They stopped first at Benson's own office, where he pulled a pair of overalls over his suit. "I sometimes put in a bit of tinkering," he explained. "Makes a nasty mess of your clothes—oil dripping all over the place."

He led the way into a spacious building where the noise of various pieces of machinery merged into a loud humming tone. Doctor Morelle and Miss Frayle followed Benson along alleyways between huge turbines and whirring dynamos. From time to time the engineer paused to give some instruction or ask a question. The Doctor noticed that on these occasions Benson assumed an unnecessarily harsh manner. The men answered him guardedly, almost sullenly; their attitude was civil, nothing more. Once or twice he climbed over the guarding rail that surrounded the machines and made some small adjustment.

Miss Frayle goggled at the ever-moving machinery from behind her spectacles. She was rather enjoying the sight-seeing tour.

"The trouble with the men here is they resent the fact that I know more about their jobs than they do themselves," Benson told the Doctor.

"Your knowledge is, no doubt, extremely comprehensive? "

"I learned in a hard school," came the reply.

It was approaching lunch-time when they returned to Howard's office. Doctor Morelle had spent most of the time listening, occasionally asking a question in his characteristically casual way. Miss Frayle had now become decidedly tired as a result of her traipsing round after the Doctor, and was thankful to sink on to a comfortable settee in the office while Howard, after Benson had quitted the office, talked to Doctor Morelle for a few minutes before they went to lunch.

"Well, what d'you make of him? " asked Howard, eyeing the Doctor hopefully.

"I prefer to reserve my opinion for the time being." The other smiled.

"All right," he said. "If you want to remain mysterious, it's up to you! Anyway let's take it easy for now. Better come and have some lunch." And he led the way to the directors' room adjoining the canteen.

"Any idea what you want to do this afternoon, Doctor? " Howard asked, as they started their soup. The Doctor glanced at the window.

"I think," he murmured, "now that the weather seems a little less inclement, a little exercise is indicated." And he looked across at Miss Frayle for her approval.

Her heart sank. She had hoped she would be able to return with the Doctor to the hotel and rest after the exertions of the morning. Howard gave Doctor Morelle a sharp glance which indicated he had expected him to devote further time to investigating the cause of the restive atmosphere at the power-house.

The Doctor interpreted the other's expression and explained: "I fear it remains for someone else to make a move before any tangible result can be achieved."

But even Doctor Morelle could not have foreseen the tragically dramatic nature of that move when it did come.

The Doctor and Miss Frayle were nearing the end of dinner that evening when the waiter hurried in to say he was wanted on the telephone.

The Doctor looked at the man with raised eyebrows.

"Indeed? Who is it waiter, do you know? "

"Gentleman gave the name of Mr. Benson."

"The chief engineer at the Power Station," said Miss Frayle helpfully. "Whatever does he want? I'd better go and see." A look of slight apprehension crossed her face: she had been anticipating being able to get to bed early, the afternoon's walk had proved as strenuous as the tour round the power station. She felt it in her bones that the telephone message might be disturbing, and her eager offer to answer it was in part a defensive measure. Perhaps she might be able to deal with the menace to her night's rest and nip it in the bud, she thought vaguely.

"Do not disturb yourself, Miss Frayle. I will ascertain the nature of Mr. Benson's requirements."

"Oh . . . thank you," she said uncertainly.

Benson's voice was agitated and urgent over the telephone. "I'm speaking from the Power Station, Doctor. I tried to get our own doctor, but he's not available—I wondered if you'd come over—there's been an accident . . ."

"What precisely has occurred? "

"One of the men has been electrocuted—I'm afraid it's all up with him, poor devil! But I thought perhaps you might— "

"I will come round immediately," Doctor Morelle cut in. "It should take me no more than fifteen minutes to reach you."

Miss Frayle looked up anxiously as the Doctor returned to the table. He had put on his overcoat and scarf.

"What is it, Doctor Morelle? " You look— "

"Benson's up at the Power Station," he snapped. "One of the men has been electrocuted. I am going along at once."

"Electrocuted? How awful! I must come with you— " He waved her back into her chair.

"No, Miss Frayle, I prefer you to remain here. The weather has turned much too inclement again for you to venture out— "

"Oh, but Doctor— "

"Please take my advice. The wind is icy and I do not wish you

155

to catch a chill. I shall feel much happier in the knowledge that you are here in this more congenial atmosphere."

His entirely unexpected consideration for her welfare in turn aroused Miss Frayle's protective instincts to the full. She fixed him with a look much as an astigmatic bird might have devoted to her newly hatched brood.

"Well, if you're sure you'll be all right? " she cooed. "I don't like you going out alone on a night like this."

He gave her a sardonic smile.

"I think I shall be able to manage, Miss Frayle! " Then he went on: "Finish your dinner, and then peruse your detective-novel until my return—I feel sure you will find the vicarious thrills therein contained much more gratifying than the comparatively uneventful expedition upon which I am setting out."

"Wrap up well," she advised him.

"I will guard myself against the elements to the best of my ability! Expect my return presently."

"I'll have a hot drink waiting for you when you get back," she called after him. "Take care, Doctor . . ."

Outside, it was snowing a little, and as Doctor Morelle came down the hotel steps a taxi drew in to drop its fare. He re-engaged it immediately, with the result that he was passing through the massive entry-gates of the Power Station a few minutes later.

A night watchman directed him to where Benson would be found, and the Doctor hurried off. The chief engineer seemed surprised to see him so soon. He was bending over a figure in blue overalls that lay on a bench.

"You're here quickly! " he remarked. "It's not a quarter-of-an-hour since I rang you."

"I said I should come without delay," replied Doctor Morelle, drawing off his gloves.

"Sorry I had to drag you out on a night like this," Benson apologised. He added: "I'm afraid there's nothing you can do."

"I regret to hear that, Mr.—ah—Benson." As he bent over the inert figure he said in a conversational tone: "The wind is immoderately chill. Snow is imminent, I should imagine."

As he examined the man, a card fell from one of his pockets. It was a club subscription card, bearing the name of John Gregory. As he replaced it the Doctor gave it a cursory glance. At length he stood up.

"Your fears are substantiated," he told Benson gravely. "Life is extinct."

"Not to be surprised at! " was the grim response. "Ten thousand volts never did anybody much good in a concentrated dose."

"The cause of death would be compatible with electrocution."

156

"I'm a bit puzzled as to how it happened," muttered the other. "Though I always said he was damned careless!"

"Perhaps I could view the scene of the accident?" suggested Doctor Morelle.

"See that High Tension wire up there." He pointed upwards. The wire he indicated was slung from one end of the building to the other, and was about fifteen feet above the ground. "He was caught on that."

"You mean, in fact, he was suspended from the wire?"

Benson nodded. "He must have slipped off that scaffolding you can see runs round the place—as you see we've some structural alterations in progress—"

"You found him there yourself, I presume?"

"Yes—I happened to be checking the instruments, when suddenly they registered a big dip. I came out, had a quick look round, and there was the poor devil!"

"No doubt you promptly switched off the electrical current in this section and extricated the unfortunate man?"

"Yes—Had to do it myself, as I thought there might still be a chance, and there was no one else handy to help me. Good job the builders had left those tall steps . . ."

"Then, it seems you were the only witness of this accident to John Gregory?" Doctor Morelle put the question in suave, almost abstract tones.

Benson shot a look at him through narrowed lids.

"What do you know about Gregory?" he said. "What's on your mind?"

"I am merely suggesting," murmured the Doctor imperturbably, "that it was no accident at all. That you have long borne this man a grudge, and that you contrived to electrocute him with malice aforethought."

A look of baffled rage showed itself on the other's face. Then he shrugged his shoulders and revealed his white teeth in a smile.

"You can't prove anything," he said.

"On the contrary, I shall be in a position when the time comes, to prove as much as is necessary to convict you of homicide."

"That time'll never come!" grated the chief engineer. As he spoke he produced a revolver and motioned the Doctor back. "I'll have to give you some of the same medicine!" His face was twisted viciously. "Back you go! . . . Back! . . ." Doctor Morelle gave ground before the menacing figure before him. He realised he was being forced towards a huge condenser.

"You'll fit very snugly between those terminals!" laughed Benson raspingly. "I'll tell them you were nosing around here—and—well—another unfortunate acccident, eh?" He waved his revolver

157

threateningly. "Back you go, Doctor Morelle! You'll find it a nice quick death—at ten thousand volts! " The Doctor realised that a few more paces would bring about his death. Suddenly he stood his ground. He leaned on his walking-stick.

"If you imagine you will escape the consequences of your crime in this way, you are greatly mistaken," he said in level tones, not taking his eyes from the other's face. "Before coming here I took the precaution of notifying the police—" he paused as if listening "—and unless I am mistaken," he went on deliberately, "I am inclined to think I hear their footsteps approaching now—"

The other listened. His eyes shifted craftily as there came the sound of running footsteps drawing nearer.

He made the mistake of turning his head in the direction from which they came. Doctor Morelle's stick struck like lightning to crack against his knuckles. With a shout of pain he dropped the gun. As he clutched his injured hand, Doctor Morelle bent swiftly and now faced him with the revolver. From the door a bewildered Miss Frayle looked questioningly from one to the other, and then came forward hesitantly, her eyes goggling.

"Kindly elevate your hands, Benson," snapped Doctor Morelle.

"Doctor, what is going on? " asked Miss Frayle in a mystified voice.

"Your appearance was quite fortuitous, Miss Frayle! This—ah—gentleman had taken a pronounced personal dislike to me and had decided to end my career with a violent and somewhat unpleasant death." His tone changed. "But I expressly ordered you to stay at the hotel," he said irritably.

"I—I brought your thick scarf, Doctor," she stammered. "You went out with the thin one, and it's started to snow."

"I feel the scarf would prove more efficacious tied round this creature's wrists! Tie them behind his back, Miss Frayle, firmly."

Miss Frayle approached Benson nervously, and while the Doctor kept the revolver trained on him menacingly, she followed his instructions. The chief engineer made no sound, but stood there, his face a white twisted mask.

"Don't blame me if you catch a cold," Miss Frayle said to Doctor Morelle as she completed her task and stepped back. She went on, surveying the scarf which she had knotted securely round Benson's wrists with approval:

"Thank goodness I felt worried about you! My intuition, I suppose, that you always jeer at! Then when I found your scarf, I had to come after you." She added brightly: "Now, would you like me to telephone the police? "

"The manner in which you divine my thoughts is little short of uncanny! " was the reply, and she hurried off.

A little while later Doctor Morelle was saying to Julian Howard:
" I have no doubt but that I have disposed of the source of your
anxiety concerning the atmosphere surrounding your employees.
Benson was most definitely a sinister influence. Few people are
insensitive, consciously or otherwise, to the presence of evil. Its
effects upon them are bound to be of a far-reaching nature . . . "

When Howard had gone, Miss Frayle picked up her detective-
novel and said she thought it was time she went off to bed. She
broke off to ask:
" Doctor Morelle, did you say what gave you the clue that Benson
was lying about the death of poor Gregory? "

" I should have imagined that would have been apparent, Miss
Frayle. Benson's story that he had taken Gregory off the High
Tension wire was an obvious fabrication for this simple reason: A
person suspended in such a manner would suffer no injury however
high the voltage, because the current would not be earthed."

She looked at him with a puzzled frown.
" But *he* must have known that too, Doctor, so why did he make
up such a story? "

" The creature was of an unbalanced mind, and my speedy arrival
at the Power Station upset his calculations and caught him somewhat unprepared."

She nodded understandingly. She glanced at the book in her hand.
" I must say," she said, with a little laugh, " I thought this was
quite an exciting story, but after the excitement we've gone through
to-night it's going to seem awfully tame! " She paused a moment,
and then with the air of one expressing a most profound *bon mot,*
observed brightly:
" But then truth *is* stronger than fiction, isn't it, Doctor Morelle? "

CHAPTER XIII

THE CASE OF THE SOLICITOR'S LEGACY

Though Doctor Morelle considered himself unique in most respects,
he had to admit he was human enough in his susceptibility to that
ubiquitous leveller, the common cold. Furthermore, in accordance
with the precepts of his profession, he accepted the axiom that once
the germ responsible has established itself, the cold must take its
course. So, at the first intimation of a chill Doctor Morelle, in this
respect at any rate, practised what he preached, and invariably took
to his bed, armed with a bottle of medicine of his own dispensing,
and proceeded to make Miss Frayle a partner in his sufferings.

Directed by his instructions issued from his sick-bed, she ran innumerable errands, placated disappointed patients who wished to see the Doctor, cancelled engagements, kept up the fire in his room, and reminded him when it was time to take his medicine. In spite of all her burdens, however, she made her characteristically conscientious efforts to carry them out and at the same time cheer up the patient.

Even when he sardonically informed her she must be under the influence of a " Florence Nightingale " fixation, she persevered with her bright smile and perhaps somewhat irritating " bedside manner." Occasionally, when one of his rebuffs was particularly bitter, her eyes behind her spectacles would blink with mortification. But pretty soon she was addressing him once more in that indulgent tone usually reserved for a very spoilt child.

She stood outside his bedroom door one morning, rather dreading the coming day. He had now passed beyond the hoarse stage of his cold, when, his voice lacking its familiar biting qualities, he had been forced to refrain from unleashing his sarcastic observations upon her efforts to play the ministering angel.

Miss Frayle was bringing him the morning papers. These, she hoped, would keep him occupied for half-an-hour at least, before he began demanding her attention to deal with the day's routine of errands and the usual variety of problems. This morning she had an added problem on her mind. There was a piece of news in the papers which she felt might upset him. She was in a quandary as to whether she should bring it to his notice. As she went into his room, she decided since it would be impossible to keep the papers from him, she must think of some way in which to break the news to him gently. Steeling herself for the coming ordeal she put on a bright and cheerful smile and advanced towards the bed.

" Miss Frayle, will you please remove that fatuous grin from your features whenever you enter the room," came the acid voice from the pillows. Its familiar incisive timbre was there, she noted with dismay. " And would you be good enough to close the door " —he added maliciously—" From the other side preferably? You may not be aware of the fact, but I am confined to bed with a chill, and if my recovery is to be expedited, I must avoid all draughts."

She closed the door and returned to the bedside. The Doctor was lying muffled in a thick bed-jacket over his pyjamas. A half-empty box of Le Sphinx cigarettes at his elbow and one between his lips indicated he had not curtailed his smoking as part of his self-imposed treatment.

" You sound much better this morning! " she said cheerfully.

He blew his nose aggressively, and stared at her through a cloud of cigarette-smoke.

" Judging by your highly complacent tone, Miss Frayle," he

rasped, "I should imagine you have something unpleasant to announce!"

He shuddered as she smiled brightly again and became busily attentive.

"Oh, dear! your eiderdown has slipped off," she chided him, as she replaced it. "Did you notice that new after-chill tonic advertised in the papers this morning?" she rattled on. "They say it's just the thing to put you on your feet after a cold."

"I am quite capable of standing on my feet when the time is opportune without any assistance of the nature you suggest!" he snapped irritably. "Not that I have had an opportunity of perusing the morning journals, which you have placed so thoughtfully out of my reach."

She handed them to him.

"I will start the day by reading the obituary column of *The Times*," he decided thoughtfully. "And reassure myself that I am fortunate enough to be in the land of the living!"

He was folding the paper when Miss Frayle interposed nervously:

"Er—Doctor—I think—that is—I ought to tell you—"

He fixed her with a mordant glare.

"As I had divined, Miss Frayle! No doubt you wish to confess to some negligence! You have possibly blown up my laboratory? Doubtless from your point of view a mere trifling mishap—"

"Oh no, no, Doctor," she interrupted in extreme agitation. "It's —it's—something in the paper!"

He eyed her shrewdly, then turned to the paper he held.

"What sensational head-line devised by the editor for the gullible public has caught your over-developed imagination?" he murmured.

"It isn't anything like that. It's—it's about Mr. Gordon."

"You mean James Horace Gordon?"

"Yes."

He suddenly snapped: "*Will* you be good enough to close that window? How often must I impress upon you the need for me to avoid draughts?"

She sighed and closed the window, which was open half-an-inch.

"You mustn't be a molly-coddle, you know," she reproved him. "After all, you've only got a chill, and you've got me to look after you. Not like poor Mr. Gordon."

"That is a debatable statement!"

"Mr. Gordon is—well, he's dead!"

The Doctor's eyebrows lifted the merest fraction.

"Dead?" he murmured.

"According to the papers," she went on, "he was gassed!"

"Are you inferring it was a case of *felo de se?*"

"Suicide, it says in the paper."

161

Doctor Morelle sighed, but made no comment. With a thoughtful expression he began to search his newspaper. He found the report, which read :
"In the early hours of this morning, James Horace Gordon, solicitor, of Quadrant Chambers, Field's Inn, was found dead in a gas-filled bedroom. The police were summoned by his man-servant, William Goodchild, who said that his employer had lately been subject to severe fits of depression . . ."
Doctor Morelle paused in his reading to give a gigantic sneeze. He blew his nose and leaned back on his pillows, his eyes closed, his face wearing an abstracted look.

He was recalling to mind the last occasion on which he had seen James Horace Gordon. He had enjoyed a very pleasant dinner with the old man at his bachelor chambers, followed by a lengthy discussion on various aspects of forensic medicine.

They had met some years ago. The Doctor had given evidence in a case as a result of which Gordon's clients had received a stiff sentence.* Out of this unpromising first encounter had developed a friendship between them based on a professional admiration for each other. They did not meet very often, for both were very busy men, respecting each other's immersion in his vocation.

But the Doctor knew he had only to telephone the little old solicitor if he required any assistance in any legal matter. In his turn Doctor Morelle was always ready to help Gordon.

He had once commented on the fact that the old man enjoyed such robust health that he never seemed to be in need of medical aid. "Moderation! That's the secret, Doctor!" the other had smiled. "I know my limits, and I never exceed 'em. Still, if ever I do, I promise you the first opportunity of diagnosing the trouble." He had paused and added: "I'll tell you something that will amuse you. Though I've spent most of my career in advising people to make wills, disentangling and contesting wills and administering 'em, I never made a will of my own till last week!" He had chuckled reminiscently. "Something seemed to tell me I'd pass the three score and ten mark. All our family have been long-livers, so I waited until I was seventy, and now I've done the job."

Then he had given the Doctor a long look, his eyes twinkling beneath his shaggy eyebrows. He had said :
"By the way, I've named you as an executor." The Doctor had expressed his appreciation of the honour, and had observed :
"I sincerely hope, however, I shall not be called upon to act in my executorial capacity for some years to come."

* See footnote to p. 85. The client in question had been a witness in the "Mayfair Poisoning Case" and had committed perjury in no small degree. (N.B.—The chapters are not necessarily placed in chronological order).

Doctor Morelle opened his eyes and regarded Miss Frayle, who was busying herself making the room tidy. He sat up in bed.

"I should be more grateful, Miss Frayle, if you would refrain from disturbing any further particles of dust, which I have repeatedly advised you is a major irritant, and instead put me into telephonic communication with Scotland Yard! "

"Scotland Yard? "

"I wish to speak to Detective-Inspector Hood immediately."

"But you know you oughtn't to have any excitement," protested Miss Frayle. "It will only send up your temperature."

"*I* am experiencing no sensation of increase in my pulse rate," he snapped.

"You're supposed to lie quiet and take some of this medicine," she insisted.

"A moment ago you were accusing me of indulging in self-pity," he accused her.

"'Phoning Scotland Yard indeed! " cried Miss Frayle, with a show of indignation. "Before we know where we are we'll be rushing off and getting mixed up with bodies—and then you'll catch pneumonia and be a body yourself! " She added by way of an afterthought: "And I shall lose my job! "

"Will you please telephone Inspector Hood? " snapped the Doctor through clenched teeth, glaring at her.

"Listen to you!" she challenged him, her voice rising to a squeak. "Why, you're looking flushed already! "

He was rapidly losing the remains of his patience. "It is you who are unable to control yourself! " he exclaimed, choking with annoyance. "I am not in the least excited! "

She eyed him uncertainly.

"Will you make that call! " he demanded, "or do I have to jump out of bed and strangle you with the telephone cord? "

He looked as if he were about to spring out of bed there and then and put his threat into operation. Miss Frayle positively dived for the telephone, on the bedside table, and began dialling. As a result of his ill-tempered agitation, the Doctor lapsed into a fit of coughing. Miss Frayle interrupted dialling to pour out his medicine. He was just gulping it down with an expression of profound distaste and she had started to dial the number again when the front-door bell rang.

Still coughing and choking, Doctor Morelle waved her to go and answer it. She returned a few minutes later with a little frown and regarded him with a look of trepidation.

"It's a Mr. Goodchild," she said. "He—he says he must see you—it's most important."

"Goodchild? " His eyebrows shot up.

163

Then his face took on an expression of interest. "Gordon's man-servant," he said half to himself. "Bring him up immediately."
"I told him you couldn't possibly see anyone," she insinuated. His gaze was baleful.
"Bring him up!" he snapped, and another paroxysm of coughing shook him. Apprehensively Miss Frayle retreated to the door.
"Very well, Doctor, but do remember you mustn't excite yourself!"
"Will you go, woman!"
She vanished.
A moment later a thin-faced man sidled apologetically into the room. He wore a shabby raincoat over a morning suit, and carried a trim black bowler hat. Miss Frayle hovered in the background and closed the door for the newcomer as he moved towards the Doctor.
"Good morning, Doctor Morelle, I'm sorry to have to trouble you like this, but it's important. Most important."
"Sit down," said the Doctor, eyeing him with his penetrative gaze. "I presume you have come to acquaint me with the facts relating to Mr. Gordon's unfortunate demise?"
Goodchild nodded sadly.
"Tell me exactly how the tragedy occurred?"
"There isn't really very much to tell, sir," the man muttered, sinking on to a chair Miss Frayle had placed for him, his bowler hat perched on his knee.
"Mr. Gordon appeared to be in fair health, except that he had seemed somewhat depressed these last few days. Unusual for him, as you know. However, he was apparently no worse when I said 'Good-night' to him last night. Soon after one o'clock this morning, I woke up suddenly. I imagined I could smell gas. I put on my dressing gown and went on to the landing. The smell was stronger there, and I traced it to Mr. Gordon's room. I knocked, but there was no reply. I went in. He was lying face downwards on the rug in front of the gas-fire. The tap was on, but the fire wasn't burning. He was dead, I could tell that at once. I tele-phoned the police, and they seem to think it is suicide."
Doctor Morelle stared at the man over his cigarette.
"And what opinion have you formed?"
"I—I don't know, Doctor."
"I am under the impression that you have not paid me this visit merely for the purpose of acquainting me with what you have?"
Goodchild shook his head. Fumbling in his inside coat pocket, he produced an envelope.
"I found this on a table in his bedroom. Addressed to you. I didn't know whether I should have given it to the police, but I thought I'd come to you first. In case it's anything private."

164

Miss Frayle saw the Doctor frown as, taking the envelope and opening it, he read:

"Dear Doctor Morelle,
    I deeply regret this step I am about to take, but feel I have lived beyond my allotted span. You will find my estate in good order, but I wish to make a small addition to my will. I want you to pay the sum of five hundred pounds to my head clerk, Jonathan Taylor, and the same amount to my man-servant, William Goodchild, in recognition of their services to me during my lifetime. Thank you, and good-bye,
                                                  James Horace Gordon."

Thoughtfully refolding the letter and replacing it in the envelope, he said:
    "Mr. Gordon gave you no hint of the contents of this letter? "
    "No, Doctor," replied Goodchild. "He never discussed his private affairs with me."
    "Quite so. I am glad you brought this communication direct to me. It may have an important bearing upon the circumstances surrounding your employer's demise."
    Goodchild nodded. He sighed heavily.
    "Yes . . . Oh, what a shocking affair. Poor Mr. Gordon. No man could have wished for a more considerate employer."
    He twisted his bowler hat round in his fingers, looked a little uncomfortable, then stood up.
    "Well— " he muttered uncertainly—" If there's nothing else, Doctor? The young lady said I wasn't to stay long— "
    "It may be desirable to get in touch with you again. No doubt you will remain at your present address for the time being? "
    "Until after the funeral, Doctor."
    "Miss Frayle will show you out."
    "Thank you, Miss. Good morning, Doctor . . ."
    When Miss Frayle re-entered the room a few minutes later, she was astonished to find the Doctor sitting up in bed, the bed clothes swathed round him and speaking into the telephone.
    "Is that Detective-Inspector Hood? " he was saying.
    "Good morning, Doctor Morelle," came the cheerful reply.
    "As a small return for the invaluable assistance I have given you on the Gardenia affair* and other cases, perhaps you would be good enough to acquaint me with one or two details concerning the late Mr. James Horace Gordon? "

    * The full story of this extraordinary case may possibly be given to the public at a later date. Doctor Morelle has intimated that he is collating the detailed facts with the intention of presenting them in a single volume.

"You mean the solicitor who committed suicide early this morning? "

"You are satisfied it *is* a case of *felo de se?* "

"Oh yes," came Hood's confident voice over the wire. "We're just conducting a routine check-up. As a matter of fact, I'm in charge of the case."

"That may be fortuitous!" remarked Doctor Morelle. "Inasmuch as I may be able to render you some further trifling assistance in its connection. Who is conducting the *post mortem ?"*

"Oh, Sir Richard'll be doing it."

"Convey my compliments to him and advise him that I should be particularly interested in the results of the blood test. Furthermore, I should be interested to know whether or no he discovers any traces of bruises. Also the position of the blood in the lungs."

"What the devil are you driving at, Doctor? " the detective queried in a puzzled tone.

"Finally," went on Doctor Morelle coolly, "would you inform me if you have found the deceased's will? "

"Yes, we've got that. I have it here on my desk."

"I desire to peruse it. You will no doubt observe that I am an executor."

"Yes, I can read English, too! " the Detective-Inspector came back at him good humouredly.

"It is a facility for *reading between the lines* which *I* find more profitable! " was the swift, sardonic retort. Kindly bring the document along immediately after the *post-mortem* has been performed. Doubtless you will let me have the results of that simultaneously? "

"All right," agreed the other. "But you talk as if it *wasn't* a plain case of suicide," he grumbled, mystified.

Doctor Morelle merely gave a sardonic chuckle and replaced the receiver. He turned to see Miss Frayle standing at his side with another glass of medicine.

"Really, Doctor," she reproved him, "you will catch your death if you go on like this."

"On the contrary, I feel very much better! " he snapped. He took a sip from the glass and choked. "Ah! What a vile concoction! "

"You mixed it yourself! " she reminded him sweetly. "Drink it up, you know it's for your own good."

With a baleful glance at her he drank it off. There followed several minutes of spluttering, coughing and groaning. When he had finally recovered from the taste of the medicine he sat upright in bed, lit a Le Sphinx, and observed thoughtfully:

"H'm . . . this affair closely resembles the famous mystery of Marie Roget."

THE CASE OF THE SOLICITOR'S LEGACY

"Who was she? "

" A young female who figured in one of Edgar Allan Poe's tales of ratiocination and detection. Marie Roget was drowned in the Seine, and— "

" But poor old Mr. Gordon wasn't drowned. He was gassed . . At least— "

He gave a ponderous sigh and shook his head hopelessly.

" If, instead of formulating theories of your own," he said through his teeth, " you would allow me to continue my speculative processes without interruption, you would be performing *some* service! "

She subsided and he went on:

" The Marie Roget affair was solved by Auguste Dupin, the fictional detective created by Edgar Allan Poe, simply by perusing the newspaper reports and documents relating to the case— "

" Oh, I see what you mean, now, Doctor! "

He ignored her interruption and proceeded in his characteristically pompous manner:

" Most authorities agree that the tale was founded on fact; that the author based it upon the mystery of a certain Mary Cecilia Rogers who was murdered in New York in 1841. The circumstances surrounding her tragic demise baffled the police authorities and the assassin was never apprehended."

He paused for a moment as a thought struck him. Then he puffed a cloud of cigarette-smoke ceilingwards, murmuring to himself:

" It would be interesting to obtain access to the newspaper files and documents relating to the Mary Rogers homicide case and, with their guidance, step back into the past and solve the mystery." He sighed. " That would be a triumph of deduction! To elucidate a homicide long since perpetrated and left unsolved— "

" I don't see that it would do much good," objected Miss Frayle. "Whoever did murder the poor girl must be dead themselves anyway, so why bother? "

He surveyed her pityingly.

" Naturally, my *dear* Miss Frayle," he said in a silky tone, " I cannot expect you, with your limited range of intelligence, to appreciate the fascination of such an achievement in the abstract. My preoccupation with criminology has little to do with the human element. The protagonists concerned are merely ciphers; what attracts me to the investigation of crime is the putting into practice of my powers of deduction, my unique aptitude for assembling the facts in their logical and relevant sequence, my— "

" That will be Detective-Inspector Hood," interrupted Miss Frayle as the front-door bell rang. With a thankful sigh and an expression

* See his article " Auguste Dupin versus Sherlock Holmes—A Study in Ratiocination," *London Archive* and *Atlantic Weekly* (New York), 1931.

of joyful release that was not lost on the Doctor, she rushed out
quickly to admit the visitor. Doctor Morelle puffed viciously at his
cigarette and made a mental note severely to reprimand Miss Frayle
at the first opportune moment for her manifest boredom when he
was discoursing so enthusiastically upon that most interesting of all
topics—himself.

Inspector Hood sat himself by the bedside, and extracted a bulky
envelope from the brief-case he was carrying.

" There you are, Doctor, that's the will." And he passed the
document over. Doctor Morelle in turn handed the detective the
letter Goodchild had delivered.

" While I peruse the will, you may care to examine this letter
consigned to me this morning by the deceased's man-servant."

Miss Frayle sat and watched breathlessly as, for a few minutes,
the only sound in the room was the rustling of papers. Then the
Doctor looked up.

" Well? "

" Looks fishy to me," said the other grimly, tapping the letter
with a stubby forefinger. " D'you think they are both in it—this
clerk chap as well as the man-servant? "

Doctor Morelle shook his head slightly, with a sardonic gleam
in his eyes.

" Why not? "

" For the simple reason that in his will, Gordon bequeaths
Jonathan Taylor the sum of one *thousand pounds*—Gordon had told
me he had mentioned this matter to Taylor and advised him on
purchasing a practice of his own in due course—Goodchild, however, was unaware of this fact, and doubtless thought it would
avert suspicion from himself if he brought in a second party."

" He's a deep 'un! " was the Detective-Inspector's comment.

The Doctor took another Le Sphinx and lit it. He went on:

" Unfortunately for himself, he made one serious mistake. He
did not realise a meticulous solicitor like Gordon would never have
written a letter containing such an injunction, for it has no validity
whatsoever. It is virtually impossible for him to have perpetrated
such an elementary legal error. He would merely have added a
codicil to his will, which was quite accessible in his office safe."

" I'll pass the letter on to the experts," said Hood. " It may not
be a forgery, of course. Goodchild may have compelled the old
chap to write it, and then murdered him."

" It is not impossible that Gordon wrote the letter himself under
intimidation," agreed Doctor Morelle, and added: " Fully conscious that what he was writing was invalid, and confident that I
should detect it and from it deduce that foul play had been
committed."

168

Miss Frayle gave a little gasp of admiration, and the Detective-Inspector looked fully impressed.

"The *post-mortem* proved it was no suicide anyway," he said. "Though how the devil you guessed— "

"I never indulge in guess-work," Doctor Morelle corrected him coldly. "I arrive at my conclusions by the process of pure reasoning and the application of logic."

"Well, you were right. Not a trace of gas in the blood. Several bruises were disclosed which might have been caused by violence. Sir Richard's theory is that the poor old chap was smothered with a pillow, and afterwards the body was laid face downwards—but the blood was found to have settled towards the back of the lungs, which would have been impossible if he *had* died in that position."

"You say Sir Richard established that several bruises had been inflicted? "

Hood nodded.

"And it seems only a little blood had leaked into 'em, so Gordon must have died very soon after they were inflicted. Another indication he couldn't have inhaled a fatal dose of gas."

"H'm," murmured the Doctor with a touch of sarcasm, "it would appear that a case for culpable homicide is conclusive! "

"And—thanks to you—the identity of the murderer established," grinned the detective amiably. He rose and produced his pipe. "Well, I'll be getting along to arrange about a warrant for the arrest of our friend, Goodchild."

He turned as he moved from the bedside and said:

"Hope you get better quickly. Next time I call, I'll bring you some grapes."

"I am deeply touched by your solicitude on my behalf," came the reply. "But I fear your generosity would be entirely wasted so far as I personally am concerned."

"Why, d'you expect to be up and about so soon? "

Doctor Morelle smiled what he hoped was his most wistful smile. "No," he sighed, ostentatiously weary. "Merely that Miss Frayle would devour the grapes while I should be permitted to lie here on my bed of pain unattended and unrefreshed by your kind offering."

"Oh, Doctor Morelle! How could you— " she protested. But she was drowned by the detective's laughter. At the door he paused.

"Well," he said admiringly, "this is the first time I've ever heard of anyone solving a murder without leaving his bedroom! "

"You should read an article of mine," murmured Doctor Morelle, "on Auguste Dupin, the detective character created by Edgar Allan Poe. It appeared in the *London Archive*. Miss Frayle will hand you a copy as you go out."

And he relaxed on his pillows and closed his eyes

CHAPTER XIV

THE CASE OF THE MAN WHO WAS TOO CLEVER

One evening Doctor Morelle had been visiting a scientist acquaintance who resided in a block of flats which the Doctor has sardonically described as "reminiscent of native cliff-dwellings." Miss Frayle had accompanied him on his visit, and they had said "Good-night" to their host and were descending the staircase from the second floor on their way out. As the distance down was so short they did not bother to call the lift. Suddenly Miss Frayle was shocked and horrified to hear the sound of what appeared to be a woman screaming. The screams came from a flat on the first floor, and the creature sounded as if she were in great agony.

Miss Frayle turned a white face to the Doctor and grasped his arm.

"Doctor, listen! That awful screaming—! It's some woman—!"

"I was not under the impression it was the squeaking of a mouse!" he replied, pausing, and glancing along the passage leading to the flats.

"It's coming from that flat along there!" gasped Miss Frayle, stepping forward as if to hurry in the direction she was indicating. "It must be someone in terrible pain—"

The Doctor's eyes narrowed speculatively. He walked quickly past her, speaking to her over his shoulder.

"I think perhaps it would be advisable to ascertain the reason for such distress."

She caught up with him and was saying breathlessly: "Perhaps we can do something—" when there came the humming of the lift ascending. The lift-gates opened with a slam and the hall-porter shot out, his eyes popping, and rushed after them.

"Here's the porter," Miss Frayle told the Doctor unnecessarily, for he had already observed the man's approach. "We'll go in with him."

"Blimey! Who's kicking up the song-and-dance?" he gulped as he joined them.

"It's from the flat along here," she said.

The screams continued, and they hurried in the direction from whence they came.

"Fancy practising scales this time o' night!" exclaimed the porter with an attempt at heavy-handed humour.

Doctor Morelle turned his head and eyed him with extreme disfavour. "I feel fewer abortive attempts at misplaced humour and more imperative action is indicated!" he snapped.

"Something awful's happening, I'm sure— " cried Miss Frayle as she ran alongside in order to keep up with the Doctor's raking strides. The porter was breathing stertoriously as he laboured after them.

Suddenly the screaming subsided, dying away into moans. Then silence.

"She's chucked it now, anyway! " grunted the porter. "Flat nineteen it sounded from. That's Mr. and Mrs. Collins— "

They reached the door which bore the number nineteen, and the porter produced his pass-key. There came no sound from within the flat as he turned the key in the lock.

Doctor Morelle and Miss Frayle found themselves in a small hall, with a glimpse of the lounge beyond. Chromium, glass and light oak predominated. There was a faint smell of perfume pervading the atmosphere. As the porter stood uncertainly in the entrance to the lounge there came a rapid movement and a youngish man appeared, wearing a blue silk dressing-gown. His face was ghastly.

"Mr. Collins! " exclaimed the porter.

"Thank heavens—! Thank heaven, you've come! " the man cried.

"What's happened? " Miss Frayle said. "We heard— "

"My wife—! " was the agitated response. "Locked herself in the bathroom! She—she's— " he broke off incoherently, and they followed him as he rushed back the way they had come. The bathroom was at the end of a short passage on either side of which two bedrooms faced each other.

"Blimey! we'd better bust the door in! " said the porter as Collins rattled vainly at the lock and called: "Diana! Diana! "

He turned to them frantically.

"We must get in! " he gasped. "Something's happened to my wife! Something's happened to her! "

"Let's shove together. Come on, sir," addressing the Doctor, "and you, Mr. Collins." Doctor Morelle murmured: "No doubt our combined efforts will prove efficacious! "

"Yes—! Yes—! " babbled Collins.

Miss Frayle stood aside as they rushed at the bathroom door together. The door was not built to withstand such vigorous treatment, and when the three of them charged at it the second time there was a sound of splintering wood.

"Once more! " shouted Collins, and after the third attempt the door crashed open. "Kindly remain in the bedroom, Miss Frayle!" Doctor Morelle said over his shoulder, as he caught sight of the crumpled figure of a woman on the bathroom floor.

"Better get a doctor! " grunted the hall-porter.

"Fortuitously," murmured Doctor Morelle, "I happen to be one —I am Doctor Morelle."

The man shot him a surprised look. "Oh? Lucky you was passing! Even though it's a bit too late by the look o' things!"

Collins cried: "The key's on the floor. Diana must have locked the door before she—she—!" He broke off and knelt down beside the woman. "She's—she's dead!" he muttered brokenly.

She was dead, the Doctor saw at a glance. Thoughtfully he stooped to pick up the fragments of a broken tumbler, which had apparently fallen from the dead woman's grasp. He sniffed at the pieces, then carried them into the lounge.

"Miss Frayle, perhaps you will kindly occupy yourself by finding something in which to wrap these fragments?" As she took them he added: "Possibly you may have noticed the aroma of poppy about them?"

"I was wondering what it was," she said sniffing.

"The poison which the unfortunate woman drank from the tumbler is undoubtedly laudanum—opium prepared in spirits of wine. Hence the aroma of poppy."

"Was it suicide—?" Miss Frayle began to ask, and then gave a sudden exclamation of pain. "Oh! I've cut my finger on one of these bits of glass."

"Tck! Tck! How careless of you! Let me observe the extent of the damage." He examined the cut.

"It's nothing much."

"Quite a superficial injury. Nevertheless it would be wiser to bandage the wound. I can use my handkerchief as a temporary measure."

"Oh Doctor, it seems a shame to spoil it." But in spite of her protest, he produced his handkerchief from his breast-pocket and proceeded to bandage the cut finger.

"How neatly you've done it!" Miss Frayle smiled up at him admiringly, as he finally tied the knot. "And so quick."

"Quite comfortable?"

"Beautiful! Thank you so much, Doctor. Er—may I have it back please?"

"Um—?" He seemed to be deep in thoughtful contemplation of her hand.

"My hand—you're holding on to it!"

He appeared to snap out of his musing.

"Ah yes! I was momentarily somewhat preoccupied. I was considering one or two questions I wish to put to Mr. Collins. Perhaps you would be good enough to acquaint him of my identity —if the porter has not already advised him—and ask him to come here. Just call him out of the bathroom, no need for you to venture inside."

172

Miss Frayle shuddered in agreement and went out of the lounge to find Collins.

In a moment he came in and sat dejectedly in an arm-chair, his head between his hands. Miss Frayle observed him with pity and glanced at the Doctor who was contemplating him with a look of calculation. Poor man, she thought, it must have been an awful shock to him. Surely the Doctor could leave the business of questioning him till later?

The porter appeared and poured a glass of whisky for Collins, but the latter, however, decided he didn't need it. The porter continued to hold the glass and took an occasional sip himself.

Doctor Morelle leaned negligently against a radiogram. He lit a cigarette thoughtfully.

"What—what could have happened—? " Collins turned to him with a haggard face. "Why should she do such a thing? "

The Doctor shook his head. "The circumstances point to the fact that your wife died from the effects of laudanum poisoning, Mr. Collins," he said quietly.

"Poor lady, what a shocking business! " muttered the porter, and Miss Frayle noticed that he consoled himself with another sip of whisky.

Collins suddenly stood up in a distracted manner and began to pace the room.

"I never dreamt she'd—she'd take her own life! " he cried. "You see, we'd quarrelled—Diana was temperamental—she was an actress on the films and radio—imagined and exaggerated all sorts of things —and when she slammed out of the bedroom, I didn't take what she said about committing suicide seriously."

"She threatened to commit *felo-de-se*? put in Doctor Morelle softly.

"Yes. But as I say, I thought she was just being melodramatic. I called out to her something to that effect, as a matter of fact, then went to bed. As you see I'm in my dressing-gown."

"I had already observed that fact."

Miss Frayle gave the Doctor a quick look and saw that his face wore an enigmatic expression.

Collins went on, speaking jerkily:

"And then suddenly I heard her screaming in terrible pain. I got out of bed, rushed to the bathroom, but the door was locked—"

At that moment the telephone rang in the hall. Collins broke off with a frown. He made as if to answer it himself, then turned to the porter. "Will you see who it is? "

When the man had gone, Doctor Morelle murmured:

"Please continue, Mr. Collins. You were describing how you hurried to the bathroom and found the door secured on the inside."

173

"Well, there's not much more to tell. I tried to force the door but couldn't, and—and—well, the rest you know."

The porter returned. He said to him:

"A lady to speak to you, sir. Wouldn't give no name."

The other's frown deepened. He hesitated and then moved towards the hall. "Perhaps I'd better answer it" he apologised, and went out. He carefully pulled the door after him, but Doctor Morelle made no attempt to overhear the conversation on the telephone ; on the contrary, he stood with his head slightly on one side, his eyes narrowed thoughtfully.

"What is it, Doctor? " began Miss Frayle in a hushed whisper.

He waved her into silence. She and the porter stood staring at him wonderingly. Suddenly he gave an exclamation of satisfaction.

"Ah! The almost imperceptible sound of some mechanical device in motion," he said.

"Eh? " grunted the porter.

"Whatever do you mean? " asked Miss Frayle.

Doctor Morelle, who had moved from the radiogram to the centre of the lounge, waved his hand casually.

"I should imagine it emanates from that radiogram."

He crossed to it with a swift movement and raised the light oak lid.

"H'm . . . As I had imagined, the turntable is still in motion."

"So it is," exclaimed the porter. "It hasn't been switched off—!"

At that moment Collins returned and saw them by the machine. He paused in the doorway, then came forward eyeing them somewhat suspiciously. The Doctor turned to him with a bland expression.

"I was admiring your radiogram," he said suavely.

The other nodded. "Yes . . . It was a present to my poor wife. She was very fond of the radio, naturally."

"The—ah—deceased also possessed a comprehensive selection of gramophone records," continued the Doctor, indicating a number which had been placed on a chair by the cabinet. He was turning them over as he spoke.

"You goin' to play us a tune, Doctor? " muttered the porter in a somewhat censorious tone. "I must say it don't seem quite the moment— "

Collins cut in, his voice high-pitched: "What's this all about? What's the radiogram got to do with my wife's suicide? "

Imperturbably the Doctor observed:

"This seems to be a somewhat unusual record." He had picked up a disc which bore a plain white label. He glanced at the inscription cursorily. An expectant silence had fallen. Miss Frayle, who had given Collins a quick look, heard Doctor Morelle murmur, as

174

if speaking to himself: "It might be interesting to hear this played . . ."

"This is fantastic!" Collins protested, stepping forward. "Horrible!"

The Doctor seemed not to hear him. He was about to place the record on the revolving turntable when there came a shout.

"Leave that record alone! Put it down—!"

The next moment the disc was almost knocked from his hand as Collins made a sudden lunge. Miss Frayle gasped with sudden apprehension as she saw the look in the man's face. The porter, too, gave an exclamation of surprise, but reacted quickly and grappled with him. There was a fierce struggle, but the porter's weight soon told. Collins was forced back and subsided, breathing heavily, into an armchair, with the porter standing over him, dour and menacing. As if nothing had happened to mar the equanimity of the proceedings, Doctor Morelle placed the record on the turntable and adjusted the volume control.

It proved to be an excerpt from what was apparently a highly dramatic playlet. But what caused the porter's jaw to drop and Miss Frayle to goggle from behind her spectacles was the part where a series of piercing screams issued from the radiogram.

"Blimey!" said the porter hoarsely. "Why, that's Mrs. Collins, and them's the screams wot we heard outside!"

"Exactly the same voice—!" gulped Miss Frayle.

"A voice raised from the grave, is it not, Mr. Collins?" said Doctor Morelle. "And accusing *you!*"

"Yes . . ." Doctor Morelle mused through a cloud of cigarette smoke, "It was patently a clear-cut case!" He gave a thin smile of self-satisfaction, and went on:

"Mrs. Collins had undoubtedly succumbed as a result of laudanum poisoning, but the drug had been administered by her husband. How exactly the police will ascertain as a result of their examination of the culprit."

He was sitting before his desk in the study of the house in Harley Street. It was some time later ; Collins had been removed by the police summoned to the flat, and he, accompanied by Miss Frayle, had returned home.

Miss Frayle asked:

"But how did the poor woman come to be found locked in the bathroom?"

He regarded her with what he imagined was an expression of extreme tolerance.

"For the simple reason," he explained carefully, "that the husband had dragged her there. He had thereupon locked the door on

175

the inside and made his exit through the window to the fire escape, closing the window after him. It was a simple manoeuvre to return to the flat through the front door. In point of fact, he aroused my suspicions somewhat in the first instance by his manner of drawing attention to the key on the floor. A shade too obviously performed, it occurred to me. Whereupon I took the precaution of ascertaining if there was easy egress from the window. That was merely a minor indicative that all might not be what it purported to be, however."

Miss Frayle duly obliged by looking at him questioningly, and he went on:

"The major clue which attracted my attention was one very obvious fact which would have been apparent to any student with the most elementary knowledge of first-aid!"

She wriggled uncomfortably under the reproach implied in his tone.

"Well, I once took a course of first-aid, Doctor," she said, making a somewhat feeble attempt not to appear intimidated.

"Then I can only presume, my *dear* Miss Frayle, that even your superior intelligence had failed to absorb the fundamental fact that laudanum is a narcotic which induces a condition of *painless stupor!*"

She blushed, fiddled with her spectacles, and stammered:

"Why yes—Yes, of course! I remember now—"

"It followed, therefore, the wife would never have screamed out as she was supposed to have done."

He flicked the ash from his cigarette.

"Why did he deliberately attract attention by playing a record of Mrs. Collins screaming like that?" Miss Frayle asked.

"His purpose was to establish a somewhat subtle alibi. He calculated that on hearing the screams the hall-porter would rush to the scene and find him attempting to force the bathroom door—"

"You mean the way we did?"

"Precisely. Thus adding colour and credence to the story he had prepared. It would appear Mr. Collins transferred his affections elsewhere. As his wife, however, was in possession of considerable wealth which would become his upon her demise, he decided to precipitate her death in order to be in a position to embark upon a second marriage." His nostrils quivered with repugnance. "A sordid sequence of events, culminating inevitably in tragedy and disaster."

"Was it the—the other woman who 'phoned?"

He nodded. "I understand it was his inamorata."

Doctor Morelle puffed at his Le Sphinx.

"Umm ..." he mused, "were I proposing to include this in a

176

collection of tales of—ah—ratiocination, I should be inclined to entitle it 'The Man who was too Clever '." He gave a thin smile of self-satisfaction. "Yes . . . a singularly appropriate title."

Miss Frayle frowned. "Oh, but surely, Doctor," she corrected him after a moment's thought, "he wasn't clever *enough?*"

He closed his eyes with a painfully elaborate sigh.

"That will be the subtle implication conveyed—to the *discerning* reader!"

"Well," she persisted obstinately, "I don't see how anyone can be too clever and not clever enough all at the same time."

He replied, his voice grating with growing irritation: "The operative word in my last observation happened to be the word, 'discerning'!"

The implication sank in and she challenged him with:

"Meaning, I suppose, that I'm not?" It was her turn to sigh, only there was nothing forced about it. Her sigh came from the heart. Then she shrugged her shoulders. "However," she said, "no doubt I should be grateful to you for thinking I can read at all!"

"I confess I often suspect it is largely a matter of guess-work on your part!"

But she was determined not to be defeated this time. With what for her must have seemed to have been an inspired riposte, she flashed back at him: "Rather in the same way that you guess at these clues you talk about . . . eh, Doctor Morelle?"

His eyebrows shot up. This was unlike Miss Frayle. For one fraction of a moment his face almost registered surprise. Then, with eyes narrowed but in a voice smooth as silk, he murmured:

"Except that *I* always happen to guess correctly, my *dear* Miss Frayle!"

Miss Frayle subsided.

CHAPTER XV

THE CASE OF THE LAST CHAPTER*

Doctor Morelle was the type of person who was at all times very content with his own company. He was, nevertheless, on terms of acquaintance with rather more people than the average person, most of them being with men with whom he shared a common interest in the field of science or medicine, or with a somewhat more varied

* The original title was " The Case of the Telbury Halt Ghost," and the above is merely a further example of Doctor Morelle's insistence on occasion of displaying his curious sense of humour

group—those individuals with whom he had come into contact upon his numerous investigations of a criminological nature.

While he would hardly be described as "rubbing shoulders with members of the underworld as well as members of the police forces in various parts of the globe "—the Doctor would have resented the description in any case for its inelegance of phrase!—he had, however, a mixed circle of acquaintances.

He received numerous invitations from these persons who were anxious—as he was quick to appreciate!—to improve the acquaintance. But he rarely accepted any of them. On the other hand, there was one he never refused if he found it possible to spare the time, and that was an invitation from old Professor Cosmo Wade. Wade lived in a delightful Georgian mansion at Telbury, a tiny village near Oxford. He telephoned one evening asking if the Doctor could come down that week-end. He had, he explained, with some excitement, just completed some interesting experiments with certain fauna obtained from the shores of the Ægean, and he was anxious for Doctor Morelle's opinion concerning them. And so, accompanied by Miss Frayle (she would be most useful in collating any notes on the Professor's work, for he was well aware that the old man failed utterly in regard to any methodical system of filing or tabulation) Doctor Morelle drove down late on Saturday to Telbury.

It had proved a pleasant week-end, the results of the Professor's research had absorbed the Doctor. True, from Miss Frayle's point of view it had hardly been a satisfactory holiday. The weather had been bitterly cold ; snow had fallen soon after they had arrived, and it was still snowing on Sunday night as they prepared to return to London.

"Are you sure you won't stay until the morning? " Wade tried to persuade the Doctor as they stood in the hall saying their " good-byes."

Doctor Morelle shook his head.

"You are most hospitable," he said, " but I have an important appointment at an early hour in the morning." And, pulling on his gloves, he urged Miss Frayle out of the front door away from the hospitable warmth and into night and the snow-storm which had now reached a considerable pitch. "Come, Miss Frayle, let us confront the elements, and refrain from shivering in that ridiculous fashion. You cannot possibly feel chilled in your thick wrappings!"

In a few moments they were in his car, nosing cautiously along the narrow country lanes which were treacherously deep in snow. They succeeded in making good progress, however, for the first few miles, and Doctor Morelle was enlarging upon his abilities as a motorist, no matter what the circumstances or conditions, when one of the cylinders began to miss. Finally the engine gave out altogether, barely giving him time to pull the car into one side of the road. He quickly switched on his dashboard light and rapidly checked the dials. They seemed to be in order. He pressed the self-starter button. There was no response from the engine.

"Oh dear!" said Miss Frayle apprehensively. "I wonder what can be wrong?"

"I fear the worst!" he snapped irritably.

She glanced at his face, shadowed and more saturnine than ever in the glow of the dashboard light. His lips were drawn in a thin bitter line.

"Can't you do anything, Doctor? You don't mean we're caught in this terrible blizzard?" And she shuddered at the idea.

He made no reply. After a moment he lit a cigarette.

"I think I may reassure you on that point," he murmured. "We would appear to have reached the main road. Doubtless a vehicle of some nature will shortly overtake us and we can obtain assistance."

It seemed, however, that this optimism was not to be realised. Very few cars appeared to be venturing out that night. For what Miss Frayle thought must be hours they sat listening to the wind whistling in the trees overhead, and watched the snow pile up steadily against the windscreen. Suddenly, during a temporary abatement of the wind, they heard the sound of an approaching car. In a few moments it drew alongside, and its driver and Doctor Morelle lowered their side-windows simultaneously. The shadowy figure of a man was at the wheel of the other car.

"Am I right for Telbury Halt?" His voice had a harsh quality, and Miss Frayle imagined that his face was white, in the dim light and bore a strained, almost anxious expression.

"I fear," Doctor Morelle began, "I have no idea as to the whereabouts of a railway station. Perhaps you could, however, assist me—?"

But the man had let in his clutch and the car was driving quickly away. Miss Frayle clutched the Doctor's arm.

"Doctor!" she gasped. "Did—did you notice there was some-one in the back seat? All muffled up so that you couldn't see who it was—?"

He laughed shortly.

"My dear Miss Frayle, your somewhat over-fertile imagination is apt to run away with you!"

"Well, he's run away from *us!*" was her quick reply.

His eyes glittered in the shadows of his face. There may have been a quirk of amusement at the corners of his mouth. She went on nervously:

179

" That shows there was something wrong! Or why did they drive off like that without waiting to answer you? "

" It certainly betrayed a lack of courtesy on his part," he conceded. " But if one suspected everyone of criminal intent merely because of their ill manners, one would be able to point to very few as being innocent! "

" Well, I've a feeling— " she was about to persist, when he interrupted her with a sardonic chuckle:

" That feminine intuition of yours! " he mocked.

Miss Frayle gave him a hurt look from behind her spectacles and said no more. They sat silently for a few minutes. Then he began to pull his coat collar up round his ears.

" What are you going to do? " she asked.

" From what I remember of this stretch of road, we should be within walking distance of a village."

" You're going to walk in this? " she indicated the falling snow.

" That is my intention. Unless you imagine I can conjure up a team of reindeer and a sleigh out of the storm and drive off in the manner of Santa Claus! "

Anyone less like that benign old gentleman she couldn't imagine! She was about to make some remark to the effect that he would look very funny as Father Christmas when she decided he might take her seriously, and refrained. She said instead:

" I'll come too. I can't stay here alone."

" My dear Miss Frayle, your footwear is quite inadequate to withstand these conditions. You would merely catch a severe cold, which would cause me considerable inconvenience. We have a busy week ahead of us. You will be perfectly safe here, I can reassure you. Lock all the doors if that affords you any satisfaction."

And, in spite of her protests at being left alone, he got out, slammed the door, and disappeared into the swirling snowflakes. She took him at his word, secured the doors and huddled in her coat, trembling with apprehension, expecting any moment that horrible menacing figures would loom up out of the storm.

It seemed hours, but actually it was only twenty minutes by the clock on the dashboard when she saw an ancient car with rather uncertain headlights come chugging along towards her. She gazed at it with a fast-beating heart as a heavily muffled little man sprang out, then her trepidation subsided when she saw the Doctor's tall gaunt shape follow him. The man lost no time in removing the bonnet of Doctor Morelle's car, making a hasty inspection with the help of a large torch. He swung the starting handle once or twice, listened, and shook his head dubiously. He grunted:

" Take more'n five minutes to fix that, I reckon! "

" You mean you can't do it to-night? " Doctor Morelle frowned.

"Not a chance! " he said with finality. "Take the best part of a working day." And he went off into a string of technical terms in explanation of what was amiss. The Doctor's face wore a bitter look. "This is very unfortunate. I particularly wish to return to London to-night."

The little man scratched his head. Then he suggested:

"Tell you what, I'll tow your car in to my garage. Then I'll run you on to Telbury Halt in my old 'bus. It's only a mile further on the station is." He glanced at his watch. "You'll just about catch the ten-twenty to London—last train up! "

Doctor Morelle had no alternative but to fall in with his suggestion which he did somewhat ungraciously. At last he and Miss Frayle had been towed with considerable difficulty through the snow into the village, safely garaged, and they set off for Telbury Halt in the little man's car. The snow had abated somewhat, but the wind blew as furiously as ever as they drove up the incline to a bleak little railway station, its entrance illuminated by two oil lamps, flickering uncertainly, which swung creakingly with every howling gust.

Miss Frayle hurried into the station while the Doctor made arrangements with the garage man concerning his car, and remunerated him for his trouble. As she passed under the corrugated roof over the station entrance she noticed a set of tyre marks in the snow indicating, apparently, that a car had pulled up and driven on again. It occurred to her casually that it might be the car with the mysterious driver which had passed them. This in turn suggested that one of the occupants might be inside the station. Which one? she wondered with mounting curiosity. She paused at the door and waited for Doctor Morelle to join her. She said nothing to him as they went in together, and the tyre-tracks seemed to have passed unnoticed by him.

The waiting-room, however, was empty. While she remained behind, the Doctor went out on to the platform. He returned after a few moments declaring he had walked the length of the platform and pronounced it deserted and the parcels-office locked.

"We would appear to be the only passengers," he said.

"You don't think the train's gone? "

He glanced at his watch. "Not unless it made its departure fifteen minutes before the time scheduled."

Miss Frayle wondered what had happened to the people in the car. Perhaps they didn't want to catch the train at all, she decided. Just wanted to make some inquiries and then continue their journey.

"Still permitting that imagination of yours to run riot! " murmured Doctor Morelle, without glancing up from a slim book he had produced and was reading. It was a scientific treatise the Professor had lent him. Miss Frayle gave him a startled look. His

181

uncanny gift for apparently divining her thoughts continued to astonish her, while at the same time it discomfited her. It wasn't natural for anyone to be able to see right into your mind like that! The Doctor chuckled sardonically at her expression and went on reading. She was silent and crossed to the fire-place. The fire, however, was almost out. The hearth was piled with ashes, which did not appear to have been removed for several days. She shivered, drew her coat closer, and gazed round the little, dimly-lit waiting room. It appeared to serve as a booking-hall also. She noticed that the door next to the ticket-window was ajar. Summoning her courage, she went over to it and cautiously put her head round the door. She was greeted with an agreeable waft of warm air from a large oil stove. The office was empty. An incandescent oil lamp glimmered somewhat fitfully, though it gave more illumination than the one in the waiting-room, and the place seemed comparatively cheerful.

"There's a much better light in here, Doctor Morelle—it's warm too," she called to him. He looked up from his book.

"Are you also implying that it is unoccupied?"

"There's no one here."

He appeared suitably impressed by the prospect of some warmth and better light and, joining her, preceded her into the office.

"I think, under the circumstances, we might presume to trespass upon the railway's hospitality!" he murmured, promptly appropriating the only chair, a large office chair under the light. Miss Frayle dragged up a stool upon which she perched, and spread her hands before the warmth from the stove. In the confined space the only sound was the sputter of the lamp and the stove and the rustle of the Doctor's book. Outside the wind howled around the little station.

"I wonder what can have become of the booking-clerk?" presently speculated Miss Frayle.

The Doctor turned a page and blew out a cloud of cigarette-smoke. "No doubt occupied in one of his other capacities—porter, stationmaster or signalman, or whatever offices he combines with that of booking-office attendant."

She nodded drowsily. The warmth from the stove was inclined to send her into a doze. She didn't hear the door open a few minutes later, though Doctor Morelle had caught the sound of soft footsteps outside, and a pair of feet and trousers moved into his line of vision. He looked up from his book to see a middle-aged man, greying slightly at the temples, standing in the doorway staring at them. He wore an official looking cap which was rather soiled, and carried a small suitcase. "Evenin'," he muttered, and Miss Frayle woke up with a start and nearly fell off her perch.

182

"Good evening" murmured the Doctor, eyeing the newcomer speculatively.

The man half closed the door and placed the suitcase beside it. Then he crossed over to the ticket-window and pushed up the flap with a sharp bang.

From his action Miss Frayle, gathering her sleep-fuddled wits about her, concluded with a twinge of embarrassment that it was in the nature of a hint that she and the Doctor were on the wrong side of the ticket-window. She glanced at Doctor Morelle who seemed, however, to have become absorbed in his book once more.

She explained to the man nervously:

"I—I hope you don't mind us warming ourselves here? But it was rather cold out in the waiting-room."

The other looked at her.

"You are very welcome," he said. His voice was low, and held a mournful note.

"If we're in the way at all, we can easily wait outside," Miss Frayle smiled at him gratefully. The man made a deprecatory gesture.

"You can wait here till the train comes—looks like being a bit late. I shall be grateful to you for your company."

Doctor Morelle made no contribution to the conversation, so she continued to make the effort.

"I suppose this must be rather a lonely job for you, isn't it?" she asked brightly.

"Lonely? . . ." The man echoed, turning his sombre gaze on her and giving a queer, mirthless laugh. "Why, you two are the first people I've spoken to since—since . . ." His voice trailed off.

Watching him somewhat apprehensively, Miss Frayle thought his eyes misted over as he stared at the stove. Then he looked up and said with a twisted little smile: "Yes, I don't have very much company."

She suppressed a shiver. There was something about him which gave her an odd uneasy sensation. His face caught the light of the flame in the stove, which gave it a yellowed, parchment-like appearance. Deep lines ran down from his nose, and the corners of his mouth had a melancholy droop. There was a distorted look about it, accentuated by the trick of flickering light and shadow. His shoulders were rounded as if bent beneath some heavy load.

Outside, the wind continued to howl round the station, rattling the doors and occasionally lifting a loose sheet of the corrugated iron roof. The atmosphere of the warm room seemed to have undergone some inexplicable change. Miss Frayle felt it had been brought about by the arrival of the man who now stood staring down at the stove with an unseeing gaze. Although, by his appear-

183

ance and manner he had awakened her sympathy, yet at the same time she felt there was something—well, something *queer* about him. She wished the train would come.

Doctor Morelle glanced up from his book and eyed the man as he bent down to tie a bootlace which had come undone. He noted the shabby trousers and their frayed turn-ups, with a jagged tear in one of them. Miss Frayle had also observed the man's shabby appearance. Poor man! she thought. He looked as if he needed someone to look after him. Perhaps that was it—she felt a surge of sympathy towards him—he hadn't got anybody. And then having to be in a lonely spot like this ; it was enough to make anyone look depressed and strange. All the same, she reflected, there was something else about him, too—

She glanced at the Doctor, who was about to return to his book, when suddenly the man said:

"Of course I always come here on this night," he was saying. "It's very important . . ." His voice trailed off once more. Again that queer look.

Doctor Morelle said condescendingly :

"Yes, one would imagine you get few trains stopping here."

The other nodded absently. Then he went on in that low, mournful tone :

"I was late once, you see," he said. "Yes, late . . . I must never be late again." He heaved a deep sigh and closed his eyes as if to shut out the sight of something he could not bear to see. Mouth agape and eyes wide behind her spectacles, Miss Frayle stared at him. The Doctor regarded him as if he might have been a specimen of some fauna possibly worthy of cursory study.

"What—what d'you mean? " Miss Frayle swallowed. There was a prickly sensation under her scalp.

"That was why it happened—my fault! " The hysterical note in the man's voice rose and was interrupted as the gale carried to them the distant whistle of an approaching train. The man tensed at once, his eyes wild, his mouth working.

"The train! " he croaked. "The train! "

While she goggled at him, Doctor Morelle calmly slipped his book in his pocket, murmuring half to himself : "It would seem the—ah—gentleman had never witnessed the arrival of a locomotive before! "

But his sarcasm was lost upon the other. The man rushed to the door, and picking up the suitcase, turned to fling back at them :

"You don't understand," he moaned, "You don't understand . . ."

"What about our tickets? " Miss Frayle remembered to gasp. But the man ignored her. He gave a wild look towards the platform as the sound of the train drew rapidly nearer.

184

"The gates! " he cried. "The level-crossing gates! . . ." And he was gone. The wind caught the door and slammed it after him. Doctor Morelle regarded Miss Frayle with a sardonic and enigmatic look. She goggled back at him and then started for the door as the train rumbled into the station. The Doctor followed her at a more leisurely pace.

As he joined her on the platform she gulped at him anxiously: "What—what shall we do about the tickets? "

"I feel confident that little matter can be adjusted quite easily, either on the train or at the terminus," he said. Adding, with a thin smile: "Rest assured there is only a slight risk of your being arrested on a charge of travelling without one! "

As the train rumbled in, the platform seemed deserted. Miss Frayle looked in all directions while she stood hesitating at the open door of the first-class compartment into which Doctor Morelle had stepped. She followed him and heard the slamming of doors further along the train, and she looked out of the window. All there was to be seen, however, was the guard's green lamp half obscured by the falling snow. Came the shrill of a whistle and the train drew out of Telbury Halt. She closed the window and huddled in a corner seat facing the Doctor.

He was complaining in acid tones:

"Why, when the train would appear to be particularly empty, did you urge me into a non-smoking compartment? "

She glanced at the notice on the window beside her.

"Oh, I'm so sorry," she apologised quickly. "I didn't see—I was so anxious about the tickets and wondering where that strange man had gone— "

He cut into her excuses.

"You may remain here if you prefer," he snapped, rising and moving to the door which led to the corridor, " but I shall seek more desirable accommodation."

"I'll come with you, of course, Doctor! "

After the disturbing events she had experienced, the last thing she looked forward to was being left alone in the empty compartment. Her imagination would soon people the corners and the corridor outside with frightening apparitions. She hurried after Doctor Morelle! Thus it was that a few minutes later she followed him into a smoking compartment where he had paused to stand and regard with saturnine amusement its only other occupant who was snoring rhythmically in a corner. It was Detective-Inspector Hood of Scotland Yard.

As she touched the Doctor's arm he turned and motioned her into the seat next to his. He sat down facing the detective.

"This is somewhat more agreeable," he observed, taking out his cigarette case and lighting a Le Sphinx. He made no attempt to lower his voice particularly, and Miss Frayle frowned and indicated the sleeping figure opposite.

"Shush! " she whispered. " You'll wake him! "

"That," he replied, " is precisely what I propose to do! "

And he leaned across and tapped the sleeper firmly upon his knee. The other awoke with a snort.

"What the devil—! " he began, then his mouth opened with surprise as he recognised the Doctor. " Well, I'll be—! "

"Indulging in a little beauty sleep? " murmured Doctor Morelle, regarding the detective's homely features. Detective-Inspector Hood blinked at him owlishly, then he grinned slowly at Miss Frayle. He sat upright in his corner and began automatically to forage in his pockets for his pipe. He found it and stuck it between his teeth, saying, as he found a match:

"Well, it is nice to meet you! But where on earth did you spring from? "

"We boarded the train at Telbury Halt," explained Doctor Morelle. " Might I inquire what coincidental circumstance causes you to be travelling by the same locomotive? "

"Yes, fancy you being on the train, too! " put in Miss Frayle.

The other sucked noisily at his old briar, slowly expelled a great cloud of somewhat acrid smoke—he went in for a powerful tobacco—apologised as the Doctor twitched his nostrils in revulsion, and explained:

"Maywood," he said.

"Maywood? " Miss Frayle said helpfully. " Isn't that about twenty miles the other side of Telbury? "

The other nodded, and his face assumed a disgruntled expression.

"And what, might I further inquire," murmured Doctor Morelle, "lured you so far afield from the precincts of Scotland Yard? "

The detective grunted

"Dragged down there on a fool's errand! " he growled.

"Some petty crime, no doubt, beneath your august consideration?"

"Well, I wouldn't describe it as petty exactly. The local police had nabbed a fellow for housebreaking, you see. By all accounts he sounded as if he might be the member of a gang I suspect are being operated from London. Thought a chat with him might lead me in the right direction towards rounding the lot up. But I got to Maywood just an hour too late. He's escaped! "

"Oh! " said Miss Frayle sympathetically. She added with a smile: " He might have waited for you! "

"Extremely annoying," agreed Doctor Morelle sardonically. "But then the criminal classes are inclined to exhibit a tendency towards a deplorable lack of any sense of etiquette! "

"H'm—may seem funny to you, but it didn't make me laugh! Half-an-hour with that chap would have saved me a lot of headaches. He could have given me quite a lot of information . . ." And he clamped his jaw so hard on his pipe-stem Miss Frayle feared it might snap.

"But surely the police will recapture him? " she asked.

Detective-Inspector Hood shrugged glumly.

"May not be as easy as all that," he grumbled. "For one thing, it's pretty certain he's got an accomplice. Not only that, he's an expert at disguise. They call him 'Rubber Face'—Riley's his real name. And he's one of the smartest men in the country at that sort of thing! "

He chewed at his pipe which had gone out, but made no effort to re-light it. "Taken all round," he said, "it's a damn nuisance! "

"Admittedly a somewhat aggravating outcome for you," the Doctor conceded.

The train drew into a station. Several bumps and jarring noises occurred as it was attached to another train waiting, and then the journey was resumed.

"Non-stop to London now," the detective explained.

"I won't be sorry to get there either! " breathed Miss Frayle in thankful anticipation. She had not altogether recovered from the earlier events of the evening. The warmth and security of the house in Harley Street was something she looked forward to.

Hood glanced at her and then at the Doctor, with a look of interrogation:

"Why, hasn't it been a nice change for you? " he queried. "I mean yours wasn't a business trip—or was it? "

Miss Frayle at once started to launch into an account of what had occurred on their way to the station and at Telbury Halt itself. She had hardly begun, however, when she was interrupted by the corridor door sliding open. They looked up to see an old lady standing there rather uncertainly.

"I do hope you won't mind me coming in here," she apologised in a thin, quavering voice. "I'm a bit nervous—and I don't like travelling alone, especially at night."

"Of course not," Miss Frayle reassured her at once, while Hood rose with alacrity, took the suitcase she was carrying and placed it carefully on the rack.

Rewarding them with a grateful glance and a murmured word of thanks, the old lady seated herself in the corner opposite Miss Frayle, folding her hands primly on her lap. She seemed very slight and worn looking, and with a tiny sigh closed her eyes wearily. Miss Frayle studied her anxiously for a moment, then went on with the story which the newcomer's entrance had interrupted. .

187

" . . . and when the strange man heard the train coming he shouted something about the gates—he was almost crazy with excitement—and rushed out."

"Gates? What gates? " The Scotland Yard man who had been listening with amused interest suddenly shot out the query.

She blinked at him.

" Why—why, the level-crossing gates, of course."

" What d'you mean? "

Something in his tone caused Doctor Morelle, who had returned again to his book, to look up sharply. Miss Frayle was goggling at the other who was eyeing her now with a puzzled frown.

" There *isn't* a crossing at Telbury Halt," he said, sucking noisily at his pipe. He added decisively: " It's a *bridge*."

She stared at him. " Bri-bridge? " she stammered, " what do *you* mean? "

The Doctor's narrowed gaze fastened itself on the detective. He made no comment. Miss Frayle shook her head in bewilderment.

" Are you sure? "

" Positive," he answered her. " Noticed it going down. And as we came back to-night. Remember it distinctly."

" But the porter? Those were his very words— " she persisted, " about the level-crossing. We both heard him, didn't we, Doctor Morelle? " And she turned to him for corroboration.

The Doctor, who had lit a Le Sphinx, blew out a spiral of cigarette-smoke thoughtfully. The Detective-Inspector glanced at Miss Frayle, then at him:

" Perhaps you only dreamt it? " he suggested genially.

" Though Miss Frayle might conceivably have been asleep at the time," said the Doctor, " it is difficult very often to know with certainty when exactly she is *awake*—I certainly was in possession of my full faculties. Furthermore," he went on, " it is hardly within the bounds of possibility that both of us had we been somnolent would have experienced a dream identical in all its features."

Hood was obviously impressed by the Doctor's pompous verbosity. He was about to ask further questions when the old lady opened her eyes and leaned forward.

" If you will pardon me for interrupting your conversation," she said tentatively in a quavering voice. " I think I might explain why the man spoke to you as he did about the level-crossing, although there is, in fact, a bridge there—I could not help overhearing what you were saying," she added with a little apologetic smile.

Hood gestured with his pipe, and said with an air of finality:

" There you are! "

" Telbury Halt used to have gates," the old lady proceeded in thin, wavering tones. " And it was the duty of the station-master

—he was porter and booking-clerk as well—to open the gates for the train to pass through." She paused, as if the exertion of speaking taxed her strength, then went on: "But about five years ago—on a Sunday night it was—"

"It's Sunday to-night" gasped Miss Frayle, her eyes wide, staring at the old lady in fascinated apprehension. The other nodded:

"Yes, I know," she said quietly, "but on this night I am speaking of five years ago, something happened to delay the poor man as he went to operate the gates. He reached them too late." Her voice sank into a whisper that could hardly be heard. "The train crashed through them and he was killed. Oh, it was a terrible business . . ." She shook her head. "Poor man, poor man! . . ."

There was a long silence, then Miss Frayle gulped:

"You—you mean that—that the man we saw to-night—the man who rushed to open the gates—you mean he was—it was a—?" She couldn't finish the question, becoming speechless with fright as the full implication of the other's story hit her.

The old lady nodded slowly. "Everybody knows there is a bridge at Telbury Halt now. It was built soon after the accident."

Miss Frayle turned her horrified gaze upon Doctor Morelle, who was leaning back in a relaxed attitude, his eyes closed. Without opening them, he puffed a spiral of cigarette smoke upwards.

Detective-Inspector Hood scratched his chin.

"Well, well!" he said, his eyebrows drawn together. "What d'you make of that, Doctor Morelle?"

The lowered eyelids condescended to flicker open for a moment and he bent their sardonic gaze upon the detective. Then they closed again, and his only reply to the question was another puff of cigarette-smoke.

"H'm . . . I've come up against some queer characters in my time," ruminated the detective, "but you two have certainly got something on me there!" He chuckled. "I've never had the pleasure of saying 'hello' to a ghost!"

Miss Frayle shivered at the remembrance. "That is," Hood added judiciously, "if it was a spook."

"Oh, other people have seen him," the old lady said with conviction. "He appears only once a year—*on this particular night, of course*—and anyone who knows about it keeps away from the station at this time on the anniversary of the awful accident."

"I expect they do!" Miss Frayle said fervently. She shivered again. "I wish we'd known."

"Oh well," Hood said cheerfully, "it doesn't seem to have done you much harm!"

The old lady had fallen silent in her corner. Her head was sunk on her shoulder as if she had fallen asleep. The detective gave her

189

a sympathetic look and then turned to the Doctor who was sitting more upright, a speculative gaze directed towards the woman.

"How do you come to be travelling by train, Doctor? I thought you got around by car?"

Doctor Morelle looked at him slowly, and then proceeded to give a brief explanation of the abandoning of his car.

"You haven't told the Inspector about that strange man who overtook us while we were waiting in the snow and drove off before you could ask him for help," Miss Frayle reminded him. "And there was that muffled figure in the back of his car—" A sudden thought struck her, and she turned, wide-eyed, to the detective. "Why, it might have been the escaped prisoner you're looking for!"

The other glanced at her sharply.

"You mean Riley?"

"Yes," she said excitedly. "You said he had an accomplice."

Hood shot a look at the Doctor whose eyes had narrowed thoughtfully.

"It is not impossible that there is a grain of probability in what Miss Frayle suggests," he conceded. "Do you know if the car went on to Telbury Halt?" the Scotland Yard man asked.

Miss Frayle was about to answer eagerly, but the Doctor spoke first.

"To judge from tyre-tracks in the snow outside the station, that would seem to be indicated."

Miss Frayle goggled at him. "Oh, you *did* notice them?" she said.

He gave her a supercilious smile. To the other he went on:

"I compared them with the tyre-tracks which led from the spot where the car had pulled alongside mine."

"Yet you saw no one at the station?"

"Only the ghost," breathed Miss Frayle. "Perhaps—perhaps he'd scared them away."

"Never mind that," the Detective-Inspector waved aside the idea. "Where did the car get to? That's the point."

"That remains to be ascertained," observed the Doctor. "Unfortunately it would have been impossible to note the vehicle's registration number inasmuch as the plate had become obscured by snow."

"Pity. Though if it was Riley I don't suppose getting the number would have helped much. He'd abandon the car as soon as he could."

Doctor Morelle nodded in agreement.

"How awful if it really was him and he's got away," put in Miss Frayle.

The other clicked his tongue. "Pity. However, I'll have a call

put out as soon as I get to London. We'll rope 'em in all right."
He re-lit his pipe and puffed at it confidently. Miss Frayle looked
across at the other occupant of the compartment. Her eyes were
closed.

Presently they steamed into the terminus. While Miss Frayle
helped the old lady to her feet, Detective-Inspector Hood rose to
lift down her suitcase. At the same time the Doctor was reaching
for his luggage.

The woman's expressions of gratitude were abruptly cut short by
a rather surprising mishap.

The Doctor was always extremely assured in his actions, but
apparently an unexpected jerk of the train as it drew to a standstill
with a final application of brakes caused him to let the end of his
suitcase slip. A corner of it caught the old lady sharply on the side
of the head. It was not a heavy blow, but sufficient to knock her
hat—*and the wig underneath*—askew. Hood had swung round,
startled by the old lady's somewhat unlady-like exclamation, and
found himself staring into a face that was, to him, familiar.

"'Rubber Face' Riley!" he grunted.

"The ghost!" cried Miss Frayle simultaneously.

The wolf in sheep's clothing tried to make a dash for it, but
Doctor Morelle obliged by neatly tripping him, followed by the
Detective-Inspector sitting heavily on the man's chest.

Some time later, as he accompanied Doctor Morelle and Miss
Frayle back from Scotland Yard to Harley Street in a police-car,
Detective-Inspector Hood was saying:

"Yes . . . that was Riley all right you saw in the back of the
car. He and the other chap—we hope to get him shortly—had
stolen it, only to find the petrol in the tank wouldn't take them far.
They were afraid to risk stopping for a fresh supply—might have
attracted attention—so they decided to try their luck at the railway-
station. They knocked out the man in charge and locked him in
the parcels-office. Riley borrowed his cap, in case anybody else
came along. His pal pushed off. Riley intended to board the train
unobserved. That was why he tried to scare you off. But,
unfortunately for him, you didn't scare so easily!"

Doctor Morelle smiled bleakly. He said: "In order that he
might enter the train unseen by us? That was his object, I presume, in pretending he had to attend to the gates?"

Hood nodded, and added: "He found an empty compartment,
drew the blinds, and made himself up as an old lady."

"But why did he deliberately come into our compartment?"
asked Miss Frayle, puzzled. "He must have realised who you were?"

"Typical of Riley. He guessed the stations would be watched

for him, as in fact they were, and was afraid he might be a bit conspicuous on his own. Some sharp-eyed policeman might have spotted that 'old lady' rig-out. But by deliberately tacking himself on to us, he hoped he'd disarm any suspicion. Of course, when I spoilt his earlier yarn to you about the level-crossing gates at Telbury Halt, he thought up his ghost story to cover his tracks."

"I must say he carried off both parts very well," said Miss Frayle, not without a hint of admiration in her voice.

"He would appear to have missed his vocation," murmured the Doctor. "I should imagine he could appear with some success on the music-hall stage!"

"Perhaps you can persuade him to try it as a new career—when he comes out of gaol!" Hood suggested with a grin.

Doctor Morelle condescended to smile thinly at the pleasantry.

"Yes. If it hadn't been for that little accident," the Detective-Inspector mused, "he'd have walked past the barrier with us as easy as kiss-your-hand. I'd have carried his suitcase, and you, Miss Frayle, would've called him a taxi!"

Doctor Morelle lit a Le Sphinx with a sardonic smile twitching at the corners of his mouth.

"I think I may say that both those eventualities would have been unlikely," he said.

"What d'you mean, Doctor?" queried Miss Frayle.

"Merely that as a result of elementary observation I perceived that the end of the—ah—gentleman's trouser-leg had become caught in the lid of his suit-case," he murmured in an elaborately casual tone. "Moreover, the turn-up in question had suffered a tear—" He paused, and then went on "—exactly similar to the tear in the trouser-leg of the—ah—'ghost' of Telbury Halt!"

Miss Frayle goggled at him from behind her spectacles.

"You—you mean—?" she gasped.

"Well, I'll be—!" Hood could find no words to express his surprise.

"You sloshed him with your suitcase deliberately!" Miss Frayle blurted out in excited astonishment and admiration.

The police-car was drawing up outside the house in Harley Street as Doctor Morelle replied through a cloud of cigarette smoke:

"Though you have hardly taken the exact words out of my mouth, my dear Miss Frayle, you have nevertheless succeeded in interpreting my implied meaning."

THE END

Printed in January 2022
by Rotomail Italia S.p.A., Vignate (MI) - Italy